Praise for *Forty Stories* by Donald Barthelme

"Barthelme's funny, ludicrous tales follow the emotional logic of a dream, and as he tells them no slice-of-life could seem more substantial . . . his stories have substance because he locates his characters—from unnamed narrators, to a generic 'playwright' to Paul Klee and Goethe—in the precise place where the weight of history intrudes on the present, where desire meets imagination."
—*The New York Times Book Review*

"What Barthelme writes aren't so much stories as acts in an almost endless vaudeville: epistemological skits, voiceless monologues, extended one-liners, intellectual shaggy-dog stories. . . . Barthelme's fiction is affected, weightless, utterly original. One wouldn't have it any other way."
—*The Boston Globe*

"Reading Barthelme is great fun. His eye and ear are quick for the absurdities of our quotidian ways and literary manners. His darts are facetiousness and wit."
—*Los Angeles Times*

"Mr. Barthelme's stories are surreal collages, witty juxtapositions of bits and pieces of contemporary life played off against the fading background of European literature, art, and philosophy. He can sound like S. J. Perelman or Groucho Marx one minute, and like Hugo or Kafka the next. He is a master of the dying fall, the blackout, and the comic operatic crescendo . . . the energy, wit, variety, beauty and high seriousness of Donald Barthelme's stories deserve all the readers and all the praise they can attract."
—*The Wall Street Journal*

"The prose of Donald Barthelme is a classy rag and bone shop of sophisticated prose, a sort of flea market of western civilization, a national resource for renewal, a kind of Save the Whales of language up on the beach of mindless overuse and clichés."
—*Houston Chronicle*

"Donald Barthelme almost single-handedly has revived the genre of the short story and made it a fresh art form. . . . This new collection provides ample evidence that there is always a playful intellect at work, and there is no such thing as a typical Barthelme story. He can, and does, write stories of every kind." —*People*

PENGUIN  CLASSICS

FORTY STORIES

DONALD BARTHELME published seventeen books, including four novels and a prize-winning children's book. He was a longtime contributor to *The New Yorker*, winner of a National Book Award, a director of PEN and the Authors Guild, and a member of the American Academy of Arts and Letters. He died in July 1989.

DAVE EGGERS is the author of *How We Are Hungry*, *You Shall Know Your Velocity*, and *A Heartbreaking Work of Staggering Genius*, a 2000 finalist for the Pulitzer prize. He is the editor of *McSweeney's*, a journal and book publishing outfit. In 2002 he founded 826 Valencia, a nonprofit writing lab and tutoring center for San Francisco youth.

BY DONALD BARTHELME

DONALD BARTHELME

Forty Stories

Introduction by
DAVE EGGERS

PENGUIN BOOKS

PENGUIN BOOKS
Published by the Penguin Group
Penguin Group (USA) Inc., 375 Hudson Street, New York, New York 10014, U.S.A.
Penguin Group (Canada), 10 Alcorn Avenue, Toronto,
Ontario, Canada M4V 3B2 (a division of Pearson Penguin Canada Inc.)
Penguin Books Ltd, 80 Strand, London WC2R 0RL, England
Penguin Ireland, 25 St Stephen's Green, Dublin 2, Ireland (a division of Penguin Books Ltd)
Penguin Group (Australia), 250 Camberwell Road, Camberwell,
Victoria 3124, Australia (a division of Pearson Australia Group Pty Ltd)
Penguin Books India Pvt Ltd, 11 Community Centre, Panchsheel Park, New Delhi – 110 017, India
Penguin Group (NZ), cnr Airborne and Rosedale Roads, Albany,
Auckland 1310, New Zealand (a division of Pearson New Zealand Ltd)
Penguin Books (South Africa) (Pty) Ltd, 24 Sturdee Avenue,
Rosebank, Johannesburg 2196, South Africa

Penguin Books Ltd, Registered Offices: 80 Strand, London WC2R 0RL, England

First published in the United States of America by G. P. Putnam's Sons 1987
Published in Penguin Books 1989
This edition published with an introduction by Dave Eggers 2005

1 3 5 7 9 10 8 6 4 2

The author gratefully acknowledges permission from Farrar, Strauss, & Giroux, Inc., to reprint
the following: "Concerning the Bodyguard" and "Great Days" from *Great Days*. Copyright © 1977,
1978, 1979 by Donald Barthelme. "Concerning the Bodyguard" originally appeared in *The New
Yorker*. "Letters to the Editore" from *Guilty Pleasures*. Copyright © 1974 by Donald Barthelme.
Originally appeared in *The New Yorker*.

The following stories first appeared in *The New Yorker*: "Chablis," "On the Deck,"
"Opening," "Sindbad," "Jaws," "Bluebeard," "Construction," and "January."

THE LIBRARY OF CONGRESS HAS CATALOGED
THE HARDCOVER EDITION AS FOLLOWS:
Barthelme, Donald.
Forty Stories / Donald Barthelme.
p.   cm.
ISBN 0 14 24.3781 6
I. Title.
PS3552.A76F6   1989
813'.54—dc19   88-28925

Printed in the United States of America
Set in Galliard

To Marion, Anne, and Katharine

Contents

Introduction

The question many people and engineers have asked recently, in board rooms and on the street, is this: If Donald Barthelme were to happen today—if he were to burst onto the scene in 2004 or 2005 or thereabouts—what would become of him? What kind of reception would he receive?

The answer is that people would be curious. Then they would probably be more or less dismissive. They might even club him in the street, using clubs meant for seals.

We live in serious times, and though this is not Donald Barthelme's fault, he would pay dearly for it. The fact is that work like Don B's—which is playful, subtle, beautiful, and more like poetry (in its perfect ambivalence toward narrative) than almost any prose we have—would be seen today as frivolous, as unserious. There is in most quarters of mainstream fiction a newspapering process going on, wherein stylistic deviations are disallowed, where innovations in style are seen as a sign of disengagement. When reading contemporary work with distinctive styles, some readers become impatient and most critics become enraged. Tell us the story, they say. Just tell it to us, get it across and get it over with. Spare us the frills.

In fact, if Donald Barthelme were to appear today, wearing corduroy and denim and a felt hat, it would be surprising if he were to find a publisher anywhere anyhow. He would be employed at a Mailboxes Etc., working the machine that sends the Styrofoam chips into the boxes to the people on the other side of the world who will have no idea how to dispose of them.

An exaggeration. In fact, all very excellent work finds a publisher sooner or later—this is the maxim that keeps us believing—so D.B. would have indeed been published. But would he have been published in some of the most robust mainstream weeklies, as he was for decades? No, no, no. Things are different in this century, thus far. There is not much time for things that don't announce themselves and make fairly clear linear sense. And how often did Barthelme make clear linear sense? How often did his stories have a beginning, middle and end? How often did he tell a story in a goddamn simple and easy way?

Maybe once or twice, when he forgot himself.

*   *   *

These are the lies and truths we know about Donald Barthelme: He was for many years a sailor on a Japanese freighter called the *Ursula Andress*. He wore a stove-pipe hat and drove a Chevy Lumina. He was wildly romantic and his prose was on par, in terms of imagery and evockery and lyricism, with Nabokov, and his sense of the absurd is rivaled only by Borges. He killed everything he ate. He dated the young Audrey Hepburn and the older Eartha Kitt.

But was Barthelme indeed the love child of Nabokov and Borges, as many have claimed? This could be so. Though, to be sure, he and V.N. were not too many years apart in age—more like contemporaries. Were they friends? It does not appear so. Rumor has it that Barthelme asked him a few questions at a party and Vlad said he would get back to him six months hence, once he could write the answers down on blue notecards. Four months later he was dead. V.N. was, that is.

That story is apocryphal.

*   *   *

How to read this book:
Put your feet in cold water. The Adriatic is recommended, in July. There will be small fish who will approach you. These fish are sort of like catfish, but much smaller, and sort of like eels. They will have faces like Wilfred Brimley and they will approach your feet as squirrels would approach a woman on a bench hold-

ing delicious nuts. These fish will not touch your feet; they will simply come near them, and will appear to be wildly content just to be near them, your feet. The water is just cold enough to be pure of heart.

With your feet in this water, read *Forty Stories*. Read the titles first and appreciate that these forty titles are among the best assemblage of titles ever assembled. Appreciate that "Some of Us Had Been Threatening Our Friend Colby" and "Porcupines at the University" have both been ranked by the relevant authorities among the top ten titles ever written, and appreciate that Barthelme has the chops to back up those titles with stories of extraordinary beauty and nuance. While you're at it, appreciate that Barthelme seems to cover more ground in these short oddities than many a novelist will cover in books twice the length.

Read in small bites. Read one story and look out on the water and wonder what the hell Donald Barthelme looked like. You love him like an uncle but you've never seen even one picture of him. Go up the beach to your bag, and retrieve some white paper and a Sharpie. Now do some renderings of what Barthelme might have looked like, in terms of physical appearance. On the next page, please find fifteen such drawings. If there are readers of this introduction who knew Mr. Barthelme or saw pictures of him, please indicate, via this publisher, which image is closest. The author of this introduction will then be awarded a check for $70 for doing such a good drawing. Thank you in advance.

*   *   *

Here is a great sentence from David Gates's introduction to *Sixty Stories*, a different but not entirely alien book, also by this author:

"Much of the pleasure in reading Barthelme comes from the way he makes you feel welcome even as he's subjecting you to a vertiginously high level of entertainment."

This is one of the most crucial things that the newcomer needs to know about Barthelme. Though his stuff is sometimes difficult to puncture, and sometimes difficult to follow, while you're finding your way, he's always grinning at you in a warm

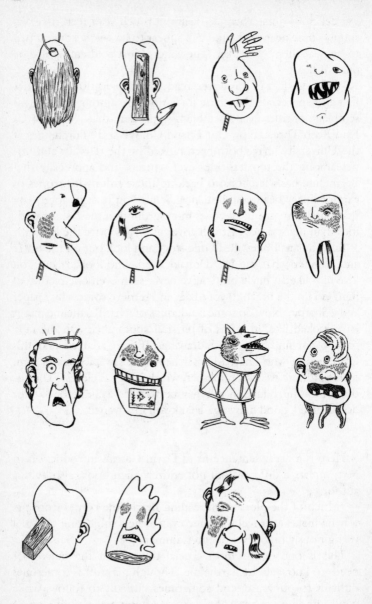

and very compassionate way. The reader gets the feeling that the author is a nice man. That he knows when he's being difficult and when he's full of shit. Knows how much of this and how much of that you can actually take. He differs from some of his contemporaries, and from many other forgers of new prose styles, in that he doesn't ever give off the impression that he takes himself overseriously, and he seems genuinely to care whether or not his work is being read by you. He is a social writer. A writer who seems to be in the next room, waiting for you to finish and tell him what you thought.

Back to David Gates: Gates's introduction is so good that you really should read it, too. It's reprinted below, in very small type.

Donald Barthelme was still alive when this volume was first published back in 1981, and he himself signed off on its modest, no-spin title. I always wondered why, since title-giving was one of his great knacks. He'd called the original books in which these stories appeared *Sadness* or *Great Days* or *Come Back, Dr. Caligari* or *Unspeakable Practices, Unnatural Acts*, and the titles of individual stories practically raise an index finger and give you the kitchy-coo: "I Bought a Little City," "Our Work and Why We Do It," "The Falling Dog," "See the Moon." Even the one-worders—"Paraguay," "Margins," "Aria"—bristle (to use one of those words Bartheleme put his brand on) with strangeness. So why settle for *Sixty Stories*? Maybe he despaired of coming up with any one title that could overarch such a various landscape, though that had never stopped him before. Or maybe, like the narrator in "I Bought a Little City," he "didn't want to be too imaginative." He might have figured sixty was a good round number—it would have been like him to make a little game of caring about good round numbers—and then picked something unpretentious and reasonably euphonious to go with it. Sixty Texts? Sixty Fictions? Not just intolerable, but unpronounceable.

But about that word "stories." Obviously Barthelme's idea of a story subverts the still-standard Chekhovian template: modest deeds of modest people leading up to a modest epiphany. He wickedly characterized such pieces in a ready-to-rumble 1964 essay as "constructed mousetrap-like to supply, at the finish, a tiny insight typically having to do with innocence violated." The parables of Kafka, the pastiches of S.J. Perelman, the monologues of Samuel Beckett, the swashbuckling absurdities of Rafael Sabatini, fairy tales, films, comic books—all these contributed as much to his sense of what a story might be as the exquisite contraptions of *Dubliners* or *In Our Time*. In later years, he could better afford to praise traditional or neotraditional fiction: he admired Updike and Cheever, Ann Beattie and Raymond Carver. But his own work continued to skitter away from any genre that seemed to spread its arms in suffocating welcome—including so-called "metafiction," the genre to which critics most often accused him of belonging. He protested against this, and pointed out that only rarely—as in *Snow White*'s mid-novel questionnaire—did he explicitly make an issue of his fiction's very fictiveness. Still, especially in such knockoffs of nineteenth-century storytelling as "Views of My Father Weeping" and "The Dolt," he seems to savor conventional narrative for its quaintness rather than for any possibility that we might drift slackjawed into a state of suspended disbelief. For Barthelme, plots and characters aren't fiction's *raison d'etre*, but good old tropes it might be fun to trot out again. More than once he described his pieces as "slumgullions": another word with the Barthelme brand, not merely pleasurable to the ear and the eye, but dead accurate. His stories are rich, dense, flavorsome throwings-together of this, that, and the other thing, concocted for the inextricable purposes of pleasure and sustenance.

Still, once he'd discovered and perfected what we think of as the Barthelme Story—"The Indian Uprising," say, which slumgullionizes the Old West, 1960s urban alienation, *Death in Venice*, and God knows what-all—he got too restless to keep cranking out the product. As the narrator of "I Bought a Little City" says: "I thought, What a nice little city, it suits me fine. It suited me fine so I started to change it." He went on to devise stories that are all dialogue ("Morning"), stories that are quasi-essays ("On Angels"), quasi-parables ("A City of Churches"), quasi-parodies ("How I Write My Songs") or quasi-legends ("The Emperor"), stories that appropriate large chunks of "found" material ("Paraguay"), stories that revert for a change to straight old-school narrative ("Bishop"), stories within stories ("The Dolt"), stories that seem to be pure freestyle riffing ("Aria"). They suited him fine. There was just one problem: terminally well-read as he was, Barthelme knew that all these forms had already been done to death. This is part of their charm for us: knowing that he knows that we know he knows it. But a writer as ambitious as Barthelme couldn't stay in any of these outmoded modes for long. So then what?

Barthelme could probably have been happy among the High Modernists: marching shoulder-to-shoulder in the vanguard with Joyce and Woolf, Eliot and Pound, making it new. Kicking over the played-out paradigms, twisting linear narrative into a Möbius strip, making the haunt and main region of his song the consciousness of his consciousness of his consciousness, cutting up Baudelaire, Wagner, Jacobean drama, and contemporary pop songs and shoring the fragments against his ruins, building Homeric/Dantean epics out of blocks of text carved from Confucius and John Adams. From *The Waste Land* to Duchamp's ready-mades—and on through *Naked Lunch* and "The Adventures of Grandmaster Flash on the Wheels of Steel"—the twentieth century's characteristic artistic procedure was (pick your term) collage, appropriation, assemblage, bricolage, or sampling. (Here's an exchange from Barthelme's "The Genius," in this book's companion volume, *Forty Stories*: "Q: What do you consider the most important tool of genius today? A: Rubber cement.") This cut-and-paste, recombinatory method of making it new, of course, implied that there *was* nothing new, though the modernists didn't go out of their way to advertise that. The hell of it was, by the time Barthelme came along, even making it new was getting old. Among the works he samples—along with *Hamlet*, Wittgenstein's *Tractatus* and Muddy Waters's "Mannish Boy"—is *The Waste Land* itself.

For Barthelme, the question of what to do after modernism had already done it all wasn't mere intellectual-careerist hand-wringing; it was also a personal agon. His father was a party-line modern architect, an admirer of Mies van der Rohe, Frank Lloyd Wright and Le Corbusier. "We were enveloped in Modernism," Barthelme said in a 1981 interview with J.D. O'Hara. "The house we lived in, which he'd designed, was Modern and the furniture was Modern and the pictures were Modern and the books were Modern." Since this house was in Houston, Texas, Barthelme also grew up enveloped in the energetically subversive Americana that such expatriate modernists as Pound and Eliot approved of on principle—think of Pound's persona as the Americodger Old Ez—and recoiled from on instinct. He told O'Hara about listening to the radio and hearing Bob Wills and his Texas Playboys, whose music was a high-spirited collage of country, jazz, blues, Mexican, and Bing Crosby pop. In the city's black jazz clubs, he heard such visiting musicians as Erskine Hawkins and Lionel Hampton rework pop songs into fresh, vernacular-modernist works by improvising on their underlying structures. "You'd hear some of these guys take a tired old tune like 'Who's Sorry Now?' and do the most incredible things with it, make it beautiful, literally make it new," he recalled. "The interest and the drama were in the formal manipulation of the rather slight material. And they were heroic figures, you know, very romantic." He may have witnessed such cutting contests as the one evoked in his story "The King of Jazz," in which the master trombonist Hokie Mokie (himself the successor to "Spicy MacLammermoor, the old king") tries to fend off a younger competitor.

So Barthelme's home and his community, as well as his reading and his writing, gave him a usefully acute case of the anxiety of influence—and the influence he seemed most anxious about was that of modernism itself. "Remember," he told O'Hara, "that I was exposed early to an almost religious crusade, the Modern movement in architecture, which, putting it as kindly as possible, has not turned out quite as expected." He was always interested in the way younger writers revere and then overthrow their forebears, sometimes by the process Harold Bloom calls "strong misreading": Blake's interpretation of Milton as a Satanic-prophetic visionary, to use one of Bloom's examples, or the high-modernist practice of willfully misappropriating and miscontextualizing fragments of canonical literature, which were threatening to the degree that they were revered. Barthelme, like Bloom, could hardly miss the Oedipal overtones: his best novel, after all, is *The Dead Father*, whose title character—a talking statue-carcass who reminds us of King Lear, Tolstoy, Jehovah, and Blake's Nobodaddy—gets dragged to his grave, protesting and orating all the way. Yet Barthelme, as he liked to remind us, was "a doubleminded man." The very baldness of that title suggests his bemusement at such an overfamiliar paradigm; no old-time modernist would have been so bathetically blunt.

Literary historians call Barthelme a postmodernist, and he didn't resist the designation as strongly as he resisted being called a metafictionist. "Critics . . . have been searching for a term that would describe fiction after the great period of modernism," he said in a 1980 interview with Larry McCaffery—" 'postmodernism,' 'metafiction,' 'surfiction,' 'superfiction.' The last two are terrible; I suppose 'postmodernism' is the least ugly, most descriptive." But in the 1987 essay "Not-Knowing," written two years before he died, he said he was "dubious" about the term and "not altogether clear as to who is supposed to be on the bus and who is not." Since the word gets applied both to works supposedly weirder-than-modern (weirder than *Finnegans Wake*?) and to works far more conservative (Raymond Carver's stories, Philip Johnson's buildings), "postmodern" is useful as a chronological marker, like "eighteenth-century," and worthless as a characterization of a particular esthetic, like "Baroque." It might be most sensible, then, simply to look at Barthelme as one more writer who came along after older writers had already done what he would like to have done—as Dante came along after Virgil who came along after Homer—and who had a hard time, as writers have always had, figuring out how to reconcile his admiration for his predecessors with his ambition to make something of his own.

Barthelme's particular Dead Father was Beckett—who had a Dead Father of his own. "I'm just overwhelmed by Beckett, as Beckett was by Joyce," he told interviewers Charles Ruas and Judith Sherman in 1975. "By the way, let me make clear that I am not proposing myself as successor or heir to Mr. Beckett, in any sense. I'm just telling you that he is a problem for me because of the enormous pull of his style. I am certainly not the only writer who has been enormously influenced by Beckett and thus wants to stay at arm's length . . . There are other lions in the path as well . . . It's just that Beckett is the largest problem for me." Here and there, Barthelme lets himself write in this or that Beckettian mode: the relentless comma-spliced monologue of "Traumerei" (cf. *The Unnamable*), the vaudevillean-stichomythic banter of such late pieces as "The Leap" (cf. *Waiting for Godot*), or the comic pedantry of "Daumier" and "A Shower of Gold" (cf. *Murphy*). What's more radically Beckettian is Barthelme's compulsion to fly blind, to approach the unknowable as an area for exploration, and his sense of the mind's cubistic noisiness. "The confusing signals, the impurity of the signal, gives you verisimilitude," he told J.D. O'Hara. "As when you attend a funeral and notice, against your will, that it's being poorly done." (This, by the way, catches almost exactly Beckett's tone and cadence—except Beckett might have used the formal "one" construction instead of the colloquial "you.")

Like Beckett, Barthelme uses his well-nurtured taste and wide-ranging erudition to point up their ultimate uselessness. "Is it really important to know that this movie is fine, and that one terrible, and to talk intelligently about the difference?" his narrator asks at the end of "The Party." "Wonderful elegance! No good at all!" Like Beckett, he's a meticulous observer and compulsive cataloguer of the things of this world, knowing that they offer no certainty or security.

> Red men in waves . . . accumulated against the barriers we had made of window dummies, silk, thoughtfully planned job descriptions . . . I analyzed the composition of the barricade closest to me and found two ashtrays, ceramic, one dark brown and one dark brown with an orange blur at the lip . . . a red pillow and blue pillow, a woven straw wastebasket . . . a Yugoslavian carved flute, wood, dark brown, and other items. I decided I knew nothing.
> —"The Indian Uprising"

Like Beckett, he's God-haunted yet unbelieving.

> —We are but poor lapsarian futiles whose preen glands are all out of kilter and who but for the grace of God—
> —Do you think He wants us to grovel quite so much?
> —I don't think He gives a rap. But it's traditional.
> —"The Leap"

And like Beckett—or like Shakespeare, for that matter—he doesn't worry much about the distinction between the dark and the comic.

Yet Barthelme would never have written a line like Nell's speech in *Endgame*: "Nothing is funnier than unhappiness, I grant you that." His is both a sunnier and a more worldly spirit. "The world is waiting for the sunrise," his narrator says in "The Sandman." (Neither the narrator's own words nor Barthelme's, of course; he's quoting the old pop song.) And while we may well wait forever—in fact, isn't that Rule One?—its failure to arrive doesn't make the sunrise less real. Barthelme has a lively sense of the absurd, but no feel for the punishingly bleak; even if all *is* vanity, he doesn't hold a little thing like that against the world and the flesh. "Anathematization of the world," he writes in *Snow White*, "is not an adequate response to the world." Both as writer and citizen, Barthelme cherished acts of political decency, like the narrator's effort, in "The Sandman," to get help for some black kids who'd been arrested for sodomizing and suffocating a little boy. "Now while I admit it sounds callous to be talking about the degree of brutality being minimal, let me tell you that it was no small matter, in that time and place, to force the cops to show the kids to the press at all. It was an achievement, of sorts." That "of sorts" undercuts the "achievement" with a Beckettian sigh; still, the achievement remains. Similarly, though physical pleasure and human connection may be hard to come by and impossible to hang onto, Barthelme never seems to feel betrayed by their absence and never doubts their absolute value. In "The Zombies," the ultimate symptom of deadening at the hands of a "bad zombie" is to "walk by a beautiful breast and not even notice." So is Barthelme wiser and more humane than Beckett? Or just whistling in the dark, punking out on the ultimate implications of what he knew?

Beckett's skepticism extends even to language itself—to the very language, that is, with which he expresses his skepticism about language. "You would do better, at least no worse," his Molloy tells us, "to obliterate texts than to blacken margins, to fill in the holes of words until all is blank and flat and the whole ghastly business looks like what it is, senseless, speechless, issueless misery." Barthelme had no inclination to follow the old man to such an extremity; when it came to language, he was a believer—even a booster. "The combinatory agility of words," he wrote in "Not-Knowing," "the exponential generation of meaning once they're allowed to go to bed together, allows the writer to surprise himself, makes art possible, reveals how much of Being we haven't yet encountered." He makes the anti-Beckettian argument that art, with its ability to "imagine alternative realities," is "fundamentally meliorative," that "the artist's effort, always and everywhere, is to attain a fresh mode of cognition"—and that the writer's particular task is "restoring freshness to a much-handled language." Doesn't this emphasis on manner rather than matter put Barthelme among literature's marginal Crazy Uncles—Firbank, Edward Lear, John Lyly—instead of among its august Dead Fathers? Doesn't it show Barthelme as deficient in moral earnestness? When O'Hara pressed him on this point, Barthelme had the answer ready. "I believe that my every sentence trembles with morality in that each attempts to engage the problematic," he said. "The change of emphasis from the what to the how seems to me to be the major impulse in art since Flaubert, and it's not merely formalism, it's not at all superficial, it's an attempt to reach truth, and a very rigorous one."

Since a writer can no more invent a new vocabulary than a painter can invent a new spectrum, Barthelme's project of restoring freshness to language—"to purify the dialect of the tribe" is how Pound put it—led him to ragpick words, phrases, tones of voice, and modes of diction from the obscure and neglected past, from the demotic present and from the surreal specialized lexicons of technology, philosophy, even the military. "Mixing bits of this and that from various areas of life to make something that did not exist before is an oddly hopeful endeavor," he wrote in a short essay about his story "Paraguay." "The sentence 'Electrolytic jelly exhibiting a capture ratio far in excess of standard is used to fix the animals in place' made me very happy—perhaps in excess of its merit. But there is in the world such a thing as electrolytic jelly; the 'capture ratio' comes from the jargon of sound technology; and the animals themselves are a salad of the real and the invented." He had a good ear for bad writing: "I'm very interested in . . . sentences that are awkward in a particular way," he said in a 1970 interview with Jerome Klinkowitz. In such pieces as "How I Write My Songs," he elevated the ungainly—the passive voice, the ill-chosen word, the clunky cadence, the banal thought—to the poetic simply by putting a frame around it. "Another type of song which is a dear favorite of almost everyone," his fictive songwriter Bill B. White tells us, "is the song that has a message, some kind of thought that people can carry away with them and think about. Many songs of this type are written and gain great acceptance every day." He was even proud of the Orwellian "loudspeaker-like tone" he achieved in this sentence from "The Rise of Capitalism": "Cultural underdevelopment of the worker, as a technique of domination, is found everywhere under late capitalism." Why? In part, as he explained to O'Hara, because its "metallic drone" undercut the truth of its assertion with a dreary countertruth: nothing will ever be done about it. But also in part because, as the modernists knew long ago, ugliness has its weird beauty if you hold it up and look at it.

In his affectionate play with language, his erudition and his lurking earnestness about the redemptive force of art, Barthelme sounds less like Beckett than like Nabokov, that other man-mountain of late modernism. Nabokov, obviously, was the better linguist, but Barthelme read at least as widely and with a more open mind: not to reinforce a set of mandarin prejudices but to explode what few he ever had. (It's hard to imagine Nabokov studying up on the conquest of Mexico, taking notes on hoodoo charms or listening to Muddy Waters.) Barthelme paid him notably, perhaps suspiciously, scant attention. (In his 1964 essay "After Joyce," he kissed off Nabokov in a single sentence along with—for some reason—Henry Green; this was almost a decade after *Lolita*.) If Beckett was Barthelme's Dead Father, Nabokov might have been his dark Uncle Claudius: uncomfortably like him, yet radically opposed in spirit. Like Nabokov, Barthelme can be clever and allusive to the point of obscurity, but he never pulls chilly practical jokes on his readers and never seeks, as Nabokov did, to misdirect them. As the narrator of "The Sandman" says of his willful, depressive, and sexy girlfriend, distance is not Barthelme's thing—"not by a long chalk." Beneath his surface of corruscating omniscience beats a kindly heart. He seems to want you to be in on his jokes, to share the joyous agility of his conceptual and linguistic leaps, the abundance of his cornucopiously stocked memory, and not to sit gazing at him from the cheap seats in mournful admiration. In essays and interviews, he explained with as little mystification as possible how he put together his pieces—considering that the process of writing is essentially mysterious—and how we might go about appreciating them. Much of the pleasure in reading Barthelme comes from the way he makes you feel welcome even as he's subjecting you to a vertiginously high level of entertainment.

My comparing Barthelme with Beckett and Nabokov suggests that I think he, too, is a King of Jazz. Can he really hold his own in a cutting session with those cats setting the tempo, and Joyce and Woolf sitting at a table in the back listening for wrong notes? Who knows? He's been gone less than fifteen years; we might have a clearer view of what he accomplished in another fifty. Certainly he's become canonical: there he is, in every anthology and on the shelves of every bookstore, right after John Barth. But a lot of unread and unreadable people get to be canonical. Unlike such co-generationists as Harold Brodkey or Don DeLillo or John Gardner or Cormac McCarthy, he doesn't do the High Seriousness thing. Which is odd, because the contemporaries he read with pleasure were folks like Thomas Bernhard, Max Frisch, William Gass, Walker Percy, García Márquez, Peter Handke—serious, some of them, to a fault. He's got all the political, sociological, literary, philosophical, and spiritual anxieties any writer could be blessed with, yet reading him never feels like a duty. That wouldn't bode well if you were bucking for King of Jazz, though it might keep you from going out of print. Neither would the shortcoming he confessed to J.D. O'Hara—"I don't offer enough emotion"—if it were really true. He never emoted, but that's a different thing. Any reader sophisticated enough to stick with Barthelme in the first place must sense the sadness he's at such pains to evade with all his funning, and feel the joy when a last line—see "Report," see "The Death of Edward Lear," see "Traumerei"—hits home.

Barthelme is a quintessential writer of the twentieth century, looking Janus-faced to both the past and future, and with a third eye turned inward. Yet he's also an anomaly. Nobody before him really reads much like him: neither Beckett or Nabokov, nor such minimalist realists as Hemingway, nor such fabulists as Kafka and Borges, nor such parodists and pasticheurs as Perelman and Firbank. Nor has he become any-body's particular Dead Father. Once in a while, George Saunders or Mark Leyner or Jim Shepherd will write something that reminds us of him. (Compare Saunders's "Pastoralia," in which faux cavepeople are trapped in a futuristic theme park, with Barthelme's "Game," whose characters are confined in the control room of a missile silo.) A few even newer jacks seem to have read him—or to have read people who've read him. The preemptively self-ironic title of Dave Eggers's *A Heartbreaking Work of Staggering Genius* sounds like Barthelme; so does the artfully broken English at the beginning of Jonathan Safran Foer's *Everything Is Illuminated*. But if there was ever a School of Barthelme, as there was a School of Carver, it's left scarcely a trace. He's too erudite, too intellectually nimble, and too many-minded. (That "doubleminded man" business is an undercount—in this book, by a factor of thirty.) An aspiring Barthelme imitator would first have to choose which Barthelme to imitate.

In "Not-Knowing," Barthelme wrote that art is "a true account of the activity of mind." These stories are reports of his expeditions into mapless worlds of language and thought, perception and memory, undertaken with no preconceptions about what he might tell us and how the reports might read—he had to go there first. Not stories of W doing X to Y with the result that Z, but stories of what goes on in a vast, various, and noisy consciousness, each story taking its unique shape from its creator's intuition of what the piece itself demands. Each one singing its own tune in its own voice. So: *Sixty Stories*. Just what the man said. It's not a modest title at all.

* * *

Personal sharing time:

1. I have not read all of Barthelme's work. And was introduced to it well after I should have known his work. As has become the pattern of my life, I was told about him because a friend recognized similarities between his work and mine. When I finally read him—starting with *Sixty Stories* and followed immediately by this book you're holding, about five years ago—I was astounded. And I felt like a thief. Or rather, that I was trodding on territory already better explored by D.B.

2. When rereading this book in the summer of 2004, I noticed more similarities, this time in stories I'd recently written, many years after first reading *Forty Stories*. Either he is my spiritual father or I am a crook.

3. I had a tough time reading this book this time around, because it's one of the few collections that inspires me to the degree that every sentence I read makes me want to stop and write something of my own. He fires all of my synapses and connects them in new ways. He sends a herd of wildebeest through my mind. It's a whole jungle full of animals, really, every color and shape, and he sends them scurrying all over my brain, screaming, defecating, fornicating.

4. That is the end of the Personal Sharing portion.

* * *

Now we will hear from Michael Silverblatt, noted and much-loved host of the syndicated American radio show *Bookworm*, and a former colleague of Donald Barthelme's. First we will ask Michael questions, then we will print his answers. Those questions:

How many people can safely eat gumbo at a table for four?
Funny you should ask. As it happens Don cooked gumbo at our house on Linwood Avenue in Buffalo. We provided the fixings; he brought The Secret Ingredient. The lack of fresh okra in Buffalo caused Don some real consternation, but we Northeasterners didn't know the difference. The Secret Ingredient worked its trick and ten people ate gumbo safely around a table for four. I don't know that this would have worked without Don. (A true story—how did you know to ask about gumbo?)

Did Donald Barthelme allow his students to call him Buck? (There are rumors to that effect.)
No one I knew ever called him Buck. This may have been a later development. I knew him well between 1971 and 1980, during those years people called him Don. Why would anyone call him Buck? I remember being too amazed to be in his presence to call him by any name at all. I remember that he never told people how to pronounce Barthelme, he would let them go on doing it the way they did the first time. I remember mumbling something or other until he told me to call him Don.

D.B's prose is gregarious. Was D.B. gregarious or was he one of those types who's funny in print but dour in person?
I'm not sure about gregarious. Don tended to vanish from parties; I remember we once searched for him in a car, sure that he would get lost one snowy taxiless night. He even disappeared at parties in his own apartment. Dour? He was a little stern, always noble, very funny—but the funny things he said were a little dour. He advised me several times that "we were put here on earth to love one another." I once heard him say, "You make my life a living hell," to a dear friend and she answered, right back, "You make my life a

living hell." I remember that this was said in the friendliest way, while Don fixed barbecued ribs for supper. He liked to cook.

Corporal punishment figures into much of D.B.'s work—not overtly, but implicitly—and I wonder if it figured into his classrooms, too?
Donald could be terrifying, but he never threatened me with corporal punishment. Sometimes he would suddenly toss out a phrase like "Me pap! Me pap!" and be utterly disappointed that I didn't know it came from "Endgame." (The pap in question was sugar pap, the "me" Beckett's Nagg.) It was a pop quiz.

How many feathers did D.B. wear in his headdress, and what did he name them?
I find this question unnerving. While I never saw the headdress in question, I do know that D.B. doctored a photograph of Henry James, providing James with a feather headdress of three feathers. I doubt they had names. This doctoring was titled *Chief Henry James* and turned up as a postcard sold in arty shops.

Did you ever meet D.B.'s father, and which of the fathers D.B. lists in "A Manual for Sons" do you suppose he was?
I never met his father, but I have spoken to one of the brothers, met two of the wives and one of the children. I can tell you that it is a remarkable family. Among writers, Don was a generous rouser of the clan, almost an activist. I think D.B. meant it when he said "Fathers are teachers of the true and not-true, and no father ever knowingly teaches what is not true. In a cloud of unknowing, then, the father proceeds with his instruction."

I can tell you this: as a teacher I never saw Don question the content of a story, only the language. And he edited word by word. He particularly dreaded conventional turns of phrase and predictable usages. Sometimes he would ask a class to vote for a better word to replace the shoddy one at hand. In other words Donald never changed a student writer's sense of truth (insofar as that concept applies to fiction), only the language in which it is dressed. In this he was singularly non-authoritarian (see question about corporal punishment above).

Tell us one of your favorite D.B. memories, in less than 150 words.
He seemed sad. A friend and I talked about getting him a dog. We gave him a collection of some of our favorite objects and he arranged them into an altar; he really did like making collage. We all began making altars, kept in the corner of the room, or on a shelf. I had a Donald altar. Once, to cheer him up, we got him to sing. (For the curious: he sang "Marching Down Broadway" from Nillson's *Harry* album—this album also had the song "City Life" which became the title of his best story collection.)

My favorite moment was going out with him visiting artists' studios, looking at new work. One of the most thrilling things he taught me was how to look at art in the presence of the artist. He was very well regarded, partly because his comments were so roundabout. I remember he told one painter that the signature at the corner of his canvas was too large. I was with him when he asked the minimalist-formalist composer Morton Feldman if he led an orderly life, and asked Feldman for more messiness in his compositions.

Now tell us another, in 75 words.

Do you agree with this introduction's assertion that if D.B. were to burst onto the scene today, that he would have a hard time finding a publisher, and could certainly not expect to appear so often in mainstream venues? (Our assertion here is that readers/critics no longer have patience for the intersection of stylistic eccentricity and meaning, that whimsy of any kind, digressiveness of any kind, is seen to indicate a lack of seriousness.)

Oh, I don't know. Of course I agree that magnificent innovation is not in abundance right now. But that's because a lot of what passes for innovativeness is rehashed Barthelme. As he wrote, about a similar circumstance (the death of postmodernism), "who can make the leap to greatness while dragging behind him the burnt-out boxcars of a dead aesthetic?" Donald's sentences went about as far as you can go hooking Hemingway declaration (a sentence which had been the previous most-imitated style in America) to dreams, nonsense, surrealism. We don't need another Donald. We need a better life.

What color were his eyes?
Brown.

Did he carry a ladder?
No

Did he eat animals?
Yes.

Did he laugh like a cheetah?
Often, or like dry leaves rustling.

*   *   *

That is the end of this introduction. The preparers hope it provided insight, but are keenly aware that it did not. This is the best book you will read this year, so please begin.

Forty Stories

CHABLIS

My wife wants a dog. She already has a baby. The baby's almost two. My wife says that the baby wants the dog.

My wife has been wanting a dog for a long time. I have had to be the one to tell her that she couldn't have it. But now the baby wants a dog, my wife says. This may be true. The baby is very close to my wife. They go around together all the time, clutching each other tightly. I ask the baby, who is a girl, "Whose girl are you? Are you Daddy's girl?" The baby says, "Momma," and she doesn't just say it once, she says it repeatedly, "Momma momma momma." I don't see why I should buy a hundred-dollar dog for that damn baby.

The kind of dog the baby wants, my wife says, is a Cairn terrier. This kind of dog, my wife says, is a Presbyterian like herself and the baby. Last year the baby was a Baptist—that is, she went to the Mother's Day Out program at the First Baptist twice a week. This year she is a Presbyterian because the Presbyterians have more swings and slides and things. I think that's pretty shameless and I have said so. My wife is a legitimate lifelong Presbyterian and says that makes it O.K.; way back when she was a child she used to go to the First Presbyterian in Evansville, Illinois. I didn't go to church because I was a black sheep. There were five children in my family and the males rotated the position of black sheep among us, the oldest one being the black sheep for a while while he was in his DWI period or whatever and then getting grayer as he maybe got a job or was in the service and then finally becoming a white sheep when he got married and had a grandchild. My sister was never a black sheep because she was a girl.

Our baby is a pretty fine baby. I told my wife for many years that she couldn't have a baby because it was too expensive. But they wear you down. They are just wonderful at wearing you down, even if it takes years, as it did in this case. Now I hang around the baby and hug her every chance I get. Her name is Joanna. She wears Oshkosh overalls and says "no," "bottle," "out," and "Momma." She looks most lovable when she's wet, when she's just had a bath and her blond hair is all wet and she's wrapped in a beige towel. Sometimes when she's watching television she forgets that you're there. You can just look at her. When she's watching television, she looks dumb. I like her better when she's wet.

This dog thing is getting to be a big issue. I said to my wife, "Well you've got the baby, do we have to have the damned dog too?" The dog will probably bite somebody, or get lost. I can see myself walking all over our subdivision asking people, "Have you seen this brown dog?" "What's its name?" they'll say to me, and I'll stare at them coldly and say, "Michael." That's what she wants to call it, Michael. That's a silly name for a dog and I'll have to go looking for this possibly rabid animal and say to people, "Have you seen this brown dog? Michael?" It's enough to make you think about divorce.

What's that baby going to do with that dog that it can't do with me? Romp? I can romp. I took her to the playground at the school. It was Sunday and there was nobody there, and we romped. I ran, and she tottered after me at a good pace. I held her as she slid down the slide. She groped her way through a length of big pipe they have there set in concrete. She picked up a feather and looked at it for a long time. I was worried that it might be a diseased feather but she didn't put it in her mouth. Then we ran some more over the parched bare softball field and through the arcade that connects the temporary wooden classrooms, which are losing their yellow paint, to the main building. Joanna will go to this school some day, if I stay in the same job.

I looked at some dogs at Pets-A-Plenty, which has birds, rodents, reptiles, and dogs, all in top condition. They showed me the Cairn terriers. "Do they have their prayer books?" I asked. This woman clerk didn't know what I was talking about. The Cairn terriers ran about two ninety-five per, with their papers. I started to ask if they had any illegitimate children at lower prices but I could see that it would be useless and the woman already didn't like me, I could tell.

What is wrong with me? Why am I not a more natural person, like my wife wants me to be? I sit up, in the early morning, at my desk on the second floor of our house. The desk faces the street. At five-thirty in the morning, the runners are already out, individually or in pairs, running toward rude red health. I'm sipping a glass of Gallo Chablis with an ice cube in it, smoking, worrying. I worry that the baby may jam a kitchen knife into an electrical outlet while she's wet. I've put those little plastic plugs into all the electrical outlets but she's learned how to pop them out. I've checked the Crayolas. They've made the Crayolas safe to eat—I called the head office in Pennsylvania. She can eat a whole box of Crayolas and nothing will happen to her. If I don't get the new tires for the car I can buy the dog.

I remember the time, thirty years ago, when I put Herman's mother's Buick into a cornfield, on the Beaumont highway. There was another car in my lane, and I didn't hit it, and it didn't hit me. I remember veering to the right and down into the ditch and up through the fence and coming to rest in the cornfield and then getting out to wake Herman and the two of us going to see what the happy drunks in the other car had come to, in the ditch on the other side of the road. That was when I was a black sheep, years and years ago. That was skillfully done, I think. I get up, congratulate myself in memory, and go in to look at the baby.

ON THE DECK

THERE is a lion on the deck of the boat. The lion looks tired, fatigued. Waves the color of graphite. A grid placed before the lion, quartering him, each quarter subdivided into sixteen squares, total of sixty-four squares through which lion parts may be seen. The lion a dirty yellow-brown against the gray waves.

Next to but not touching the lion, members of a Christian motorcycle gang (the gang is called Banditos for Jesus and has nineteen members but only three are on the deck of the boat) wearing their colors which differ from the colors of other gangs in that the badges, insignia, and so on have Christian messages, "Jesus is LORD" and the like. The bikers are thick-shouldered, gold earrings, chains, beards, red bandannas, a sweetness expressed in the tilt of their bodies toward the little girl wearing shiny steel leg braces who stands among them and smiles—they have chosen her as their "old lady" and are collecting money for her education.

To the right of the Christian bikers and a bit closer to the coils of razor wire forward of the lion is a parked Camry (in profile) covered with a tarp and tied down with bright new rope, blocks under the wheels, the lower half of its price sticker visible on the window not completely covered by canvas. The motor is running, exhaust from the twin tailpipes touching the thirty-five burlap-wrapped bales stacked at the back of the car. There is someone inside the car, behind the wheel. This person is named Mitch. The exhaust from the car irritates the lion, whose head rolls from side to side, yellow teeth bared.

In front of the tied-down red Camry, a man with a nosebleed holding a steel basin under his chin. The basin is full of brown blood, brown-stained blooms of gauze. He holds the basin with one hand and clutches his nose with the other. His blue-and-red-striped shirt is bloody. "Hello," he says, "hello, hello!" Gray institutional pants and brown shoes. There's a tree, an eight-foot western fir, in a heavy terra-cotta pot between his legs. He appears to be trying to avoid bleeding on the tree. "They don't have anything I want," he says. A basketball wedged between the upper branches on the left side. Immediately to the left and forward of the fir tree, a yellow fifty-five-gallon drum labeled in black letters PRISMATEX, a hose coiled on top of it; bending over the PRISMATEX, her back turned, a young woman with black hair in a thin thin yellow dress. Concentrate on the hams.

The tilting of the deck increases; spray. The captain, a red-faced man in a blue blazer, sits in an armchair before the young woman, a can of beer in his right hand. He says: "I would have done better work if I'd had some kind of encouragement. I've met a lot of people in my life. I let my feelings carry me along." At the captain's knee is the captain's dog, a black-and-white Scottie. The dog is afraid of the lion, keeps looking back over his shoulder at the lion. The captain kisses the hem of the young woman's yellow dress. There's a rolled Oriental rug bound with twine in front of the Scottie, and in front of that a child's high chair with a peacock sitting in it, next to that a Harley leaning on its kickstand (HONK IF YOU LOVE JESUS in script on the gas tank). The owner of the boat, sister of the woman in the yellow dress, is squatting by the Harley cooking hot dogs on a hibachi, a plastic bag of buns by her right foot. A boyfriend lies next to her, playing with the bottom edge of her yellow shorts. "Sometimes she's prim," he says. "Don't know when you wake up in the morning what you're going to get. I'm really not interested just now. At some point you get into it pretty far, then it becomes frightening."

"A smooth flight isn't totally dependent on the pilot," says the next man. There's a bucket of raw liver between his knees, liver for the lion, he's up to his elbows in liver. Next, a shuffleboard court and two men shoving the brightly colored disks this way and that with old battered M-1 rifles. "I put two forty-pound sacks of cat food in the bed and covered them neatly with a blanket but she still didn't get the message." Further along, a marble bust of Hadrian on a bamboo plant stand, Hadrian's marble curls curling to meet Hadrian's marble beard, next to that someone delivering the mail, a little canvas pushcart containing mail pushed in front of her, blue uniform, two shades of blue, red hair. "Everyone likes mail, except those who are afraid of it." Everyone gets mail. The captain gets mail, the Christian bikers get mail, Liverman gets mail, the woman in the scandal-dress gets mail. Many copies of *Smithsonian*. A man sitting in a red wicker chair.

Winter on deck. All of the above covered with snow. Christmas music.

Then, spring. A weak sun, then a stronger sun.

You came and fell upon me, I was sitting in the wicker chair. The wicker exclaimed as your weight fell upon me. You were light, I thought, and I thought how good it was of you to do this. We'd never touched before.

THE GENIUS

His assistants cluster about him. He is severe with them, demanding, punctilious, but this is for their own ultimate benefit. He devises hideously difficult problems, or complicates their work with sudden oblique comments that open whole new areas of investigation—yawning chasms under their feet. It is as if he wishes to place them in situations where only failure is possible. But failure, too, is a part of mental life. "I will make you failure-proof," he says jokingly. His assistants pale.

Is it true, as Valéry said, that every man of genius contains within himself a false man of genius?

"This is an age of personal ignorance. No one knows what others know. No one knows enough."

The genius is afraid to fly. The giant aircraft seem to him . . . flimsy. He hates the takeoff and he hates the landing and he detests being in the air. He hates the food, the stewardesses, the voice of the captain, and his fellow passengers, especially those who are conspicuously at ease, who remove their coats, loosen their ties, and move up and down the aisles with drinks in their hands. In consequence, he rarely travels. The world comes to him.

Q: What do you consider the most important tool of the genius of today?
A: Rubber cement.

He has urged that America be divided into four smaller countries. America, he says, is too big. "America does not look where it puts its foot," he says. This comment, which, coming from anyone else, would have engendered widespread indignation, is greeted with amused chuckles. The Chamber of Commerce sends him four cases of Teacher's Highland Cream..

The genius defines "inappropriate response":
"Suppose my friend telephones and asks, 'Is my wife there?' 'No,' I reply, 'they went out, your wife and my wife, wearing new hats, they are giving themselves to sailors.' My friend is astounded at this news. 'But it's Election Day!' he cries. 'And it's beginning to rain!' I say."

The genius pays close attention to work being done in fields other than his own. He is well read in all of the sciences (with the exception of the social sciences); he follows the arts with a connoisseur's acuteness; he is an accomplished amateur musician. He jogs. He dislikes chess. He was once photographed playing tennis with the Marx Brothers.

He has devoted considerable thought to an attempt to define the sources of his genius. However, this attempt has led approximately nowhere. The mystery remains a mystery. He has therefore settled upon the following formula, which he repeats each time he is interviewed: "Historical forces."

The government has decided to award the genius a few new medals—medals he has not been previously awarded. One medal is awarded for his work prior to 1956, one for his work from 1956 to the present, and one for his future work.

"I think that this thing, my work, has made me, in a sense, what I am. The work possesses a consciousness which shapes that of the worker. The work flatters the worker. Only the strongest worker can do this work, the work says. You must be a fine fellow, that you can do this work. But disaffection is also possible. The worker grows careless. The worker pays slight regard to the work, he ignores the work, he is *unfaithful* to the work. The work is insulted. And perhaps it finds little ways of telling the worker. . . . The work slips in the hands of the worker—a little cut on the finger. You understand? The work becomes slow, sulky, consumes more time, becomes more tiring. The gaiety that once existed between the worker and the work has evaporated. A fine situation! Don't you think?"

The genius has noticed that he does not interact with children successfully. (Anecdote)

Richness of the inner life of the genius:
(1) Manic-oceanic states
(2) Hatred of children
(3) Piano playing
(4) Subincised genitals
(5) Subscription to *Harper's Bazaar*
(6) Stamp collection

The genius receives a very flattering letter from the University of Minnesota. The university wishes to become the depository of his papers, after he is dead. A new wing of the Library will be built to house them.

The letter makes the genius angry. He takes a pair of scissors, cuts the letter into long thin strips, and mails it back to the Director of Libraries.

He takes long walks through the city streets, noting architectural details—particularly old ironwork. His mind is filled with ideas for a new— But at this moment a policeman approaches him. "Beg pardon, sir. Aren't you—" "Yes," the genius says, smiling. "My little boy is an admirer of yours," the policeman says. He pulls out a pocket notebook. "If it's not too much trouble . . ." Smiling, the genius signs his name.

The genius carries his most important papers about with him in a green Sears toolbox.

He did not win the Nobel Prize again this year.

It was neither the year of his country nor the year of his discipline. To console him, the National Foundation gives him a new house.

The genius meets with a group of students. The students tell the genius that the concept "genius" is not, currently, a popular one. Group effort, they say, is more socially productive than the isolated efforts of any one man, however gifted. Genius by its very nature sets itself over against the needs of the many. In answering its own imperatives, genius tends toward, even embraces, totalitarian forms of social organization. Tyranny of the gifted over the group, while bringing some advances in the short run, inevitably produces a set of conditions which—

The genius smokes thoughtfully.

A giant brown pantechnicon disgorges the complete works of the Venerable Bede, in all translations, upon the genius's lawn—a gift from the people of Cincinnati!

Q: Is America a good place for genius?
A: I have found America most hospitable to genius.

"I always say to myself, 'What is the most important thing I can be thinking about at this minute?' But then I don't think about it."

His driver's license expires. But he does nothing about renewing it. He is vaguely troubled by the thought of the expired license (although he does not stop driving). But he loathes the idea of taking the examination again, of going physically to the examining station, of waiting in line for an examiner. He decides that if he writes a letter to the License Bureau requesting a new license, the bureau will grant him one without an examination, because he is a genius. He is right. He writes the letter and the License Bureau sends him a new license, by messenger.

In the serenity of his genius, the genius reaches out to right wrongs—the sewer systems of cities, for example.

The genius is reading *The Genius,* a 736-page novel by Theodore Dreiser. He arrives at the last page:

> ". . . What a sweet welter life is—how rich, how tender, how grim, how like a colorful symphony."
>   Great art dreams welled up into his soul as he viewed the sparkling deeps of space. . . .

The genius gets up and looks at himself in a mirror.

An organization has been formed to appreciate his thought: the Blaufox Gesellschaft. Meetings are held once a month, in a room over a cafeteria in Buffalo, New York. He has always refused to have anything to do with the Gesellschaft, which reminds him uncomfortably of the Browning Society. However, he cannot prevent himself from glancing at the group's twice-yearly *Proceedings,* which contains such sentences as "The imbuement of all reaches of the scholarly community with Blaufox's views must, *ab ovo,* be our . . ."
He falls into hysteria.

Moments of self-doubt . . .
"Am I really a—"
"What does it *mean* to be a—"
"Can one *refuse* to be a—"

His worst moment: He is in a church, kneeling in a pew near the back. He is gradually made aware of a row of nuns, a half-dozen, kneeling twenty feet ahead of him, their heads bent over their beads. One of the nuns however has turned her head almost completely around, and seems to be staring at him. The genius glances at her, glances away, then looks again: she is still staring at him. The genius is only visiting the church in the first place because the nave is said to be a particularly fine example of Burgundian Gothic. He places his eyes here, there, on the altar, on the stained glass, but each time they return to the nuns, *his* nun is still staring. The genius says to himself, *This is my worst moment.*

He is a drunk.

"A truly potent abstract concept avoids, resists closure. The ragged, blurred outlines of such a concept, like a net in which the fish have eaten large, gaping holes, permit entry and escape equally. What does one catch in such a net? The sea horse with a Monet in his mouth. How did the Monet get there? Is the value of the Monet less because it has gotten wet? Are there tooth marks in the Monet? Do sea horses have teeth? How large is the Monet? From which period? Is it a water lily or group of water lilies? Do sea horses eat water lilies? Does Parke-Bernet know? Do oil and water mix? Is a mixture of oil and water bad for the digestion of the sea horse? Should art be expensive? Should artists wear beards? Ought beards to be forbidden by law? Is underwater art better than overwater art? What does the expression 'glad rags' mean? Does it refer to Monet's paint rags? In the Paris of 1878, what was the average monthly rent for a north-lit, spacious studio in an unfashionable district? If sea horses eat water lilies, what percent of their daily work energy, expressed in ergs, is generated thereby? Should the holes in the net be mended? In a fight between a sea horse and a flittermouse, which would you bet on? If I mend the net, will you forgive me? Do water rats chew upon the water lilies? Is there a water buffalo in the water cooler? If I fill my water gun to the waterline, can I then visit the watering place? Is fantasy an adequate substitute for correct behavior?"

The genius proposes a world inventory of genius, in order to harness and coordinate the efforts of genius everywhere to create a better life for all men.

Letters are sent out . . .

The response is staggering!

Telegrams pour in . . .

Geniuses of every stripe offer their cooperation.

The *Times* prints an editorial praising the idea . . .

Three thousand geniuses in one hall!

The genius falls into an ill humor. He refuses to speak to anyone for eight days.

But now a brown UPS truck arrives at his door. It contains a ceremonial sword (with inscription) forged in Toledo, courtesy of the Mayor and City Council of Toledo, Spain. The genius whips the blade about in the midmorning air, signing the receipt with his other hand. . . .

OPENING

THE actors feel that the music played before the curtain rises will put the audience in the wrong mood. The playwright suggests that the (purposefully lugubrious) music be played at twice-speed. This peps it up somewhat while retaining its essentially dark and gloomy character. The actors listen carefully, and are pleased.

The director, in white overalls and a blue work shirt, whispers to the actors. The director is tender with the actors, like a good father, calms them, solicits their opinions, gives them aspirin. The playwright regards the actors with the greatest respect. How sweetly they speak! They have discovered meanings in his lines far beyond anything he had imagined possible.

ARDIS: But it's always that way, always.
PAUL: Not necessarily, dear friend. Not necessarily.

The rug on the set was done by a famous weaver, indeed is a modern classic, and costs four thousand dollars. It has been lent to the production (for program credit) as has the chrome-and-leather sofa. No one steps on the rug (or sits on the sofa) oftener than necessary.

The playwright studies the empty set for many hours. Should

the (huge, magnificent) plant be moved a few inches to the left? The actors are already joking about being upstaged by the plant. The actors are gentle, amusing people, but also very tough, and physically strong. Many of their jokes involve scraps of dialogue from the script, which become catchphrases of general utility: "Not necessarily, dear friend. Not necessarily."

In the rehearsal room the costume designer spreads out his sketches over a long table. The actors crowd around to see how they will look in the first act, in the second act. The designs sparkle, there is no other word for it. Also, the costume designer is within the budget, whereas the set designer was eighteen thousand over and the set had to be redesigned, painfully.

An actor whispers to the playwright. "A playwright," he says, "is a man who has decided that the purpose of human life is to describe human life. Don't you find that odd?" The playwright, who has never thought about his vocation in quite this way, does find it odd. He worries about it all day.

The playwright loves the theatre when it is empty. When it has people in it he does not love it so much; the audience is a danger to his play (although it's only sometimes he feels this). In the empty theatre, as in a greenhouse, his play grows, thrives. Rehearsals, although tedious in the extreme and often disheartening—an actor can lose today something he had yesterday—are an intelligent process charged with hope.

The actors tell stories about other shows they've been in, mostly concerning moments of disaster onstage. "When I did *Charity* in London—" In the men's dressing room, one of the actors tells a long story about a female colleague whose hair caught fire during a production of *Saint Joan*. "I poured Tab on it," he says. Photographs are taken for the newspapers. The playwright goes alone for lunch to a Chinese restaurant which has a bar. He is the only one in the group who drinks at lunchtime. The temperate, good-natured actors vote in all elections and vehemently support a nuclear freeze.

> PAUL: You've got to . . . transcend . . . the circumstances.
> Know what I mean?

REGINA: Easier said than done, boyo.

The playwright makes a shocking discovery. One of his best exchanges—

ARDIS: The moon is beautiful now.
PAUL: You should have seen it before the war.

—freighted with the sadness of unrecapturable time, is also to be found, almost word for word, in Oscar Wilde's *Impressions of America*. How did this happen? Has he written these lines, or has he remembered them? He honestly cannot say. In a fit of rectitude, he cuts the lines.

The producer slips into a seat in the back of the house and watches a scene. Then he says, "I love this material. I *love* it." The playwright asks that the costume worn by one of the actresses in the second act be changed. It makes her look too little-girlish, he feels. The costume designer disagrees but does not press the point. *Now my actress looks more beautiful*, the playwright thinks.

The opening is at hand. The actors bring the playwright small, thoughtful gifts: a crock of imported mustard, a finely printed edition of Ovid's *Art of Love*. The playwright gives the actors, men and women, little cloth sacks containing gold-wrapped chocolates.

The notices are good, very good.

LIGHTS UP THE SKY OVER
OFF-BROADWAY AND STIMULATES
MEN'S MINDS
—Cue

The actors are praised, warmly and with discrimination. People attend the play in encouraging numbers. At intermission the lobby is filled with well-dressed, enthusiastic people, discussing the play. The producer, that large, anxious man, steams with enthusiasm. The critics, he tells the playwright, are unreliable. But sometimes one has good fortune. The play, he tells the playwright, will remain forever in the history of the theatre.

After the show closes, the director purchases the big, spiky plant that appeared, burning with presence, throughout the second act. The actors, picking up their gear, pause to watch the plant being loaded onto a truck. "Think he can teach it to go to the corner for coffee and a Danish?" "Easier said than done, boyo."

In his study, the playwright begins his next play, which will explore the relationship between St. Augustine and a Carthaginian girl named Luna and the broken bones of the heart.

SINDBAD

THE BEACH: Sindbad, drowned animal, clutches at the sand of still another island shore.

His right hand, marvelous upon the pianoforte, opens and closes. His hide is roasted red, his beard white with crusted salt. The broken beam to which he clung to escape his shattered vessel lies nearby.

He hears waltzes from the trees.

He should, of course, rouse himself, get to his feet, gather tree fruits, locate a spring, build a signal fire, or find a stream that will carry him toward the interior of this strange new place, where he will encounter a terrifying ogre of some sort, outwit him, and then take possession of the rubies and diamonds, big as baseballs, which litter the ogre's domains, wonderfully.

Stir your stumps, sir.

Classroom: It's true that the students asked me to leave. I had never taught in the daytime before, how was I to know how things were done in the daytime?

I guess they didn't like my looks. I was wearing shades (my eyes unused to so much light) and a jacket that was, admittedly, too big for me. I was rather prominently placed toward the front of the room, *in* the front of the room to be precise, sitting on the desk that faced their desks, fidgeting.

"Would you just, please, leave?" the students said.

The chair had asked me, "How'd you like to teach in the daytime? Just this once?" I said that I could not imagine such a thing but that I would do my very best. "Don't get carried away, Robert," she said, "it's only one course, we've got too many people on leave and now this damnable flu . . ." I said I would prepare myself carefully and buy a new shirt. "That's a good idea," she said, looking closely at my shirt, which had been given to me by my younger brother, the lawyer. He was throwing out shirts.

Sindbad's wives look back: "I knew him, didn't you know that I knew him?"

"I didn't think that a person such as you could have known him."

"Intimately. That's how well I knew him. I was his ninth wife."

"Well of course you were more in the prime of life then. It was more reasonable to expect something."

"He treated me well, on the whole. In the years of our intimacy. Many gowns of great costliness."

"You'd never know it to look at you. I mean now."

"Well I have other things besides these things. I don't wear my better things all the time. Besides gowns, he gave me frocks. Shoes of beaten lizard."

"Maybe jewels?"

"Rubies and diamonds big as baseballs. I seem to remember a jeweled horsewhip. To whip my horses with. I rode, in the early mornings, on the cliffs, the cliffs overlooking the sea."

"You had a sea."

"Yes, there was a sea, adjacent to the property. He was fond of the sea."

"He must have been very well-off then. When I knew him he was just a merchant. A small merchant."

"Yes, he'd begun as a poor person, tried that for a while, didn't like it, and then ventured forth. Upon the sea."

The Beaux-Arts Ball: At the Beaux-Arts Ball given by the Art and Architecture Departments I saw a young woman wearing what appeared to be men's cotton underwear. The undershirt was sleeveless and the briefs, cut very high on the sides, had the designer's name ("EGIZIO") in half-inch red letters stitched around the waist-band.

"Who are you?" I asked.

She raised her hands, which were encased in red rubber gloves. "Lady Macbeth," she said. Then she asked me to leave.

So I went out into the parking lot carrying my costume, a brightly polished English horn. If anyone had asked me who I was I had intended saying I was one of Robin Hood's merry men. One of the students followed me, wanted to know if I had a wife. I answered honestly that I did not, and told her that if you taught at night you weren't allowed to have a wife. It was a sort of unwritten law, understood by all. "You're not allowed to have a wife and you're not allowed to have a car," I told her honestly.

"Then what are you doing in this parking lot?" she asked. I showed her my old blue bicycle, parked between a Camaro and a Trans Am. "Do you have a house?" she asked, and I said that I had a room somewhere, with a radio in it and one of those little re-frigerators that sit upon a table.

Sindbad's first emporium in Baghdad: When we opened Sindbad's we did not anticipate the good results we obtained almost imme-diately.

The people leaped over the counters and wrested the goods from our hands and from the shelves behind the counters.

Stock boys ran back and forth between the stockrooms and the counters. We had developed patterns of running back and forth so that Stock Boy A did not collide with Stock Boy B. Some warped, some woofed.

We had always wanted a store and had as children played "store" with tiny cedar boxes replicating real goods. Now we had an actual store, pearl-colored with accents of saturated jade.

Every day, people leaped over the counters and wrested goods from the hands of our brave, durable clerks. Our store was glorious, glorious. The simple finest of everything, that was what we pur-veyed. Often people had been wandering around for years trying to find the finest, lost, uncertain. Then they walked through our great bronze doors resonant with humming filigree. There it was, the finest.

Even humble items were the finest of their kind. Our straight pin was straighter than any other straight pin ever offered, and pinned better, too.

Once, a little girl came into the store, alone. She had only a few gold coins, and we took them from her, and made her happy. We had never, in our entire careers as merchants, seen a happier little girl as she left the store, carrying in her arms the particular goods she had purchased with her few, but real, gold coins.

Once, a tall man came into the store, tall but bent, arthritis, he was bent half-double, but you could tell that he was tall, or had been tall before he became bent, three or four lines of physical suffering on his forehead. He asked for food. We furnished him with foodstuffs from Taillevent in Paris, the finest, and not a centime did we charge him. Because he was bent.

In our pearl-colored store we had a pearl beyond price, a tulip bulb beyond price, and a beautiful slave girl beyond price. These were displayed behind heavy glass set in the walls. No offer for these items was ever accepted. They were beyond price. Idealism ruled us in these matters.

The students: "Would you please leave now?" they asked. "Would you please just leave?"

Then they all started talking to each other, they turned in their seats and began talking to each other, the air grew loud, it was rather like a cocktail party except that everybody was sitting down, the door opened and a waiter came in with drinks on a tray followed by another waiter with water chestnuts wrapped in bacon on a tray and another waiter with more drinks. It was exactly like a cocktail party except that everybody was sitting down. So I took a drink from a tray and joined one of the groups and tried to understand what they were saying.

Tennis: Yes, he could do this sort of thing all day. Something he can go home and talk about (assuming that he gets back to Baghdad alive), how he played tennis with two ogres tall as houses and brought them to their knees. Each ogre has a single red eye in the middle of his forehead and a single wire-rimmed lens framing the eye. He can sucker the one on the left out of position merely by glancing at the one on the right before he serves, and anything placed to the left of the one on the right is invariably missed, the one on the right has no backhand whatsoever. So how-he-played-tennis-with-two-ogres will be added to the repertoire, two female ogres following the game intently, their two staring eyes with the single tinted lenses turning right, left, right, left, the sun bursting off the lenses like the beams of two lighthouses. . . .

At night: At night, the Department's offices are empty. The cleaning women make their telephone calls, in Spanish, from Professor This's office, from Professor That's office, taking care of business. The parking lots are infernos of yellow light.

Sitting one night on the steps of the power plant I saw a man carrying a typewriter, an IBM Selectric III. I judged him to be one of those people who stole typewriters from the university at night. "Can you type?" I asked him. He said, "Shit, man, don't be a fool." I asked him why he stole typewriters and he said, "Them mothers ain't got nothin' else worth stealin'." I was going to suggest that he return the typewriter, when another man came out of the darkness carrying another typewriter. "This mother's *heavy*," he said to the first, and they went off together, cursing. An IBM Selectric III weighs approximately forty pounds.

The students, no doubt, whispered about me:

"I heard this is the first time he's taught in the daytime."

"They wouldn't *let* that sucker teach in sunlight 'cept that all the real teachers are dead."

"Did you get a shot of that coat? Tack-eeee."

I stood in the corridor gazing at them from behind my shades. What a good-looking group! I thought. In the presto of the morning, as Stevens puts it.

Experience: Sindbad learns nothing from experience.

A prudent man, after the first, second, third, fourth, fifth, sixth, and seventh voyages, would never again set foot on a ship's deck. Every vessel upon which he has ever embarked has either headed for the bottom not two days out of port or marooned him, has been stove in by a gigantic whale (first voyage), seduced into distraction by jubilant creatures of the air (second voyage), stolen by apelike savages no more than three feet high (third voyage), crushed by a furious squall (fourth voyage), bombed from the air by huge birds carrying huge rocks (fifth voyage), or dashed against a craggy shore (sixth voyage) by the never-sleeping winds.

But there is always a sturdy (wooden trough, floating beam, stray piece of wreckage from the doomed vessel) to cling to, and an island (garnished with rubies and diamonds, large quantities of priceless pearls, bales of the choicest ambergris) to pillage. Sindbad never fails to return to Baghdad richer than before, with many sumptuous presents for the friends and relatives who gather at his house to hear the news of his latest heroic impertinence.

Sindbad is not a prudent but a daring man. In *Who's Who at Sea* he is listed, disapprovingly, as an "adventurer."

Water cannon: The graduates don't wish to leave the campus. We'll have to blast them out. I say "we" because I identify with the administration although no member of the administration has asked my opinion on the matter. I think water cannon are the means of choice. I have never seen a water cannon except in TV news reports from East Germany but it seems to be an effective and relatively humane means of blasting people out of there. I wouldn't mind having a water cannon of my own. There are certain people I wouldn't mind blasting.

The grounds crew was standing at the edge of the field, waiting to fold the folding chairs. The band was putting away its instruments. The graduates must have had some boards stashed away among the trees. They began building lean-tos, many of them leaned against the Science Building, some against the Student Center. Cooking fires were lit, the graduates squatted around the cooking fires, roasting corn on spits. Totem poles were erected before the lean-tos. The provost went to the microphone. "Time to go, time to go," he said. The graduates refused to leave.

Waltzes: Sindbad gets to his feet, shakes himself, and heads toward the tree line. Waltzes? The music is exotic to him, he has never heard such music before. He congratulates himself that on his eighth voyage the world can still reward him with new enchantments.

Teaching: I reentered the classroom and fixed them with my fiercest glare. I began to teach. They had to put down their drinks and shrimp on toothpicks and listen.

It was true, I said, that I had never taught in the daytime before, and that my refrigerator was small and my jacket far, far too baggy.

Nonetheless, I said, I have something to teach. Be like Sindbad! Venture forth! Embosom the waves, let your shoes be sucked from your feet and your very trousers enticed by the frothing deep. The ambiguous sea awaits, I told them, marry it!

There's nothing out there, they said.

Wrong, I said, absolutely wrong. There are waltzes, sword canes, and sea wrack dazzling to the eyes.

What's a sword cane? they asked, and with relief I plunged into the Romantics.

THE EXPLANATION

Q: Do you believe that this machine could be helpful in changing the government?

A: Changing the government . . .

Q: Making it more responsive to the needs of the people?

A: I don't know what it is. What does it do?

Q: Well, look at it.

A: It offers no clues.
Q: It has a certain . . . reticence.
A: I don't know what it does.
Q: A lack of confidence in the machine?

Q: Is the novel dead?
A: Oh yes. Very much so.
Q: What replaces it?
A: I should think that it is replaced by what existed before it was invented.
Q: The same thing?
A: The same sort of thing.
Q: Is the bicycle dead?

Q: You don't trust the machine?
A: Why should I trust it?
Q: (States his own lack of interest in machines)

Q: What a beautiful sweater.
A: Thank you. I don't want to worry about machines.

Q: What do you worry about?

A: I was standing on the corner waiting for the light to change when I noticed, across the street among the people there waiting for the light to change, an extraordinarily handsome girl who was looking at me. Our eyes met, I looked away, then I looked again, she was looking away, the light changed. I moved into the street as did she. First I looked at her again to see if she was still looking at me, she wasn't but I was aware that she was aware of me. I decided to smile. I smiled but in a curious way—the smile was supposed to convey that I was interested in her but also that I was aware that the situation was funny. But I bungled it. I smirked. I dislike even the word "smirk." There was, you know, the moment when we passed each other. I had resolved to look at her directly in that moment. I tried but she was looking a bit to the left of me, she was looking fourteen inches to the left of my eyes.

Q: This is the sort of thing that—

A: I want to go back and do it again.

Q: Now that you've studied it for a bit, can you explain how it works?

A: Of course. (Explanation)

Q: Is she still removing her blouse?

A: Yes, still.

Q: Do you want to have your picture taken with me?

A: I don't like to have my picture taken.

Q: Do you believe that, at some point in the future, one will be able to achieve sexual satisfaction, "complete" sexual satisfaction, for instance by taking a pill?

A: I doubt that it's impossible.

Q: You don't like the idea.

A: No. I think that under those conditions, we would know less than we do now.

Q: Know less about each other.

A: Of course.

Q: It has beauties.

A: The machine.

Q: Yes. We construct these machines not because we confidently expect them to do what they are designed to do—change the government in this instance—but because we intuit a machine, out there, glowing like a shopping center. . . .

A: You have to contend with a history of success.

Q: ˙Which has gotten us nowhere.

A: (Extends consolation)

Q: What did you do then?

A: I walked on a tree. For twenty steps.

Q: What sort of tree?

A: A dead tree. I can't tell one from another. It may have been an oak. I was reading a book.

Q: What was the book?

A: I don't know, I can't tell one from another. They're not like films. With films you can remember, at a minimum, who the actors were. . . .

Q: What was she doing?

A: Removing her blouse. Eating an apple.

Q: The tree must have been quite large.

A: The tree must have been quite large.

Q: Where was this?

A: Near the sea. I had rope-soled shoes.

Q: I have a number of error messages I'd like to introduce here and I'd like you to study them carefully . . . they're numbered. I'll go over them with you: undefined variable . . . improper sequence of operators . . . improper use of hierarchy . . . missing operator . . . mixed mode, that one's particularly grave . . . argument of a function is fixed-point . . . improper character in constant . . . improper fixed-point constant . . . improper floating-point constant . . . invalid character transmitted in sub-program statement, that's a bitch . . . no END statement.

A: I like them very much.

Q: There are hundred of others, hundreds and hundreds.

A: You seem emotionless.

Q: That's not true.

A: To what do your emotions . . . adhere, if I can put it that way?

Q: Do you see what she's doing?

A: Removing her blouse.

Q: How does she look?

A: . . . Self-absorbed.

Q: Are you bored with the question-and-answer form?

A: I am bored with it but I realize that it permits many valuable omissions: what kind of day it is, what I'm wearing, what I'm thinking. That's a very considerable advantage, I would say.

Q: I believe in it.

Q: She sang and we listened to her.

A: I was speaking to a tourist.

Q: Their chair is here.

A: I knocked at the door; it was shut.

Q: The soldiers marched toward the castle.

A: I had a watch.

Q: He has struck me.

A: I have struck him.

Q: Their chair is here.

A: We shall not cross the river.

Q: The boats are filled with water.

A: His father will strike him.

Q: Filling his pockets with fruit.

Q: The face . . . the machine has a face. This panel here . . .

A: That one?

Q: Just as the human face developed . . . from fish . . . it's traceable, from, say, the . . . The first mouth was that of a jellyfish. I can't remember the name, the Latin name. . . . But a mouth, there's more to it than just a mouth, a mouth alone is not a face. It went on up through the sharks . . .

A: Up through the sharks . . .

Q: ... to the snakes. ...

A: Yes.

Q: The face has *three* main functions, detection of desirable energy sources, direction of the locomotor machinery toward its goal, and capture. ...

A: Yes.

Q: Capture and preliminary preparation of food. Is this too ...

A: Not a bit.

Q: The face, a face, also serves as a lure in mate acquisition. The broad, forwardly directed nose—

A: I don't see that on the panel.

Q: Look at it.

A: I don't—

Q: There is an analogy, believe it or not. The ... We use industrial designers to do the front panels, the controls. Designers, artists. To make the machines attractive to potential buyers. Pure cosmetics. They told us that knife switches were masculine. Men felt ... So we used a lot of knife switches. ...

A: I know that a great deal has been written about all this but when I come across such articles, in the magazines or in a newspaper, I don't read them. I'm not interested.

Q: What are your interests?

A: I'm a director of the Schumann Festival.

Q: What is she doing now?

A: Taking off her jeans.

Q: Has she removed her blouse?

A: No, she's still wearing her blouse.

Q: A yellow blouse?

A: Blue.

Q: Well, what is she doing now?

A: Removing her jeans.

Q: What is she wearing underneath?

A: Pants. Panties.

Q: But she's still wearing her blouse?

A: Yes.

Q: Has she removed her panties?

A: Yes.

Q: Still wearing the blouse?

A: Yes. She's walking along a log.

Q: In her blouse. Is she reading a book?

A: No. She has sunglasses.

Q: She's wearing sunglasses?

A: Holding them in her hand.

Q: How does she look?

A: Quite beautiful.

Q: What is the content of Maoism?

A: The content of Maoism is purity.

Q: Is purity quantifiable?

A: Purity has never been quantifiable.

Q: What is the incidence of purity worldwide?

A: Purity occurs in .004 percent of all cases.

Q: What is purity in the pure state often consonant with?

A: Purity in the pure state is often consonant with madness.

Q: This is not to denigrate madness.

A: This is not to denigrate madness. Madness in the pure state offers an alternative to the reign of right reason.

Q: What is the content of right reason?

A: The content of right reason is rhetoric.

Q: And the content of rhetoric?

A: The content of rhetoric is purity.

Q: Is purity quantifiable?

A: Purity is not quantifiable. It *is* inflatable.

Q: How is our rhetoric preserved against attacks by other rhetorics?

A: Our rhetoric is preserved by our elected representatives. In the fat of their heads.

Q: There's no point in arguing that the machine is wholly successful, but it has its qualities. I don't like to use anthropomorphic language in talking about these machines, but there is one quality . . .

A: What is it?

Q: It's brave.

A: Machines are braver than art.

Q: Since the death of the bicycle.

Q: There are ten rules for operating the machine. The first rule is turn it on.

A: Turn it on.

Q: The second rule is convert the terms. The third rule is rotate the inputs. The fourth rule is you have made a serious mistake.

A: What do I do?

Q: You send the appropriate error message.

A: I will never remember these rules.

Q: I'll repeat them a hundred times.

A: I was happier before.

Q: You imagined it.

A: The issues are not real.

Q: The issues are not real in the sense that they are touchable. The issues raised here are equivalents. Reasons and conclusions exist although they exist elsewhere, not here. Reasons and conclusions are in the air and simple to observe even for those who do not have the leisure to consult or learn to read the publications of the specialized disciplines.

A: The situation bristles with difficulties.

Q: The situation bristles with difficulties but in the end young people and workers will live on the same plane as old people and government officials, for the mutual good of all categories. The phenomenon of masses, in following the law of high numbers, makes possible exceptional and rare events, which—

A: I called her then and told her that I had dreamed about her, that she was naked in the dream, that we were making love. She didn't wish to be dreamed about, she said—not now, not later, not ever, when would I stop. I suggested that it was something over which I had no control. She said that it had all been a long time ago and that she was married to Howard now, as I knew, and that she didn't want . . . irruptions of this kind. Think of Howard, she said.

Q: He has struck me.
A: I have struck him.
Q: We have seen them.
A: I was looking at the window.
Q: Their chair is here.
A: She sang and we listened to her.
Q: Soldiers marching toward the castle.
A: I spoke to a tourist.
Q: I knocked at the door.
A: We shall not cross the river.
Q: The river has filled the boats with water.
A: I think that I have seen her with my uncle.
Q: Getting into their motorcar, I heard them.
A: He will strike her if he has lost it.

A (concluding): There's no doubt in my mind that the ball-players today are the greatest ever. They're brilliant athletes, extremely well coordinated, tremendous in every department. The ballplayers today are so magnificent that scoring is a relatively simple thing for them.

Q: Thank you for confiding in me.

Q: . . . show you a picture of my daughter.

A: Very nice.
Q: I can give you a few references for further reading.
A: (Claps hand to ear)

Q: What is she doing now?
A: There is a bruise on her thigh. The right.

CONCERNING
THE BODYGUARD

DOES the bodyguard scream at the woman who irons his shirts? Who has inflicted a brown burn on his yellow shirt purchased expensively from Yves St. Laurent? A great brown burn just over the heart?

Does the bodyguard's principal make conversation with the bodyguard, as they wait for the light to change, in the dull gray Citroën? With the second bodyguard, who is driving? What is the tone? Does the bodyguard's principal comment on the brown young women who flock along the boulevard? On the young men? On the traffic? Has the bodyguard ever enjoyed a serious political discussion with his principal?

Is the bodyguard frightened by the initials D.I.T.?

Is the bodyguard frightened by the initials C.N.D.?

Will the bodyguard be relieved, today, in time to see the film he has in mind—*Emmanuelle Around the World*? If the bodyguard is relieved in time to see *Emmanuelle Around the World*, will there be a queue for tickets? Will there be students in the queue?

Is the bodyguard frightened by the slogan *Remember 17 June*? Is the bodyguard frightened by black spray paint, tall letters ghostly at the edges, on this wall, on this wall? At what level of education did the bodyguard leave school?

Is the bodyguard sufficiently well-paid? Is he paid as well as a machinist? As well as a foreman? As well as an army sergeant? As well as a lieutenant? Is the Citroën armored? Is the Mercedes armored? What is the best speed of the Mercedes? Can it equal that of a BMW? A BMW motorcycle? Several BMW motorcycles?

Does the bodyguard gauge the importance of his principal in terms of the number of bodyguards he requires? Should there not be other cars leading and following his principal's car, these also filled with bodyguards? Are there sometimes such additional precautions, and does the bodyguard, at these times, feel himself part of an ocean of bodyguards? Is he exalted at these times? Does he wish for even more bodyguards, possibly flanking cars to the right and left and a point car far, far ahead?

After leaving technical school, in what sort of enterprises did the bodyguard engage before accepting his present post? Has he ever been in jail? For what sort of offense? Has the bodyguard acquired a fondness for his principal? Is there mutual respect? Is there mutual contempt? When his principal takes tea, is the bodyguard offered tea? Beer? Who pays?

Can the bodyguard adduce instances of professional success? Had he a previous client?

Is there a new bodyguard in the group of bodyguards? Why?

How much does *pleasing* matter? What services does the bodyguard provide for his principal other than the primary one? Are there services he should not be asked to perform? Is he nevertheless asked from time to time to perform such services? Does he refuse? Can he refuse? Are there, in addition to the bodyguard's agreed-upon compensation, tips? Of what size? On what occasions?

In the restaurant, a good table for his principal and the distinguished gray man with whom he is conferring. Before it (between the table with the two principals and the door), a table for the four bodyguards. What is the quality of the conversation between the two sets of bodyguards? What do they talk about? Soccer, perhaps, Holland vs. Peru, a match which they have all seen. Do they rehearse the savaging of the Dutch goalkeeper Piet Schrijvers by the bastard Peruvian? Do they discuss Schrijvers's replacement by the brave Jan

Jongbloed, and what happened next? Has the bodyguard noted the difference in quality between his suit and that of his principal? Between his shoes and those of his principal?

In every part of the country, large cities and small towns, bottles of champagne have been iced, put away, reserved for a celebration, reserved for a special day. Is the bodyguard aware of this?

Is the bodyguard tired of waking in his small room on the Calle Caspe, smoking a Royale Filtre, then getting out of bed and throwing wide the curtains to discover, again, eight people standing at the bus stop across the street in postures of depression? Is there on the wall of the bodyguard's small room a poster showing Bruce Lee in a white robe with his feet positioned in such-and-such a way, his fingers outstretched in such-and-such a way? Is there a rosary made of apple beads hanging from a nail? Is there a mirror whose edges have begun to craze and flake, and are there small blurrish Polaroids stuck along the left edge of the mirror, Polaroids of a woman in a dark-blue scarf and two lean children in red pants? Is there a pair of dark-blue trousers plus a long-sleeved white shirt (worn once already) hanging in the dark-brown wardrobe? Is there a color foldout of a naked young woman torn from the magazine VIR taped inside the wardrobe door? Is there a bottle of Long John Scotch atop the cheese-colored mini-refrigerator? Two-burner hotplate? Dull-green ceramic pot on the windowsill containing an unhealthy plant? A copy of *Explication du Tai Chi,* by Bruce Tegner? Does the bodyguard read the newspaper of his principal's party? Is he persuaded by what he reads there? Does the bodyguard know which of the great blocs his country aligned itself with during the Second World War? During the First World War? Does the bodyguard know which countries are the preeminent trading partners of his own country, at the present time?

Seated in a restaurant with his principal, the bodyguard is served, involuntarily, turtle soup. Does he recoil, as the other eats? Why is this near-skeleton, his principal, of such importance to the world that he deserves six bodyguards, two to a shift with the shifts changing every eight hours, six bodyguards of the first competence plus supplementals on occasion, two armored cars, stun grenades ready to hand under the front seat? What has he meant to the world? What are his plans?

Is the retirement age for bodyguards calculated as it is for other citizens? Is it earlier, fifty-five, forty-five? Is there a pension? In what amount? Those young men with dark beards staring at the Mercedes, or staring at the Citroën, who are they? Does the bodyguard pay heed to the complaints of his fellow bodyguards about the hours spent waiting outside this or that Ministry, this or that Headquarters, hours spent propped against the fenders of the Mercedes while their principal is within the (secure) walls? Is the thick glass of these specially prepared vehicles thick enough? Are his fellow bodyguards reliable? Is the new one reliable?

Is the bodyguard frightened by young women of good family? Young women of good family whose handbags contain God knows what? Does the bodyguard feel that the situation is *unfair*? Will the son of the bodyguard, living with his mother in a city far away, himself become a bodyguard? When the bodyguard delivers the son of his principal to the school where all of the children are delivered by bodyguards, does he stop at a grocer's on the way and buy the child a peach? Does he buy himself a peach?

Will the bodyguard, if tested, be equal to his task? Does the bodyguard know which foreign concern was the successful bidder for the construction of his country's nuclear reprocessing plant? Does the bodyguard know which sections of the National Bank's yearly report on debt service have been falsified? Does the bodyguard know that the general amnesty of April coincided with the rearrest of sixty persons? Does the bodyguard know that the new, liberalized press laws of May were a provocation? Does the bodyguard patronize a restaurant called The Crocodile? A place packed with young, loud, fat Communists? Does he spill a drink, to disclose his spite? Is his gesture understood?

Are the streets full of stilt-walkers? Stilt-walkers weaving ten feet above the crowd in great papier-mâché bird heads, black and red costumes, whipping thirty feet of colored cloth above the heads of the crowd, miming the rape of a young female personage symbolizing his country? In the Mercedes, the bodyguard and his colleague stare at the hundreds, men and women, young and old, who move around the Mercedes, stopped for a light, as if it were a rock in a river. In the rear seat, the patron is speaking into a telephone. He looks up, puts down the telephone. The people pressing around the car cannot be counted, there are too many of them; they cannot be known, there are too many of them; they cannot be predicted, they have volition. Then, an opening. The car accelerates.

Is it the case that, on a certain morning, the garbage cans of the city, the garbage cans of the entire country, are overflowing with empty champagne bottles? Which bodyguard is at fault?

RIF

LET me tell you something. New people have moved into the apartment below me and their furniture is, shockingly, identical to mine, the camelback sofa in camel-colored tweed is there as are the two wrong-side-of-the-blanket sons of the Wassily chair and the black enamel near-Mackintosh chairs, they have the pink-and-purple dhurries and the brass quasi-Eames torchères as well as the fake Ettore Sottsass faux-marble coffee table with cannonball legs. I'm shocked, in a state of shock—

—I taught you that. Overstatement. You're shocked. You reel, you fall, you collapse in Rodrigo's arms, complaining of stress. He slowly begins loosening your stays, stay by stay, singing the great *Ah, je vois le jour, ah, Dieu*, and the second act is over.

—You taught me that, Rhoda. You, my mentor in all things.

—You were apt Hettie very apt.

—I was apt.

—The most apt.

—Cold here in the garden.

—You were complaining about the sun.

—But when it goes behind a cloud—

—Well, you can't have everything.

—The flowers are beautiful.

—Indeed.

—Consoling to have the flowers.

—Half-consoled already.

—And these Japanese rocks.

—Artfully placed, most artfully.

—You must admit, a great consolation.

—And our work.

—A great consolation.

—God, aren't these flowers beautiful.

—Only three of them. But each remarkable, of its kind.

—What are they?

—Some kind of Japanese dealies, I don't know.

—Lazing here in the garden. This is really most luxurious.

—I think that they provide, the company provides, a space like this, in the middle of this vast building, it's—

—Most enlightened.

—It drains away. The tensions.

—We still haven't decided what color to paint the trucks.

—I said blue.

—Surely not your last word on the subject.

—I have some swatches. If you'd care to take a gander.

—Not now. This sun is blistering.

—New skin. You're going to complain?

—Those new people. Upstairs. They make me feel bad. Wouldn't you feel bad?

—It's not my furniture that's being replicated in every detail. Every last trite detail. So I don't feel bad. The implications don't—

—I have something to tell you, Rhoda.

—What, Hettie?

—We're having a thirteen-percent reduction-in-force. A rif. You're in line to be riffed, Rhoda.

—I am?

—If you take early retirement voluntarily you get a better package. If I have to release you, you get less.

—How much less?

—Rounds out at about forty-two percent. Less.

—Well.

—Yes.

—I'll need something to do with myself. I am young yet Hettie. Relatively speaking.

—Very relatively very.

—What about the windows?

—What about them?

—They need washing. Badly in want of washing.

—You? Washing windows?

—Maybe work my way up through the ranks. Again.

—Your delicate hands in the ammonia-bright bucket—I can't see it.

—Is cheese alive when it's killed? My daughter asked me that she's beginning to get the hang of things.

—Perhaps too early?

—On schedule I would say. The windows radiate filth, building-wide. I can do it.

—I will plunge the dagger into my breast before I send you to Support Services.

—All part of the program, Hettie.

—Will I be okay without you, Rhoda?

—Fine, Hettie, fine. My parting advice is, cut the dagger.

—The only person I ever stuck with it was Bruce.

—He smiled slightly as he slid to the floor, a vivid pinkness obscuring the Polo emblem on his chest.

—He was most gracious about it, called it a learning experience.

—Most gracious. Above and beyond.

—I remember the year we got the two-percent increase.

—Then the four-percent increase.

—Then the eight-percent across-the-board cut.

—The year the Easter bonus came through.

—Our ups and downs.

—Wonderful memories, wonderful.

—Bruce. Mentor-at-large. First he was your Bruce. Then he was my Bruce.

—Taught me much, Bruce.

—That's what they're for. To teach. That's how I regarded him. That's why I took him.

—A good poke too, not a bad poke, fair poke not too bad a poke.

—Mentoring away. Through dark and dank.

—Yes.

—He always said you cast him off like an old spreadsheet.

—I remember a night in California. I've always hated California. But on this night, in California, he by God taught me lost-horse theory. Where you have a lost horse and have to find it. Has to do with the random movement of markets and the taming of probability. I was by God *entranced*.

—Well we've moved beyond that now haven't we?

—If you say so Hettie.

—I mean we don't want to get hung up on the Bruce question at this late date.

—What good would it do? He's gone.

—He thought he could cook.

—He prided himself upon his cooking.

—He couldn't cook.

—He could do gizzards. Something about gizzards that engaged his attention.

—Nothing he could do I couldn't do better. In addition, I could luxuriously stretch out my naked, golden leg. He couldn't do that.

—His, a rather oaklike leg covered with lichen.

—Oh he was a sturdy boy. Head like a chopping block. Many's the time I tried to bash the new into it.

—Your subtle concept shattered upon the raw butchered surface.

—And when it was necessary to put him out to pasture—

—Did we flinch? We did not flinch.

—Grazing now with all the other former vice-presidents in Kentucky.

—Muzzle-deep in the sweetest clover.

—I have the greatest of expectations, still.

—Of course you do. Part of the program.

—My expectations are part of the program?

—The soul of the program.

—No no no no. My expectations come from within.

—I think not. Blown into being, as it were, by the program.

—My expectations are a function of my thinking. My own highly individuated thinking which includes elements of the thought of Immanuel Kant and Harry S. Truman.

—Absolutely. Unique to you.

—Furthermore I'm going to bust out of this constraining smothering retrograde environment at the first opportunity. I give you fair warning.

—Why tell me? I'm the mere window person.

—To me, Rhoda, you will always be the rock upon which my church is founded.

—Why you ragged kid, you ain't got no church.

—I ain't?

—At most, a collection plate.

—I circulate among the worshipers, taking tithes.

—It's a living. Put a bunch of tithes one on top of another, you have a not inconsiderable sum.

—The priestly function, mine. The one who understands the arcanum, me.

—Also you get to herd the flock. Tell the flock to flock here, to flock there.

—Divine inspiration. That's all it is. Nothing to it.

—You yourself awash in humility all the while.

—I can do humility.

—Don't wave the dagger. The argument of the third act, as it spreads itself before us, is perfectly plain: If we recognize ourselves to be part of a larger whole with which we are in relations, those relations and that whole cannot be created by the finite self but must be produced by an absolute all-inclusive mind of which our minds are parts and of which the world-process in its totality is the experience. Don't wave the dagger.

—I'll bare my breast, place the point of the knife upon its plump surface. Then explain the issues.

—I tell you people lust for consummation. They see a shining dagger poised above a naked breast, they want it shoved in.

—I wonder what it would have been like. If I'd had another mentor. One less sour, perhaps.

—You'd be a different person, Hettie.

—I would, wouldn't I. Strange to think.

—Are you satisfied? You needn't answer.

—No, I'm not. You taught me that. Not to be satisfied.

—The given can always be improved upon. Screwed around with.

—You were a master. Are a master. Wangling and diddling, fire and maneuver.

—I can sit and watch my daughter. Scrape the city off her knees and tell her to look both ways when she crosses the street.

—They have to learn. Like everybody else.

—Maybe I'll teach her to look only to the left. Not both ways.

—That's wrong. That's not right. It's unsafe.

—The essence of my method.

—You were a wild old girl, Rhoda. I'll remember.

—I was, wasn't I.

—We still haven't decided what color to paint the trucks.

—Blue?

THE PALACE AT FOUR A.M.

MY father's kingdom was and is, all authorities agree, large. To walk border to border east-west, the traveler must budget no less than seventeen days. Its name is Ho, the Confucian term for harmony. Confucianism was an interest of the first ruler (a strange taste in our part of the world), and when he'd cleared his expanse of field and forest of his enemies, two centuries ago, he indulged himself in an *hommage* to the great Chinese thinker, much to the merriment of some of our staider neighbors, whose domains were proper Luftlunds and Dolphinlunds. We have an economy based upon truffles, in which our forests are spectacularly rich, and electricity, which we were exporting when other countries still read by kerosene lamp. Our army is the best in the region, every man a colonel—the subtle secret of my father's rule, if the truth be known. In this land every priest is a bishop, every ambulance-chaser a robed justice, every peasant a corporation and every street-corner shouter Hegel himself. My father's genius was to promote his subjects, male and female, across the board, ceaselessly; the people of Ho warm themselves forever in the sun of Achievement. I was the only man in the kingdom who thought himself a donkey.

—From the *Autobiography*

I am writing to you, Hannahbella, from a distant country. I daresay you remember it well. The King encloses the opening pages of his autobiography. He is most curious as to what your response to them will be. He has labored mightily over their composition, working without food, without sleep, for many days and nights.

The King has not been, in these months, in the best of spirits. He has read your article and declares himself to be very much impressed by it. He begs you, prior to publication in this country, to do him the great favor of changing the phrase "two disinterested and impartial arbiters" on page thirty-one to "malign elements under the ideological sway of still more malign elements." Otherwise, he is delighted. He asks me to tell you that your touch is as adroit as ever.

Early in the autobiography (as you see) we encounter the words: "My mother the Queen made a mirror pie, a splendid thing the size of a poker table . . ." The King wishes to know if poker tables are in use in faraway lands, and whether the reader in such places would comprehend the dimensions of the pie. He continues: " . . . in which reflections from the kitchen chandelier exploded when the crew rolled it from the oven. We were kneeling side-by-side, peering into the depths of a new-made mirror pie, when my mother said to me, or rather her celestial image said to my dark, heavy-haired one, 'Get out. I cannot bear to look upon your donkey face again.' "

The King wishes to know, Hannahbella, whether this passage seems to you tainted by self-pity, or is, rather, suitably dispassionate.

He walks up and down the small room next to his bedchamber, singing your praises. The decree having to do with your banishment will be rescinded, he says, the moment you agree to change the phrase "two disinterested and impartial arbiters" to "malign elements," etc. This I urge you to do with all speed.

The King has not been at his best. Peace, he says, is an unnatural condition. The country is prosperous, yes, and he understands that the people value peace, that they prefer to spin out their destinies in placid, undisturbed fashion. But *his* destiny, he says, is to alter the map of the world. He is considering several new wars, small ones, he says, small but interesting, complex, dicey, even. He would very much like to consult with you about them. He asks you to change, on page forty-four of your article, the phrase "egregious usurpations" to "symbols of benign transformation." Please initial the change on the proofs, so that historians will not accuse us of bowdlerization.

Your attention is called to the passage in the pages I send which runs as follows: "I walked out of the castle at dusk, not even the joy of a new sunrise to console me, my shaving kit with its dozen razors (although I shaved a dozen times a day, the head was still a donkey's) banging against the Walther .22 in my rucksack. After a time I was suddenly quite tired. I lay down under a hedge by the side of the road. One of the bushes above me had a shred of black cloth tied to it, a sign, in our country, that the place was haunted (but my head's enough to frighten any ghost)." Do you remember that shred of black cloth, Hannahbella? "I ate a slice of my mother's spinach pie and considered my situation. My princeliness would win me an evening, perhaps a fortnight, at this or that noble's castle in the vicinity, but my experience of visiting had taught me that neither royal blood nor novelty of aspect prevailed for long against a host's natural preference for folk with heads much like his own. Should I en-zoo myself? Volunteer for a traveling circus? Attempt the stage? The question was most vexing.

"I had not wiped the last crumbs of the spinach pie from my whiskers when something lay down beside me, under the hedge.

" 'What's this?' I said.

" 'Soft,' said the new arrival, 'don't be afraid, I am a bogle, let me abide here for the night, your back is warm and that's a mercy.'

" 'What's a bogle?' I asked, immediately fetched, for the creature was small, not at all frightening to look upon and clad in female flesh, something I do not hold in low esteem.

" 'A bogle,' said the tiny one, with precision, 'is not a black dog.'

" 'Well, I thought, now I know.

" 'A bogle,' she continued, 'is not a boggart.'

" 'Delighted to hear it,' I said.

" 'Don't you ever *shave*?' she asked. 'And why have you that huge hideous head on you, that could be mistaken for the head of an ass, could I see better so as to think better?'

" 'You may lie elsewhere,' I said, 'if my face discountenances you.'

" 'I am fatigued,' she said, 'go to sleep, we'll discuss it in the morning, move a bit so that your back fits better with my front, it will be cold, later, and this place is cursed, so they say, and I hear that the Prince has been driven from the palace, God knows what that's all about but it promises no good for us plain folk, police, probably, running all over the fens with their identity checks and making you blow up their great balloons with your breath—'

"She was confusing, I thought, several issues, but my God! she was warm and shapely. Yet I thought her a strange piece of goods, and made the mistake of saying so.

" 'Sir,' she answered, 'I would not venture upon what's strange and what's not strange, if I were you,' and went on to say that if I did not abstain from further impertinence she would commit sewer-pipe. She dropped off to sleep then, and I lay back upon the ground. Not a child, I could tell, rather a tiny woman. A bogle."

The King wishes you to know, Hannahbella, that he finds this passage singularly moving and that he cannot read it without being forced to take snuff, violently. Similarly the next:

"What, precisely, is a donkey? As you may imagine, I have re-searched the question. My *Larousse* was most delicate, as if the editors thought the matter blushful, but yielded two observations of interest: that donkeys came originally from Africa, and that they, or we, are 'the result of much crossing.' This urges that the parties to the birth must be ill-matched, and in the case of my royal parents, 'twas thunderously true. The din of their calamitous conversations reached every quarter of the palace, at every season of the year. My mother named me Duncan (var. of Dunkey, clearly) and went into spasms of shrinking whenever, youthfully, I'd offer a cheek for a kiss. My father, in contrast, could sometimes bring himself to scratch my head between the long, weedlike ears, but only, I suspect, by means of a mental shift, as if he were addressing one of his hunting dogs, the which, incidentally, remained firmly ambivalent about me even after long acquaintance.

"I explained a part of this to Hannahbella, for that was the bogle's name, suppressing chiefly the fact that I was a prince. She in turn gave the following account of herself. She was indeed a bogle, a semispirit generally thought to be of bad character. This was a libel, she said, as her own sterling qualities would quickly persuade me. She was, she said, of the utmost perfection in the female line, and there was not a woman within the borders of the kingdom so beautiful as herself, she'd been told it a thousand times. It was true, she went on, that she was not of a standard size, could in fact be called small, if not minuscule, but those who objected to this were louts and fools and might profitably be stewed in lead, for the entertainment of the countryside. In the matter of rank and precedence, the meanest bogle outweighed the greatest king, although the kings of this earth, she conceded, would never acknowledge this but in their dotty solipsism conducted themselves as if bogles did not even exist. And would I like to see her all unclothed so that I might glean some rude idea as to the true nature of the sublime?

"Well, I wouldn't have minded a bit. She was wonderfully crafted, that was evident, and held in addition the fascination surrounding any perfect miniature. But I said, 'No, thank you. Perhaps another day, it's a bit chill this morning.'

" 'Just the breasts then,' she said, 'they're wondrous pretty,' and before I could protest further she'd whipped off her mannikin's tiny shirt. I buttoned her up again meanwhile bestowing buckets of extravagant praise. 'Yes,' she said in agreement, 'that's how I am all over, wonderful.' "

The King cannot reread this section, Hannahbella, without being reduced to tears. The world is a wilderness, he says, civilization a folly we entertain in concert with others. He himself, at his age, is beyond surprise, yet yearns for it. He longs for the conversations he formerly had with you, in the deepest hours of the night, he in his plain ermine robe, you simply dressed as always in a small scarlet cassock, most becoming, a modest supper of chicken, fruit and wine on the sideboard, only the pair of you awake in the whole palace, at four o'clock in the morning. The tax evasion case against you has been dropped. It was, he says, a hasty and ill-considered undertaking, even spiteful. He is sorry.

The King wonders whether the following paragraphs from his autobiography accord with your own recollections: "She then began,

as we walked down the road together (an owl pretending to be
absent standing on a tree limb to our left, a little stream snapping
and growling to our right), explaining to me that my father's administration of the realm left much to be desired, from the bogle point
of view, particularly his mad insistence on filling the forests with
heavy-footed truffle hounds. Standing, she came to just a hand
above my waist; her hair was brown, with bits of gold in it; her
quite womanly hips were encased in dun-colored trousers. 'Duncan,'
she said, stabbing me in the calf with her sharp nails, 'do you know
what that man has done? Nothing else but ruin, absolutely ruin,
the whole of the Gatter Fen with a great roaring electric plant that
makes a thing that who in the world could have a use for I don't
know. I think they're called volts. Two square miles of first-class
fen paved over. We bogles are being squeezed to our knees.' I had
a sudden urge to kiss her, she looked so angry, but did nothing,
my history in this regard being, as I have said, infelicitous.

   " 'Duncan, *you're not listening!*' Hannahbella was naming the chief
interesting things about bogles, which included the fact that in the
main they had nothing to do with humans, or nonsemispirits; that
although she might seem small to me she was tall, for a bogle,
queenly, in fact; that there was a type of blood seas superior to
royal blood, and that it was bogle blood; that bogles had no magical
powers whatsoever, despite what was said of them; that bogles were
the very best lovers in the whole world, no matter what class of
thing, animal, vegetable, or insect, might be under discussion; that
it was not true that bogles knocked bowls of mush from the tables
of the deserving poor and caused farmers' cows to become pregnant
with big fishes, out of pure mischief; that female bogles were the
most satisfactory sexual partners of any kind of thing that could
ever be imagined and were especially keen for large overgrown
things with ass's ears, for example; and that there was a something
in the road ahead of us to which it might, perhaps, be prudent to
pay heed.

   "She was right. One hundred yards ahead of us, planted squarely
athwart the road, was an army."

   The King, Hannahbella, regrets having said of you, in the journal

Vu, that you have two brains and no heart. He had thought he was talking not-for-attribution, but as you know, all reporters are scoundrels and not to be trusted. He asks you to note that *Vu* has suspended publication and to recall that it was never read by anyone but serving maids and the most insignificant members of the minor clergy. He is prepared to give you a medal, if you return, any medal you like—you will remember that our medals are the most gorgeous going. On page seventy-five of your article, he requires you, most humbly, to change "monstrous over-reaching fueled by an insatiable if still childish ego" to any kinder construction of your choosing.

The King's autobiography, in chapters already written but which I do not enclose, goes on to recount how you and he together, by means of a clever stratagem of your devising, vanquished the army barring your path on that day long, long ago; how the two of you journeyed together for many weeks and found that your souls were, in essence, the same soul; the shrewd means you employed to place him in power, against the armed opposition of the Party of the Lily, on the death of his father; and the many subsequent campaigns which you endured together, mounted on a single horse, your armor banging against his armor. The King's autobiography, Hannahbella, will run to many volumes, but he cannot bring himself to write the end of the story without you.

The King feels that your falling-out, over the matter of the refugees from Brise, was the result of a miscalculation on his part. He could not have known, he says, that they had bogle blood (although he admits that the fact of their small stature should have told him something). Exchanging the refugees from Brise for the twenty-three Bishops of Ho captured during the affair was, he says in hindsight, a serious error; more bishops can always be created. He makes the point that you did not tell him that the refugees from Brise had bogle blood but instead expected him to know it. Your outrage was, he thinks, a pretext. He at once forgives you and begs your forgiveness. The Chair of Military Philosophy at the university is yours, if you want it. You loved him, he says, he is convinced of it, he still cannot believe it, he exists in a condition of doubt. You are both old; you are both forty. The palace at four A.M. is silent. Come back, Hannahbella, and speak to him.

JAWS

How is William to prove to Natasha that he still loves her? That's the problem I'm working on, mentally, as I check the invoices and get the big double-parked trucks from the warehouses unloaded and deal with all the people bringing in aluminum cans for redemption. Benny, this black Transit cop who had ordered a hot pastrami on rye with mustard from our deli and then had to rush out on a call, is now eating his hot pastrami and telling me about this woman who was hanging out of a sixth-floor window over on Second Avenue where he and his partner couldn't get at her. "She wouldn't come in," Benny says. "I said, go ahead and fly, Loonytunes. I shouldn't have said that. I made an error."

I understand how that could be. This woman wanted to blend her head with Second Avenue and mess up the honor of the Transit Police, probably because somebody didn't love her anymore. Mutilation, actual or verbal, is usually taken as an earnest of sincere interest in another person. Verbal presentations, with William and Natasha, are no good. So many terrible sentences drift in the poisoned air between them, sentences about who is right and sentences about who works hardest and sentences about money and even sentences about physical appearance—the most ghastly of known sentences. That's why Natasha bites, I'm convinced of it. She's trying to say something. She opens her mouth, then closes it (futility) on William's arm (sudden eloquence).

I like them both, so they both tell me about these incidents and I rationalize and say, well, that's not so terrible, maybe she's under stress, or maybe he's under stress. I neglect to mention that most people in New York are under some degree of stress and few of them, to my knowledge, bite each other. People always like to hear that they're under stress, makes them feel better. You can imagine what they'd feel if they were told they weren't under stress.

Natasha is a small woman with dark hair and a serious, concerned face. Good teeth. She wears trusty Canal Street–West Broadway pants and shirts and is maybe twenty-six. I met her three years ago when she came over to my little cubicle at the A&P at Twelfth Street and Seventh to cash a check, one that William had signed. Of course she didn't have the proper ID, since she wasn't William. But she was so embarrassed that I decided she was okay. "He's a little peculiar about money," she told me, and *I* was embarrassed. I thought, what's with this guy? I thought he was probably some kind of monster, in a minor way. Then one day he came in to cash a check himself. "Why don't you put your wife on your account?" I asked him. "I cash her checks because I know her, but sometimes I'm not here. Also, she must have trouble other places. I mean, I'm not telling you how to run your life."

William blushed. You don't see that much blushing at A&P Twelfth Street. He was wearing a suit, a gray Barney's pin-striped number, and had obviously just come from work. "She has a tendency to overspend," he said. "It's not her fault. She was born to wealth and her habits never left her, even when she married me. When we had a joint account she never entered the checks in her checkbook. So we were always overdrawn and I finally closed the account and now we do it this way."

When Natasha found out about William's affair with the girl at the office, I should say woman at the office, she came straight to me and told me everything. "It was at the office picnic in Central Park," she said. "Everybody was playing badminton, okay? In bare feet. William was playing and I noticed that he had a piece of silver duct tape around his big toe. He had a cut, he said. William uses duct tape for everything. Our place is practically held together with duct tape. And then later on I noticed that this rather pretty girl was playing with a piece of duct tape on her ankle. She'd scraped her ankle. And that told me the story, right there. I confronted him with it and he admitted it. It was as simple as that."

Well, romance is not unknown at the A&P. We are an old and wise organization and have seen much. We are not called The Great Atlantic and Pacific for nothing, we contain multitudes and sometimes people lock gazes across the frozen rabbit parts and the balloon goes up, figuratively speaking. I counseled forbearance. "Don't come down too hard on him," I said. "William is clearly in the wrong in this matter, that gives you a certain edge. Don't harangue or threaten or cry and weep. Calm, rational understanding is your mode. Politically, you're way out in front. Act accordingly."

I think this was psychologically acute advice. It was the best I had to offer. What she did was, she bit him again. On the shoulder, in the shower. He was in the shower, he told me, and suddenly there was this horrible pain in his left shoulder and this time she did break the skin. He had to slug her in the hipbone to make her let go. "It's the only time I've ever hit her," he said. He poured Johnnie Walker Black over the wound and slapped a piece of duct tape on it and took a room at the Mohawk Motor Inn, on Tenth Avenue.

William has not only not proved to Natasha that he still loves her but alienated her still further, because of the thing with Patricia, who he's not seeing anymore, in that way. Furthermore he's been in the Mohawk Motor Inn for a week, and that can get to you. Nothing breaks down a man accustomed to at least some degree of domestic felicity more than a week at a Motor Inn, however welcoming. He walks over in the mornings from the Mohawk for a bagel with dilled cream cheese and to find out if Natasha's been around. I have to be, and have been, strictly impartial. "She was in," I say. "She's butterflying a leg of lamb tonight. Marinating it for six hours in soy sauce and champagne. I don't myself think the champagne is a good idea but she got some recipe from somewhere—"

"From her sister," William says. "Danni spreads champagne on hot dog buns. Rex, what do you think?"

"Go home," I say. "Praise the lamb."

"How do I know it won't be the spinal cord next?"

"Hard to get to. Probably couldn't even dent it."

"I feel like I'm married to some kind of animal."

"Our animal nature is part of us and we are part of it."

So he goes back to their apartment on Charles Street and they have a festive evening with the lamb and candles. They go to bed together and in the middle of the night she bites him on the back of the leg, severing a tendon just above the knee. A real gorilla bite. I can't understand it. She's a really nice woman, and pretty, too.

"You can't bite your way through life," I say to her. She's just seen William in his semi-private room at St. Vincent's.

"The physical therapist says there'll be a slight limp," she says, "forever. How could I have done that?"

"Passion, I guess. Feeling run rampant."

"Will he ever speak to me again?"

"What'd he say at the hospital?"

"Said the food was lousy."

"That's a beginning."

"He doesn't feel for me anymore. I know it."

"He keeps coming back. However chewed upon. That's got to prove something."

"I guess."

I don't believe that we are what we do although many thinkers argue otherwise. I believe that what we do is, very often, a poor approximation of what we are—an imperfect manifestation of a much better totality. Even the best of us sometimes bite off, as it were, less than we can chew. When Natasha bites William she's saying only part of what she wants to say to him. She's saying, *William! Wake up! Remember!* But that gets lost in a haze of pain, his. I'm trying to help. I give her a paper bag of bagels and a plastic container of cream cheese with shallots to take to him, and for herself, an A&P check-cashing application with my approval already initialed in the upper right-hand corner. I pray that they will be successful together, eventually. Our organization stands behind them.

CONVERSATIONS WITH GOETHE

November 13, 1823

I was walking home from the theatre with Goethe this evening when we saw a small boy in a plum-colored waistcoat. Youth, Goethe said, is the silky apple butter on the good brown bread of possibility.

December 9, 1823

Goethe had sent me an invitation to dinner. As I entered his sitting room I found him warming his hands before a cheerful fire. We discussed the meal to come at some length, for the planning of it had been an occasion of earnest thought to him and he was in quite good spirits about the anticipated results, which included sweetbreads prepared in the French manner with celery root and paprika. Food, said Goethe, is the topmost taper on the golden candelabrum of existence.

January 11, 1824

Dinner alone with Goethe. Goethe said, "I will now confide to you some of my ideas about music, something I have been considering for many years. You will have noted that although certain members of the animal kingdom make a kind of music—one speaks of the 'song' of birds, does one not?—no animal known to us takes part in what may be termed an organized musical performance. Man alone does that. I have wondered about crickets—whether their evening cacophony might be considered in this light, as a species of performance, albeit one of little significance to our ears. I have asked Humboldt about it, and Humboldt replied that he thought not, that it is merely a sort of tic on the part of crickets. The great point here, the point that I may choose to enlarge upon in some future work, is not that the members of the animal kingdom do not unite wholeheartedly in this musical way but that man does, to the eternal comfort and glory of his soul."

Music, Goethe said, is the frozen tapioca in the ice chest of History.

March 22, 1824

Goethe had been desirous of making the acquaintance of a young Englishman, a Lieutenant Whitby, then in Weimar on business. I conducted this gentleman to Goethe's house, where Goethe greeted us most cordially and offered us wine and biscuits. English, he said, was a wholly spendid language, which had given him the deepest pleasure over many years. He had mastered it early, he told us, in order to be able to savor the felicities and tragic depths of Shakespeare, with whom no author in the world, before or since, could rightfully be compared. We were in a most pleasant mood and continued to talk about the accomplishments of the young Englishman's countrymen until quite late. The English, Goethe said in parting, are the shining brown varnish on the sad chiffonier of civilization. Lieutenant Whitby blushed most noticeably.

April 7, 1824

When I entered Goethe's house at noon, a wrapped parcel was standing in the foyer. "And what do you imagine this may be?" asked Goethe with a smile. I could not for the life of me fathom what the parcel might contain, for it was most oddly shaped. Goethe explained that it was a sculpture, a gift from his friend van den Broot, the Dutch artist. He unwrapped the package with the utmost care, and I was seized with admiration when the noble figure within was revealed: a representation, in bronze, of a young woman dressed as Diana, her bow bent and an arrow on the string. We marveled together at the perfection of form and fineness of detail, most of all at the indefinable aura of spirituality which radiated from the work. "Truly astonishing!" Goethe exclaimed, and I hastened to agree. Art, Goethe said, is the four-percent interest on the municipal bond of life. He was very pleased with this remark and repeated it several times.

June 18, 1824

Goethe had been having great difficulties with a particular actress at the theatre, a person who conceived that her own notion of how her role was to be played was superior to Goethe's. "It is not enough," he said, sighing, "that I have mimed every gesture for the poor creature, that nothing has been left unexplored in this character I myself have created, willed into being. She persists in what she terms her 'interpretation,' which is ruining the play." He went on to discuss the sorrows of managing a theatre, even the finest, and the exhausting detail that must be attended to, every jot and tittle, if the performances are to be fit for a discriminating public. Actors, he said, are the Scotch weevils in the salt pork of honest effort. I loved him more than ever, and we parted with an affectionate handshake.

September 1, 1824

Today Goethe inveighed against certain critics who had, he said, completely misunderstood Lessing. He spoke movingly about how such obtuseness had partially embittered Lessing's last years, and speculated that it was because Lessing was both critic and dramatist that the attacks had been of more than usual ferocity. Critics, Goethe said, are the cracked mirror in the grand ballroom of the creative spirit. No, I said, they were, rather, the extra baggage on the great cabriolet of conceptual progress. "Eckermann," said Goethe, "*shut up.*"

AFFECTION

How do you want to cook this fish? How do you want to cook this fish? Harris asked.

What?

Claire heard: How do you want to cook this fish?

Breaded, she said.

Fine, Harris said.

What?

Fine!

We have not slept together for three hundred nights, she thought. We have not slept together for three hundred nights.

His rough, tender hands not wrapped around me.

Lawnmower. His rough, tender hands wrapped around the handles of the lawnmower. Not around me.

What?

Where did you hide the bread crumbs?

What?

The bread crumbs!

Behind the Cheerios!

Claire telephoned her mother. Her mother's counsel was broccoli, mostly, but who else was she going to talk to?

What?

You have to be optimistic. Be be be. Optimistic.

What?

Optimistic, her mother said, they go through phases. As they get older. They have less tolerance for monotony.

I'm monotony?

They go through phases. As they grow older. They like to think that their futures are ahead of them. This is ludicrous, of course—

Oh oh oh oh.

Ludicrous, of course, but I have never yet met one who didn't think that way until he got played out then they sink into a comfortable lassitude take to wearing those horrible old-geezer hats . . .

What?

Hats with the green plastic bills, golf hats or whatever they are—

Harris, Claire said to her husband, you've stopped watering the plants.

What?

You've stopped watering the plants my mother always said that when they stopped watering the plants that was a sure sign of an impending marital breakup.

Your mother reads too much.

What?

Sarah decided that she and Harris should not sleep together any longer.

Harris said, What about hugging?

What?

Hugging.

Sarah said that she would have a ruling on hugging in a few days and that he should stand by for further information. She pulled the black lace mantilla down to veil her face as they left the empty church.

I have done the right thing the right thing. I am right.

Claire came in wearing her brown coat and carrying a large brown paper bag. Look what I got! she said excitedly.

What? Harris said.

She reached into the bag and pulled out a smeary plastic tray with six frozen shell steaks on it. The steaks looked like they had died in the nineteenth century.

Six dollars! Claire said. This guy came into the laundromat and said he was making deliveries to restaurants and some of the restaurants already had all the steaks they needed and now he had these left over and they were only six dollars. Six dollars.

You spent six dollars on *these*?

Other people bought some too.

Diseased, stolen steaks?

He was wearing a white coat, Claire said. He had a truck.

I'll bet he had a truck.

Harris went to see Madam Olympia, a reader and advisor. Her office was one room in a bad part of the city. Chicken wings burned in a frying pan on the stove. She got up and turned them off, then got up and turned them on again. She was wearing a t-shirt that had "Buffalo, City of No Illusions" printed on it.

Tell me about yourself, she said.

My life is hell, Harris said. He sketched the circumstances.

I am bored to tears with this sort of thing, Madam Olympia said. To tears to tears.

Well, Harris said, me too.

Woman wakes up in the middle of the night, Madam Olympia said, she goes, what you thinkin' about? You go, the float. She goes, is the float makin' us money or not makin' us money? You go, it depends on what happens Wednesday. She goes, that's nice. You go, what do you mean, you don't understand *dick* about the float, woman. She goes, well you don't have to be nasty. You go, I'm *not* being nasty, you just don't *understand*. She goes, so why don't you tell me? Behind this, other agendas on both sides.

The float is a *secret,* Harris said. Many *men* don't even know about the float.

To tears to tears to tears.

Right, Harris said. How much do I owe you?

Fifty dollars.

The community whispered: Are they still living? How many times a week? What is that symbol on your breast? Did they consent to sign it? Did they refuse to sign it? In the rain? Before the fire? Has there been weight loss? How many pounds? What is their favorite color? Have they been audited? Was there a his side of the bed and a her side of the bed? Did she make it herself? Can we have a taste? Have they stolen money? Have they stolen stamps? Can he ride a horse? Can he ride a steer? What is his best time in the calf scramble? Is there money? Was there money? What happened to the money? What will happen to the money? Did success come early or late? Did success come? A red wig? At the Junior League? A red dress with a red wig? Was she ever a Fauve? Is that a theoretical position or a real position? Would they do it again? Again and again? How many times? A thousand times?

Claire met Sweet Papa Cream Puff, a new person. He was the house pianist at Bells, a club frequented by disconsolate women in the early afternoons.

He was a huge man and said that he was a living legend.

What?

Living legend, he said.

I didn't name the "Sweet Papa Cream Puff Blues" by that name, he said. It was named by the people of Chicago.

Oh my oh my oh my, Claire said.

This musta been 'bout nineteen twenty-one, twenty-two, he said. Those was wonderful days.

There was one other man, at that time, who had part of my fame. Fellow named Red Top, he's dead now.

He was very good, scared me a little bit.

I studied him.

I had two or three situations on the problem.

I worked very hard and bested him in nineteen twenty-three. June of that year.

Wow, Claire said.

Zum, Sweet Papa Cream Puff sang, zum zum zum zum *zum.*

Six perfect bass notes in the side pocket.

Sarah calls Harris from the clinic in Detroit and floors him with the news of her "miscarriage." Saddened by the loss of the baby, he's nevertheless elated to be free of his "obligation." But when Harris rushes to declare his love for Claire, he's crushed to learn that she is married to Sarah. Hoping against hope that Harris will stay with her, Sarah returns. Harris is hung over from drinking too much the night before when Sarah demands to know if he wants her. Unable to decide at first, he yields to Sarah's feigned helplessness and tells her to stay. Later, they share a pleasant dinner at the Riverboat, where Claire is a waiter. Harris is impressed to learn that Sarah refused to join in his mother's plan to dissuade him from becoming a policeman. Claire is embracing Harris before his departure when Sarah enters the office. When Harris is caught shoplifting, Claire's kid sister, terrified at having to face a court appearance, signs for his release. Missing Sarah terribly, Harris calls her from New Orleans; when she tells him about becoming chairwoman of Claire's new bank, he hangs up angrily. Although they've separated, his feelings for Claire haven't died entirely, and her growing involvement with his new partner, Sarah, is a bitter pill for him to swallow, as he sits alone drinking too much brandy in Sarah's study. Sarah blazes with anger when she finds Claire in the hotel's banquet office making arrangements for Harris's testimonial dinner, as Sarah, her right leg in a cast, walks up the steps of the brownstone and punches Claire's bell, rage clearly burning in her eyes.

Sarah visited Dr. Whorf, a good psychiatrist.

Cold as *death,* she said.

What?

Cold as *death*.

Good behavior is frequently painful, Dr. Whorf said. Shit you know that.

Sarah was surprised to find that what she had told Dr. Whorf was absolutely true. She was fully miserable.

Harris drunk again and yelling at Claire said that he was not drunk.

I feel worse than you feel, she said.

What?

Worse, she said, woooooooorrrssse.

You know what I saw this morning? he asked. Eight o'clock in the morning. I was out walking.

Guy comes out of this house, wearing a suit, carrying an attaché case.

He's going to work, right?

He gets about ten steps down the sidewalk and this woman comes out. Out of the same house.

She says, "James?"

He turns around and walks back toward her.

She's wearing a robe. Pink and orange.

She says, "James, *I . . . hate . . . you.*"

Maybe it's everywhere, Claire said. A pandemic.

I don't think that, Harris said.

This is the filthiest phone booth I've ever been in, Harris said to Sarah.

What?

The *filthiest phone booth* I have ever been in.

Hang up darling hang up and find another phone booth thank you for the jewels the pearls and the emeralds and the onyx but I haven't changed my mind they're quite quite beautiful just amazing but I haven't changed my mind you're so kind but I have done the right thing painful as it was and I haven't changed my mind—

He remembered her standing over the toothpaste with her face two inches from the toothpaste because she couldn't see it without her contacts in.

Freud said, Claire said, that in the adult, novelty always constitutes the condition for orgasm.

Sweet Papa looked away.

Oh me oh my.

Well you know the gents they don't know what they after they own selves, very often.

When do they find out?

At the eleventh hour let me play you a little thing I wrote in the early part of the century I call it "Verklärte Nacht" that means "stormy weather" in German, I played there in Berlin oh about—

Claire placed her arms around Sweet Papa Cream Puff and hugged the stuffing out of him.

What?
What?
What?
What?
By a lucky stroke Harris made an amount of money in the market. He bought Claire a beautiful black opal. She was pleased.
He looked to the future.
Claire will continue to be wonderful.
As will I, to the best of my ability.
The New York Times will be published every day and I will have to wash it off my hands when I have finished reading it, every day.
What? Claire said.
Smile.
What?
Smile.

THE NEW OWNER

WHEN he came to look at the building, with a real-estate man hissing and oozing beside him, we lowered the blinds, muted or extinguished lights, threw newpapers and dirty clothes on the floor in piles, burned rubber bands in ashtrays, and played Buxtehude on the hi-fi—shaking organ chords whose vibrations made the plaster falling from the ceiling fall faster. The new owner stood in profile, refusing to shake hands or even speak to us, a tall thin young man suited in hopsacking with a large manila envelope under one arm. We pointed to the plaster, to the crevasses in the walls, sagging ceilings, leaks. Nevertheless, he closed.

Soon he was slipping little rent bills into the mailboxes, slip slip slip slip. In sixteen years we'd never had rent bills but now we have rent bills. He's raised the rent, and lowered the heat. The new owner creeps into the house by night and takes the heat away with him. He wants us out, out. If we were gone, the building would be decontrolled. The rents would climb into the air like steam.

Bicycles out of the halls, says the new owner. Shopping carts out of the halls. My halls.

The new owner stands in profile in the street in front of our building. He looks up the street, then down the street—this wondrous street where our friends and neighbors have lived for decades in Christian, Jewish, and, in some instances, Islamic peace. The new owner is writing the Apartments Unfurn. ads of the future, in his head.

The new owner fires the old super, simply because the old super is a slaphappy, widowed, shot-up, black, Korean War-sixty-five-percent-disability drunk. There is a shouting confrontation in the basement. The new owner threatens the old super with the police. The old super is locked out. A new super is hired who does not put out the garbage, does not mop the halls, does not, apparently, exist. Roaches prettyfoot into the building because the new owner has stopped the exterminating service. The new owner wants us out.

We whisper to the new owner, through the walls. Go away! Own something else! Don't own this building! Try the Sun Belt! Try Alaska, Hawaii! Sail away, new owner, sail away!

The new owner arrives, takes out his keys, opens the locked basement. The new owner is standing in the basement, owning the basement, with its single dangling light bulb and the slightly busted souvenirs of all our children's significant progress. He is taking away the heat, carrying it out with him under his coat, a few pounds at a time, and bringing in with him, a few hundred at a time, his hired roaches.

The new owner stands in the hall, his manila envelope under his arm, owning the hall.

The new owner wants our apartment, and the one below, and the two above, and the one above them. He's a bachelor, tall thin young man in cheviot, no wife, no children, only buildings. He's covered the thermostat with a locked clear-plastic case. His manila envelope contains estimates and floor plans and draft Apartment Unfurn. ads and documents from the Office of Rent and Housing Preservation which speak of Maximum Base Rents and Maximum Collectible Rents and under what circumstances a Senior Citizen Rent Increase Exemption Order may be voided.

Black handprints all over the green of the halls where the new owner has been feeling the building.

The new owner has informed the young cohabiting couple on

the floor above us (rear) that they are illegally living in sin and that for this reason he will give them only a month-to-month lease, so that at the end of each and every month they must tremble.

The new owner has informed the old people in the apartment above us (front) that he is prepared to prove that they do not actually live in their apartment in that they are old and so do not, in any real sense, live, and that they are thus subject to a Maximum Real Life Estimate Revision, which, if allowed by the City, will award him their space. Levon and Priscilla tremble.

The new owner stands on the roof, where the tomato plants are, owning the roof. May a good wind blow him to hell.

ENGINEER-PRIVATE
PAUL KLEE MISPLACES
AN AIRCRAFT BETWEEN
MILBERTSHOFEN AND
CAMBRAI, MARCH 1916

P<small>AUL</small> Klee said:

"Now I have been transferred to the Air Corps. A kindly sergeant effected the transfer. He thought I would have a better future here, more chances for promotion. First I was assigned to aircraft repair, together with several other workers. We presented ourselves as not just painters but artist-painters. This caused some shaking of heads. We varnished wooden fuselages, correcting old numbers and adding new ones with the help of templates. Then I was pulled off the painting detail and assigned to transport. I escort aircraft that are being sent to various bases in Germany and also (I understand) in occupied territory. It is not a bad life. I spend my nights racketing across Bavaria (or some such) and my days in switching yards. There is always bread and wurst and beer in the station restaurants. When I reach a notable town I try to see the notable paintings there, if time allows. There are always unexpected delays, reroutings, back-trackings. Then the return to the base. I see Lily fairly often. We meet in hotel rooms and that is exciting. I have never yet lost an aircraft or failed to deliver one to its proper destination. The war seems interminable. Walden has sold six of my drawings."

The Secret Police said:

"We have secrets. We have many secrets. We desire all secrets.

We do not have your secrets and that is what we are after, your secrets. Our first secret is where we are. No one knows. Our second secret is how many of us there are. No one knows. Omnipresence is our goal. We do not even need real omnipresence. The theory of omnipresence is enough. With omnipresence, hand-in-hand as it were, goes omniscience. And with omniscience and omnipresence, hand-in-hand-in-hand as it were, goes omnipotence. We are a three-sided waltz. However our mood is melancholy. There is a secret sigh that we sigh, secretly. We yearn to be known, acknowledged, admired even. What is the good of omnipotence if nobody knows? However that is a secret, that sorrow. Now we are everywhere. One place we are is here watching Engineer-Private Klee, who is escorting three valuable aircraft, B.F.W. 3054/16-17-18, with spare parts, by rail from Milbertshofen to Cambrai. Do you wish to know what Engineer-Private Klee is doing at this very moment, in the baggage car? He is reading a book of Chinese short stories. He has removed his boots. His feet rest twenty-six centimeters from the baggage-car stove."

Paul Klee said:

"These Chinese short stories are slight and lovely. I have no way of knowing if the translation is adequate or otherwise. Lily will meet me in our rented room on Sunday, if I return in time. Our destination is Fighter Squadron Five. I have not had anything to eat since morning. The fine chunk of bacon given me along with my expense money when we left the base has been eaten. This morning a Red Cross lady with a squint gave me some very good coffee, however. Now we are entering Hohenbudberg."

The Secret Police said:

"Engineer-Private Klee has taken himself into the station restaurant. He is enjoying a hearty lunch. We shall join him there."

Paul Klee said:

"Now I emerge from the station restaurant and walk along the line of cars to the flatcar on which my aircraft (I think of them as *my* aircraft) are carried. To my surprise and dismay, I notice that one of them is missing. There had been three, tied down on the flatcar and covered with canvas. Now I see with my trained painter's eye that instead of three canvas-covered shapes on the flatcar there are only two. Where the third aircraft had been there is only a puddle of canvas and loose rope. I look around quickly to see if anyone else has marked the disappearance of the third aircraft."

The Secret Police said:

"We had marked it. Our trained policemen's eyes had marked the fact that where three aircraft had been before, tied down on the flatcar and covered with canvas, now there were only two. Unfortunately we had been in the station restaurant, lunching, at the moment of removal, therefore we could not attest as to where it had gone or who had removed it. There is something we do not know. This is irritating in the extreme. We closely observe Engineer-Private Klee to determine what action he will take in the emergency. We observe that he is withdrawing from his tunic a notebook and pencil. We observe that he begins, very properly in our opinion, to note down in his notebook all the particulars of the affair."

Paul Klee said:

"The shape of the collapsed canvas, under which the aircraft had rested, together with the loose ropes—the canvas forming hills and valleys, seductive folds, the ropes the very essence of looseness, lapsing—it is irresistible. I sketch for ten or fifteen minutes, wondering the while if I might not be in trouble, because of the missing aircraft. When I arrive at Fighter Squadron Five with less than the number of aircraft listed on the manifest, might not some officious person become angry? Shout at me? I have finished sketching. Now I will ask various trainmen and station personnel if they have seen anyone carrying away the aircraft. If they answer in the negative, I will become extremely frustrated. I will begin to kick the flatcar."

The Secret Police said:

"Frustrated, he begins to kick the flatcar."

Paul Klee said:

"I am looking up in the sky, to see if my aircraft is there. There are in the sky aircraft of several types, but none of the type I am searching for."

The Secret Police said:

"Engineer-Private Klee is searching the sky—an eminently sound procedure, in our opinion. We, the Secret Police, also sweep the Hohenbudberg sky, with our eyes. But find nothing. We are debating with ourselves as to whether we ought to enter the station restaurant and begin drafting our preliminary report, for forwarding to higher headquarters. The knotty point, in terms of the preliminary report, is that we do not have the answer to the question 'Where is the aircraft?' The damage potential to the theory of omniscience, as well as potential to our careers, dictates that this point be omitted from the preliminary report. But if this point is omitted, might not some officious person at the Central Bureau for Secrecy note the omission? Become angry? Shout at us? Omissiveness is not rewarded at the Central Bureau. We decide to observe further the actions of Engineer-Private Klee, for the time being."

Paul Klee said:

"I who have never lost an aircraft have lost an aircraft. The aircraft is signed out to me. The cost of the aircraft, if it is not found, will be deducted from my pay, meager enough already. Even if Walden sells a hundred, a thousand drawings, I will not have enough money to pay for this cursed aircraft. Can I, in the time the train remains in the Hohenbudberg yards, construct a new aircraft or even the simulacrum of an aircraft, with no materials to work with or indeed any special knowledge of aircraft construction? The situation is ludicrous. I will therefore apply Reason. Reason dictates the solution. I will diddle the manifest. With my painter's skill which is after all not so different from a forger's, I will change the manifest to reflect conveyance of *two* aircraft, B.F.W. 3054/16 and 17, to Fighter Squadron Five. The extra canvas and ropes I will conceal in an empty boxcar—this one, which according to its stickers is headed for Essigny-le-Petit. Now I will walk around town and see if I can find a chocolate shop. I crave chocolate."

The Secret Police said:

"Now we observe Engineer-Private Klee concealing the canvas and ropes which covered the former aircraft in an empty boxcar bound for Essigny-le-Petit. We have previously observed him diddling the manifest with his painter's skill which resembles not a little that of the forger. We applaud these actions of Engineer-

Private Klee. The contradiction confronting us in the matter of the preliminary report is thus resolved in highly satisfactory fashion. We are proud of Engineer-Private Klee and of the resolute and manly fashion in which he has dealt with the crisis. We predict he will go far. We would like to embrace him as a comrade and brother but unfortunately we are not embraceable. We are secret, we exist in the shadows, the pleasure of the comradely/brotherly embrace is one of the pleasures we are denied, in our dismal service."

Paul Klee said:

"We arrive at Cambrai. The planes are unloaded, six men for each plane. The work goes quickly. No one questions my altered manifest. The weather is clearing. After lunch I will leave to begin the return journey. My release slip and travel orders are ready, but the lieutenant must come and sign them. I wait contentedly in the warm orderly room. The drawing I did of the collapsed canvas and ropes is really very good. I eat a piece of chocolate. I am sorry about the lost aircraft but not overmuch. The war is temporary. But drawings and chocolate go on forever."

TERMINUS

SHE agrees to live with him for "a few months"; where? probably at the Hotel Terminus, which is close to the Central Station, the blue coaches leaving for Lyons, Munich, the outerlands . . . Of course she has a Gold Card, no, it was not left at the florist's, absolutely not. . . .

The bellmen at the Hotel Terminus find the new arrival odd, even furtive; her hair is cut in a funny way, wouldn't you call it funny? and her habits are nothing but odd, the incessant pumping of the huge accordion, "Malagueña" over and over again, at the hour usually reserved for dinner. . . .

The yellow roses are delivered, no, white baby orchids, the cream-colored walls of the room are severe and handsome, tall windows looking down the avenue toward the Angel-Garden. Kneeling, with a sterilized needle, she removes a splinter from his foot; he's thinking, *clothed, and in my right mind,* and she says, now I lay me down to sleep, I mean it, Red Head—

They've agreed to meet on a certain street corner; when he arrives, early, she rushes at him from a doorway; it's cold, she's wearing her long black coat, it's too thin for this weather; he gives her his scarf, which she wraps around her head like a babushka; tell me, she says, how did this happen?

When she walks, she slouches, or skitters, or skids, catches herself and stands with one hip tilted and a hand on the hip, like a cowboy; she's twenty-six, served three years in the Army, didn't like it and got out, took a degree in statistics and worked for an insurance company, didn't like it and quit and fell in love with him and purchased the accordion. . . .

Difficult, he says, difficult, difficult, but she is trying to learn "When Irish Eyes Are Smiling," the sheet music propped on the cream marble mantelpiece, in two hours' time the delightful psychiatrist will be back from his Mexican vacation, which he spent in perfect dread, speaking to spiders—

Naked, she twists in his arms to listen to a sound outside the door, a scratching, she freezes, listening; he's startled by the beauty of her tense back, the raised shoulders, tilted head, there's nothing, she turns to look at him, what does she see? The telephone rings, it's the delightful psychiatrist (hers), singing the praises of Cozumel, Cancun. . . .

He punches a hole in a corner of her Gold Card and hangs it about her neck on a gold chain.

What are they doing in this foreign city? She's practicing "Cherokee," and he's plotting his next move, up, out, across, down. . . . He's wanted in Flagstaff, at a succulent figure, more consulting, but he doesn't want to do that anymore, they notice a sullen priest reading his breviary in the Angel-Garden, she sits on a bench and opens the *Financial Times* (in which his letter to the editor has been published, she consumes it with intense comprehension); only later, after a game of billiards, does he begin telling her how beautiful she is, no, she says, no, no—

I'll practice for eighteen hours a day, she says, stopping only for a little bread soaked in wine; he gathers up the newspapers, including the *Financial Times,* and stacks them neatly on the cream-colored radiator; and in the spring, he says, I'll be going away.

She's setting the table and humming "Vienna"; yes, she says, it will be good to have you gone.

They're so clearly in love that cops wave at them from passing cruisers; what has happened to his irony, which was supposed to protect him, keep him clothed, and in his right mind? I love you so much, so much, she says, and he believes her, sole in a champagne sauce, his wife is skiing in Chile—

And while you sit by the fire, tatting, he says. . . . .

She says, no tatting for me, Big Boy. . . .

In the night, he says, alone, to see of me no more, your good fortune.

Police cars zip past the Hotel Terminus in threes, sirens hee-hawing. . . .

No one has told him that he is *a husband;* he has learned nothing from the gray in his hair; the additional lenses in the lenses of his spectacles have not educated him; the merriment of dental assistants has not brought him the news; he behaves as if *something* were possible, still; there's whispering at the Hotel Terminus.

He decides to go to a bar and she screams at him, music from the small radio, military marches, military waltzes; she's confused, she says, she really didn't mean that, but meant, rather, that the bell captain at the Hotel Terminus had said something she thought offensive, something about "Malagueña," it was not the words but the tone—

Better make the bed, he says, the bed in which you'll sleep, chaste and curly, when I'm gone. . . .

Yes, she says, yes that's what they say. . . .

True, he's lean; true, he's not entirely stupid; yes, he's given up cigarettes; yes, he's given up saying "forgive me," no longer uses the phrase "as I was saying"; he's mastered backgammon and sleeping with the radio on; he's apologized for his unkind remark about the yellow-haired young man at whom she was not staring— And when a lover drifts off while being made love to, it's a lesson in humility, right?

He looks at the sleeping woman; how beautiful she is! He touches her back, lightly.

The psychiatrist, learned elf, calls and invites them to his party, to be held in the Palm Room of the Hotel Terminus, patients will dance with doctors, doctors will dance with receptionists, receptionists will dance with detail men, a man who once knew Ferenczi will be there in a sharkskin suit, a motorized wheelchair— Yes, says the psychiatrist, *of course* you can play "Cherokee," and for an encore, anything of Victor Herbert's—

She, grimly: I don't like to try to make nobody bored, Hot Stuff. Warlike music in all hearts, she says, why are we together?

But on the other hand, she says, *that which exists is more perfect than that which does not*. . . .

This is absolutely true. He is astonished by the quotation. In the Hotel Terminus coffee shop, he holds her hand tightly.

Thinking of getting a new nightie, she says, maybe a dozen.

Oh? he says.

He's a whistling dog this morning, brushes his teeth with tequila thinking about *Geneva,* she, dying of love, shoves him up against a cream-colored wall, biting at his shoulders. . . . Little teed off this morning, aren't you, babe? he says, and she says, fixin' to prepare to get mad, way I'm bein' treated, and he says, oh darlin', and she says, way I'm bein' jerked around—

Walking briskly in a warm overcoat toward the Hotel Terminus, he stops to buy flowers, yellow freesias, and wonders what "a few months" can mean: three, eight? He has fallen out of love this morning, feels a refreshing distance, an absolution— But then she calls him *amigo,* as she accepts the/flowers, and says, *not bad, Red Head,* and he falls back into love again, forever. She comes toward him fresh from the bath, opens her robe. Goodbye, she says, goodbye.

THE EDUCATIONAL
EXPERIENCE

 M USIC from somewhere. It is Vivaldi's great work, *The Semesters.*

The students wandered among the exhibits. The Fisher King was there. We walked among the industrial achievements. A good-looking gas turbine, behind a velvet rope. The manufacturers described themselves in their literature as "patient and optimistic." The students gazed, and gaped. Hitting them with ax handles is no longer permitted, hugging and kissing them is no longer permitted, speaking to them is permitted but only under extraordinary circumstances.

The Fisher King was there. In *Current Pathology* by Spurry and Entemann, the King is called "a doubtful clinical entity." But Spurry and Entemann have never caught him, so far as is known. Transfer of information from the world to the eye is permitted if you have signed oaths of loyalty to the world, to the eye, to *Current Pathology.*

We moved on. The two major theories of origin, evolution and creation, were argued by bands of believers who gave away buttons, balloons, bumper stickers, pieces of the True Cross. On the walls, photographs of stocking masks. The visible universe was doing very well, we decided, a great deal of movement, flux—unimpaired vitality. We made the students add odd figures, things like 453498*23:J and 8977?22MARY. This was part of the educational experience, we told them, and not even the hard part—just one side of a many-sided effort. But what a wonderful time you'll have, we told them, when the experience is over, done, completed. You will all, we told them, be more beautiful than you are now, and more employable too. You will have a grasp of the total situation; the total situation will have a grasp of you.

Here is a diode, learn what to do with it. Here is Du Guesclin, constable of France 1370–80—learn what to do with him. A divan is either a long cushioned seat or a council of state—figure out at which times it is what. Certainly you can have your dangerous drugs, but only for dessert—first you must chew your cauliflower, finish your fronds.

Oh they were happy going through the exercises and we told them to keep their tails down as they crawled under the wire, the wire was a string of quotations, Tacitus, Herodotus, Pindar. . . . Then the steady-state cosmologists, Bondi, Gold, and Hoyle, had to be leaped over, the students had to swing from tree to tree in the Dark Wood, rappel down the sheer face of the Merzbau, engage in unarmed combat with the Van de Graaf machine, sew stocking masks. See? Unimpaired vitality.

We paused before a bird's lung on a pedestal. "But the mammalian lung is different!" they shouted. "A single slug of air, per hundred thousand population . . ." Some fool was going to call for "action" soon, citing the superiority of praxis to pale theory. A wipe-out requires thought, planning, coordination, as per our phoncon of 6/8/75. Classic film scripts were stretched tight over the destruction of indigenous social and political structures for dubious ends, as per our phoncon of 9/12/75. "Do you think intelligent life exists outside this bed?" one student asked another, confused as to whether she was attending the performance, or part of it. Unimpaired vitality, yes but—

And Sergeant Preston of the Yukon was there in his Sam Browne belt, he was copulating violently but copulating with no one, that's always sad to see. Still it was a "nice try" and in that sense inspirational, a congratulation to the visible universe for being what it is. The group leader read from an approved text. "I have eaten from the tympanum, I have drunk from the cymbals." The students shouted and clashed their spears together, in approval. We noticed that several of them were off in a corner playing with animals, an ibex, cattle, sheep. We didn't know whether we should tell them to stop, or urge them to continue. Perplexities of this kind are not infrequent in our business. The important thing is the educational experience itself—how to survive it.

We moved them along as fast as we could, but it's difficult, with all the new regulations, restrictions. The Chapel Perilous is a bomb farm now, they have eight thousand acres in guavas and a few hundred head of white-faced enlisted men who stand around with buckets of water, buckets of sand. We weren't allowed to smoke, that was annoying, but necessary I suppose to the preservation of our fundamental ideals. Then we taught them how to put stamps on letters, there was a long line waiting in front of that part of the program, we lectured about belt buckles, the off/on switch, and putting out the garbage. It is wise not to attempt too much all at once—perhaps we weren't wise.

The best way to live is by not knowing what will happen to you at the end of the day, when the sun goes down and the supper is to be cooked. The students looked at each other with secret smiles. Rotten of them to conceal their feelings from us, we who are doing the best we can. The invitation to indulge in emotion at the expense of rational analysis already constitutes a political act, as per our phoncon of 11/9/75. We came to a booth where the lessons of 1914 were taught. There were some wild strawberries there, in the pool of blood, and someone was playing the piano, softly, in the pool of blood, and the Fisher King was fishing, hopelessly, in the pool of blood. The pool is a popular meeting place for younger people but we aren't younger anymore so we hurried on. "Come and live with me," that was something somebody said to someone else, a bizarre idea that was quickly scotched—we don't want that kind of idea to become general, or popular.

"The world is everything that was formerly the case," the group leader said, "and now it is time to get back on the bus." Then all of the guards rushed up and demanded their bribes. We paid them with soluble traveler's checks and hoped for rain, and hoped for rodomontade, braggadocio, blare, bray, fanfare, flourish, tucket.

BLUEBEARD

"Never open that door," Bluebeard told me, and I, who knew his history, nodded. In truth I had a very good idea of what lay on the other side of the door and no interest at all in opening it. Bluebeard was then in his forty-fifth year, quite vigorous, the malaise that later claimed him—indeed enfeebled him—not yet in evidence. When he had first attempted to put forward his suit, my father, who knew him slightly (they were both clients of Dreyer, the American art dealer), refused him admittance, saying only, "Not, I think, a good idea." Bluebeard sent my father a small Poussin watercolor, a study for *The Death of Phocion;* me he sent, with astonishing boldness, a black satin remarque nightgown.

Events progressed. My father could not bring himself to part with the Poussin, and in very short order Bluebeard was a fixture in our sitting room, never without some lavish gift—a pair of gold cruets attributed to Cellini, a cut-pile Aubusson fire-extinguisher cover. I admit I found him very attractive despite his age and his nose, the latter a black rocklike object threaded with veins of silver, a feature I had never before seen adorning a human countenance. The sheer energy of the man carried all before it, and he was as well most thoughtful. "The history of architecture is the history of the struggle for light," he said one day. I have latterly seen this remark attributed to the Swiss Le Corbusier, but it was first uttered, to my certain knowledge, in our sitting room, Bluebeard paging through a volume of Palladio. In fine, I was taken; I became his seventh wife.

"Have you tried to open the door?" he asked me, in the twelfth month of our (to that point) happy marriage. I told him I had not, that I was not at all curious by nature and was furthermore obedient to the valid proscriptions my husband might choose to impose vis-à-vis the governance of the household. This seemed to irritate him. "I'll know, you know," he said. "If you try." The silver threads in his black nose pulsated, light from the chandelier bouncing from them. He had at that time a project in view, a project with which I was fully in sympathy: the restoration of the south wing of the castle, bastardized in the eighteenth century by busybodies who had overlaid its Georgian pristinity with Baroque rickrack in the manner of Vanbrugh and Hawksmoor. Striding here and there in his big India-rubber boots, cursing the trembling masons on the scaffolding and the sweating carpenters on the ground, he was all in all a fine figure of a man—a thing I have never forgotten.

I spent my days poring over motorcar catalogues (the year was 1910). Karl Benz and Gottlieb Daimler had produced machines capable of great speed and dash and I longed to have one, just a little one, but could not bring myself to ask my husband (my ever-generous husband) for so considerable a gift. Where did I want to go, my husband would ask, and I would be forced to admit that *going somewhere* was a conception alien to our rich, full life at the castle, only forty kilometers from Paris, to which I was allowed regular visits. My husband's views on marriage—old-fashioned if you will—were not such as to encourage promiscuous wanting. If I could have presented the Daimler phaeton as a toy, something to tootle about the grounds in, something that enabled him to laugh at my inadequacies as a pilot of the machine (decimation of the rosebushes), then he might have, with a toss of his full, rich head of hair, acceded to my wish. But I was not that intelligent.

"Will you never attempt the door?" he asked one morning over coffee in the sunroom. He had just returned from a journey—he always returned suddenly, unexpectedly, a day or two before he had planned to do so—and had brought me a Buen Retiro white biscuit clock two meters high. I repeated what I had told him previously: that I had no interest in the door or what lay behind it, and that I would gladly return the silver key he had given me if his mind would be eased thereby. "No, no," he said, "keep the key, you must have the key." He thought for a moment. "You are a peculiar woman," he said. I did not know what he meant by this remark and I fear I did not take it kindly, but I had no time to protest or plead my ordinariness, for he abruptly left the room, slamming the door behind him. I knew I had angered him in some way but I could not for the life of me understand precisely how I had erred. Did he *want* me to open the door? To discover, in the room behind the door, hanging on hooks, the beautifully dressed carcasses of my six predecessors? But what if, contrary to informed opinion, the beautifully dressed carcasses of my six predecessors were not behind the door? What was? At that moment I became curious, and at the same time, one part of my brain contesting another, I contrived to lose the key, in the vicinity of the gazebo.

I had trusted my husband to harbor behind the door nothing more than rotting flesh, but now that the worm of doubt had inched its way into my consciousness I became a different person. On my hands and knees on the brilliant green lawn behind the gazebo I searched for the key; looking up I saw, in a tower window, that great black nose, with its veins of silver, watching me. My hands moved nervously over the thick grass and only the thought of the three duplicate keys I had had made by the locksmith in the village, a M. Necker, consoled me. What was behind the door? Whenever I placed my hands on it the thick carved oak gave off a slight chill (although this may have been the result of an inflamed imagination). Exhausted, I gave up the search; Bluebeard now knew that I had lost something and could readily surmise what it was—advantage to me, in a sense. At dusk, from a tower window, I saw him trolling in the grass with a horseshoe magnet dangling from a string.

I had taken care that the duplicate keys manufactured for me by M. Necker had also been coated with silver, were in every way exact replicas of the original, and could with confidence present one on

demand if my husband required it. But if he had been successful
in finding the one I had lost but concealed that fact (and conceal-
ment was the very essence of his nature), and I presented one of
the duplicates as the original when the original lay in his pocket,
this would constitute proof that I had reproduced the key, a clear
breach of trust. I could, of course, simply maintain that I had in
fact lost it—this had the virtue of being true—meanwhile concealing from him the existence of the counterfeits. This seemed the
better course.

He sat that night at the dining table slicing a goose with a prune-
and-foie-gras stuffing (taking the best parts for himself, I observed)
and said without preamble, "Where do you meet your lover, Doroteo Arango?"

Doroteo Arango, the Mexican revolutionary leader known to the
world as Pancho Villa, was indeed in Paris at that moment, raising
funds for his sacred and just cause, but I had had little contact with
him and was certainly not yet his lover although he had pressed my
breasts and tried to insinuate his hand underneath my skirt at the
meeting of 23 July at my aunt Thérèse Perrault's house in the
Sixteenth at which he had spoken so eloquently. The strange Mexican spirit tequila had been served, golden in brandy snifters. I had
not taken exception to his behavior, assuming that all Mexican
revolutionary leaders behaved in this way, but he had persisted in
sending me, hand-delivered by hard-riding vaqueros in Panhards,
bottles of the pernicious liquor, one of which my husband was now
waving in my face.

I told him I had purchased a few bottles to assist the cause, much
as one might buy paper flowers from schoolchildren, and that Arango
was a well-known celibate with a special devotion to St. Erasmus
of Delft, the castrate. "You gave him my machine gun," Bluebeard
said. This was true; the Maxim gun that usually rested in a dusty
corner of the castle's vast attic had been transferred, under cover of
night, to one of the Panhards not long before. I had a truly frightful
time wrestling the thing down the winding stairs. "A loan only," I
said. "You weren't using it and he is pledged to rid Mexico of Díaz's
vile and corrupt administration by spring at the latest."

My husband had no love for the Díaz regime—held, in fact, a

portfolio of Mexican railroad bonds of the utmost worthlessness.
"Well," he growled, "next time, ask me first." This was the end of
the matter, but I could see that his trust in me, not absolute in the
best of seasons, was fraying.

My involvement with Père Redon, the castle's chaplain, was then,
I blush to confess, at its fiery height. The handsome young priest,
with his auburn locks and long, straight, white nose . . . It was to
him that I had entrusted the three duplicate keys to the locked door
and the eleven additional duplicate keys that I had caused to be
made by the village's second locksmith, a M. Becque. Redon had
hidden one key behind each of the Bronzino plaques marking the
chapel's fourteen Stations of the Cross, and since the chapel was
visited by my husband only at Christmas and Easter and on his own
name day, I felt them safe there. Still, the cache of my letters that
Redon kept in a small crypt carved out of the reverse side of the
altar table worried me, even though he replastered the opening
most skillfully each time he added a letter. The nun's habit that I
wore during the midnight Sabbats organized by the notorious Bishop
of Troyes, in which we, Redon and I, participated (my shame and
my delight, my husband drunk and dreaming all the while), hung
chastely in the same closet that held Constantin's Mass vestments—
cassock and chasuble, alb and stole. The ring Constantin had given
me, unholy yet cherished symbol of our love, remained in its tiny
velvet casket on the altar itself, within the tabernacle, stuffed behind
pyx, chalice, and ciborium. The chapel was in the truest sense a
sanctuary, all thanks to a living and merciful God.

"You must open the door," Bluebeard said to me one afternoon
at croquet—I had just hit his ball off into the shrubbery—"even
though I forbid it." What was I to make of this conundrum?

"Dear husband," I said, "I cannot imagine opening the door
against your wishes. Why then do you say I *must* open it?"

"I change the exhibit from time to time," he said, grimacing.
"You may not find, behind the door, what you expect. Furthermore,
if you are to continue as my wife, you must occasionally be strong
enough to go against my wishes, for my own good. Even the bluest

beard amongst us, even the blackest nose, needs on occasion the correction of connubial give-and-take." And he hung his head like a lycée boy.

"Very well then," I said. "Give me the key, for as you know I have lost mine."

He withdrew from his waistcoat pocket a silver key, and, leaving the game, I entered the castle and walked up the grand staircase to the third étage. Before I could reach the cursed portal, a house servant flourishing a telegram intercepted me. "For you, Madame," she said, all rosy and out of breath from running. The message read "930177 1886445 88156031 04344979" and was signed "EVERLAST." Coded of course, and the codebook far from me at this moment, recorded on fragile cigarette papers tightly rolled and concealed within the handlebars of my favorite yellow bicycle, "A" to "M" in the left handlebar, "N" to "Z" in the right handlebar, in the bicycle shed. "Everlast" was M. Grévy, the Finance Minister. What calamity was he announcing, and was he telling me to buy or sell? My entire fortune, as distinct from my husband's, rested upon the Bourse; Everlast's timely information, which had increased the value of my holdings in most satisfactory fashion, was vital to its continued existence. I'm finished, I thought; I'll wear rags and become secretary to a cat-seller. I longed to rush to the bicycle shed, yet my intense curiosity about the contents of the prohibited chamber exerted the stronger sway. I turned the key in the lock and plunged through the door.

In the room, hanging on hooks, gleaming in decay and wearing Coco Chanel gowns, seven zebras. My husband appeared at my side. "Jolly, don't you think?" he said, and I said, "Yes, jolly," fainting with rage and disappointment. . . .

DEPARTURES

MILAN, Tenn., Feb. 14 (AP)—The Army is planning to freeze to death three million or so blackbirds that took up residence two years ago at the Milan Arsenal.

Paul Lefebvre of the U.S. Department of the Interior, which is also working on the plan, said yesterday that the birds would be sprayed with two chemicals, resulting in a rapid loss of body heat. This will be done on a night with sub-freezing temperatures, he said.

THERE is an elementary school, P.S. 421, across the street from my building. The Board of Education is busing children from the bad areas of the city to P.S. 421 (our area is thought to be a good area) and busing children from P.S. 421 to schools in the bad areas, in order to achieve racial balance in the schools. The parents of the P.S. 421 children do not like this very much, but they are all good citizens and feel it must be done. The parents of the children in the bad areas may not like it much, either, having their children so far from home, but they too probably feel that the process makes somehow for a better education. Every morning the green buses arrive in front of the school, some bringing black and Puerto Rican children to P.S. 421 and others taking the local, mostly white, children away. Presiding over all this is the loadmaster.

The loadmaster is a heavy, middle-aged white woman, not fat but heavy, who wears a blue cloth coat and a scarf around her head and carries a clipboard. She gets the children into and out of the buses, briskly, briskly, shouting, "Let's go, let's go, *let's go!*" She has a voice that is louder than the voices of forty children. She gets a bus filled up, gives her clipboard a fast once-over, and sends the driver on his way: "O.K., José." The bus has been parked in the middle of the street, and there is a long line of hungup cars behind it, unable to pass, their drivers blowing their horns impatiently. When the drivers of these cars honk their horns too vigorously, the loadmaster steps away from the bus and yells at them in a voice louder than fourteen stacked-up drivers blowing their horns all at once: *"Keep your pants on!"* Then to the bus driver: "O.K., José." As the bus starts off, she stands back and gives it an authoritative smack on its rump (much like a coach sending a fresh player into the game) as it passes. Then she waves the stacked-up drivers on their way, one authoritative wave for each driver. She is making authoritative motions long after there is any necessity for it.

My grandfather once fell in love with a dryad—a wood nymph who lives in trees and to whom trees are sacred and who dances around trees clad in fine leaf-green tutu and who carries a great silver-shining ax to whack anybody who does any kind of thing inimical to the well-being and mental health of trees. My grandfather was at that time in the lumber business.

It was during the Great War. He'd got an order for a million board feet of one-by-ten of the very poorest quality, to make barracks out of for the soldiers. The specifications called for the dark red sap to be running off it in buckets and for the warp on it to be like the tops of waves in a distressed sea and for the knotholes in it to be the size of an intelligent man's head for the cold wind to whistle through and toughen up the (as they were then called) doughboys.

My grandfather headed for East Texas. He had the timber rights to ten thousand acres there, Southern yellow pine of the loblolly family. It was third-growth scrub and slash and shoddy—just the thing for soldiers. Couldn't be beat. So he and his men set up operations and first crack out of the box they were surrounded by threescore of lovely dryads and hamadryads all clad in fine leaf-green tutus and waving great silver-shining axes.

"Well now," my grandfather said to the head dryad, "wait a while, wait a while, somebody could get hurt."

"That is for sure," says the girl, and she shifts her ax from her left hand to her right hand.

"I thought you dryads were indigenous to oak," says my grandfather, "this here is pine."

"Some like the ancient tall-standing many-branched oak," says the girl, "and some the white-slim birch, and some take what they can get, and you will look mighty funny without any legs on you."

"Can we negotiate," says my grandfather, "it's for the War, and you are the loveliest thing I ever did see, and what is your name?"

"Megwind," says the girl, "and also Sophie. I am Sophie in the night and Megwind in the day and I make fine whistling ax-music night or day and without legs for walking your life's journey will be a pitiable one."

"Well Sophie," says my grandfather, "let us sit down under this tree here and open a bottle of this fine rotgut here and talk the thing over like reasonable human beings."

"Do not use my night-name in the light of day," says the girl, "and I am not a human being and there is nothing to talk over and what type of rotgut is it that you have there?"

"It is Teamster's Early Grave," says my grandfather, "and you'll cover many a mile before you find the beat of it."

"I will have one cupful," says the girl, "and my sisters will have each one cupful, and then we will dance around this tree while you still have legs for dancing and then you will go away and your men also."

"Drink up," says my grandfather, "and know that of all the women

I have interfered with in my time you are the absolute top woman."

"I am not a woman," says Megwind, "I am a spirit, although the form of the thing is misleading I will admit."

"Wait a while," says my grandfather, "you mean that no type of mutual interference between us of a physical nature is possible?"

"That is a thing I could do," says the girl, "if I chose."

"Do you choose?" asks my grandfather, "and have another wallop."

"That is a thing I will do," says the girl, and she has another wallop.

"And a kiss," says my grandfather, "would that be possible do you think?"

"That is a thing I could do," says the dryad, "you are not the least prepossessing of men and men have been scarce in these parts in these years, the trees being as you see mostly scrub, slash, and shoddy."

"Megwind," says my grandfather, "you are beautiful."

"You are taken with my form which I admit is beautiful," says the girl, "but know that this form you see is not necessary but contingent, sometimes I am a fine brown-speckled egg and sometimes I am an escape of steam from a hole in the ground and sometimes I am an armadillo."

"That is amazing," says my grandfather, "a shape-shifter are you."

"That is a thing I can do," says Megwind, "if I choose."

"Tell me," says my grandfather, "could you change yourself into one million board feet of one-by-ten of the very poorest quality neatly stacked in railroad cars on a siding outside of Fort Riley, Kansas?"

"That is a thing I could do," says the girl, "but I do not see the beauty of it."

"The beauty of it," says my grandfather, "is two cents a board foot."

"What is the *quid pro quo*?" asks the girl.

"You mean spirits engage in haggle?" asks my grandfather.

"Nothing from nothing, nothing for nothing, that is a law of life," says the girl.

"The *quid pro quo*," says my grandfather, "is that me and my men will leave this here scrub, slash, and shoddy standing. All you have to do is to be made into barracks for the soldiers and after the War you will be torn down and can fly away home."

"Agreed," says the dryad, "but what about this interference of a physical nature you mentioned earlier? For the sun is falling down and soon I will be Sophie and human men have been scarce in these parts for ever so damn long."

"Sophie," says my grandfather, "you are as lovely as light and let me just fetch another bottle from the truck and I will be at your service."

This is not really how it went. I am fantasizing. Actually, he just plain cut down the trees.

I was on an operating table. My feet were in sterile bags. My hands and arms were wrapped in sterile towels. A sterile bib covered my beard. A giant six-eyed light was shining in my eyes. I closed my eyes. There was a doctor on the right side of my head and a doctor on the left side of my head. The doctor on the right was my doctor. The doctor on the left was studying the art. He was Chinese, the doctor on the left. My doctor spoke to the nurse who was handing him tools. *"Rebecca! You're not supposed to be holding conversations with the circulating nurse, Rebecca. You're supposed to be watching me, Rebecca!"* We had all gathered here in this room to cut out part of my upper lip, into which a basal-cell malignancy had crept.

In my mind, the basal-cell malignancy resembled a tiny truffle.

"Most often occurs in sailors and farmers," the doctor had told me. "The sun." But I, I sit under General Electric light, mostly. "We figure you can lose up to a third of it, the lip, without a bad result," the doctor had told me. "There's a lot of stretch." He had demonstrated upon his own upper lip, stretching it with his two forefingers. The doctor a large handsome man with silver spectacles. In my hospital room, I listened to my Toshiba transistor, Randy Newman singing "Let's Burn Down the Cornfield." I was waiting for the morning, for the operation. A friendly Franciscan entered in his brown robes. "Why is it that in the space under 'Religion' on your form you entered 'None'?" he asked in a friendly way. I considered the question. I rehearsed for him my religious history. We discussed the distinguishing characteristics of the various religious orders—the Basilians, the Capuchins. Recent outbreaks of Enthusiasm among the Dutch Catholics were touched upon. "Rebecca!" the doctor said, in the operating room. *"Watch me, Rebecca!"*

I had been given a morphine shot along with various locals in the lip. I was feeling very good! The Franciscan had lived in the Far East for a long time. I too had been in the Far East. The Army band had played, as we climbed the ramp into the hold of the troopship, "Bye Bye Baby, Don't Forget That You're My Baby." "We want a good result," my original doctor had said, "because of the prominence of the—" He pointed to my upper lip. "So I'm sending you to a good man." This seemed sensible. I opened my eyes. The bright light. "Give me a No. 10 blade," the doctor said. "Give me a No. 15 blade." Something was certainly going on there, above my teeth. "Gently, gently," my doctor said to his colleague. The next morning a tiny Thai nurse came in bringing me orange juice, orange Jell-O, and an orange broth. "Is there any pain?" she asked.

My truffle was taken to the pathologist for examination. I felt the morphine making me happy. I thought: What a beautiful hospital.

A handsome nurse from Jamaica came in. "Now you put this on," she said, handing me a wrinkled white garment without much back to it. "No socks. No shorts."

No shorts!

I climbed onto a large moving bed and was wheeled to the operating table, where the doctors were preparing themselves for the improvement of my face. My doctor invited the Chinese doctor to join him in a scrub. I was eating my orange Jell-O, my orange broth. My wife called and said that she had eaten a superb Beef Wellington for dinner, along with a good bottle. Every time I smiled the stitches jerked tight.

I was standing outside the cashier's window. I had my pants on and was feeling very dancy. "Udbye!" I said. "Hank you!"

*   *   *

I went to a party. I saw a lady I knew. "Hello!" I said. "Are you pregnant?" She was wearing what appeared to be maternity clothes.

"No," she said, "I am not."

"Cab!"

But where are you today?

Probably out with your husband for a walk. He has written another beautiful poem, and needs the refreshment of the air. I admire him. Everything he does is successful. He is wanted for lectures in East St. Louis, at immense fees. I admire him, but my admiration for you is . . . Do you think he has noticed? What foolishness! It is as obvious as a bumper sticker, as obvious as an abdication.

Your Royal Canadian Mounted Police hat set squarely across the wide white brow . . .

Your white legs touching each other, under the banquet table . . .

Probably you are walking with your husband in SoHo, seeing what the new artists are refusing to do there, in their quest for a scratch to start from.

The artists regard your brown campaign hat, your white legs. "Holy God!" they say, and return to their lofts.

I have spent many message units seeking your voice, but I always get Frederick instead.

"Well, Frederick," I ask cordially, "what amazing triumphs have you accomplished today?"

He has been offered a sinecure at Stanford and a cenotaph at CCNY. Bidding for world rights to his breath has begun at $500,000.

But I am wondering—

When you placed your hand on my napkin, at the banquet, did that mean anything?

When you smashed in the top of my soft-boiled egg for me, at the banquet, did that indicate that I might continue to hope?

I will name certain children after you. (People often ask my advice about naming things.) It will be suspicious, so many small

Philippas popping up in our city, but the pattern will become visible only with the passage of time, and in the interval, what satisfaction!

I cannot imagine the future. You have not made your intentions clear, if indeed you have any. Now you are climbing aboard a great ship, and the hawsers are being loosed, and the flowers in the cabins arranged, and the dinner gong sounded. . . .

VISITORS

It's three o'clock in the morning.

Bishop's daughter is ill, stomach pains. She's sleeping on the couch.

Bishop too is ill, chills and sweating, a flu. He can't sleep. In bed, he listens to the occasional groans from two rooms away. Katie is fifteen and spends the summer with him every year.

Outside on the street, someone kicks on a motorcycle and revs it unforgivingly. His bedroom is badly placed.

He's given her Pepto-Bismol, if she wakes again he'll try Tylenol. He wraps himself in the sheet, pulls his t-shirt away from his damp chest.

There's a radio playing somewhere in the building, big-band music, he feels rather than hears it. The steady, friendly air conditioner hustling in the next room.

Earlier he'd taken her to a doctor, who found nothing. "You've got a bellyache," the doctor said, "stick with fluids and call me if it doesn't go away." Katie is beautiful, tall with dark hair.

In the afternoon they'd gone, groaning, to a horror movie about wolves taking over the city. At vivid moments she jumped against him, pressing her breasts into his back. He moved away.

When they walk together on the street she takes his arm, holding on tightly (because, he figures, she spends so much of her time away, away). Very often people give them peculiar looks.

He's been picking up old ladies who've been falling down in front of him, these last few days. One sitting in the middle of an intersection waving her arms while dangerous Checkers curved around her. The old ladies invariably display a superb fighting spirit. "Thank you, young man!"

He's forty-nine. Writing a history of 19th Century American painting, about which he knows a thing or two.

Not enough.

A groan, heartfelt but muted, from the other room. She's awake.

He gets up and goes in to look at her. The red-and-white cotton robe she's wearing is tucked up under her knees. "I just threw up again," she says.

"Did it help?"

"A little."

He once asked her what something (a box? a chair?) was made of and she told him it was made out of tree.

"Do you want to try a glass of milk?"

"I don't want any milk," she says, turning to lie on her front. "Sit with me."

He sits on the edge of the couch and rubs her back. "Think of something terrific," he says. "Let's get your mind off your stomach. Think about fishing. Think about the time you threw the hotel keys out of the window." Once, in Paris, she had done just that, from a sixth-floor window, and Bishop had had visions of some Frenchman walking down the Quai des Grands-Augustins with a set of heavy iron hotel keys buried in his brain. He'd found the keys in a potted plant outside the hotel door.

"Daddy," she says, not looking at him.

"Yes?"

"Why do you live like this? By yourself?"

"Who am I going to live with?"

"You could find somebody. You're handsome for your age."

"Oh very good. That's very neat. I thank you."

"You don't try."

This is and is not true.

"How much do you weigh?"

"One eighty-five."

"You could lose some weight."

"Look, kid, gimme a break." He blots his forehead with his arm. "You want some cambric tea?"

"You've given up."

"Not so," he says. "Katie, go to sleep now. Think of a great big pile of Gucci handbags."

She sighs and turns her head away.

Bishop goes into the kitchen and turns on the light. He wonders what a drink would do to him, or for him—put him to sleep? He decides against it. He turns on the tiny kitchen TV and spends a few minutes watching some kind of Japanese monster movie. The poorly designed monster is picking up handfuls of people and, rather thoughtfully, eating them. Bishop thinks about Tokyo. He was once in bed with a Japanese girl during a mild earthquake, and he's never forgotten the feeling of the floor falling out from underneath him, or the woman's terror. He suddenly remembers her name, Michiko. "You no butterfly on me?" she had asked, when they met. He was astonished to learn that "butterfly" meant, in the patois of the time, "abandon." She cooked their meals over a charcoal brazier and they slept in a niche in the wall closed off from the rest of her room by sliding paper doors. Bishop worked on the copy desk at *Stars & Stripes*. One day a wire photo came in showing the heads of the four (then) women's services posing for a group portrait. Bishop slugged the caption LEADING LADIES. The elderly master sergeant who was serving as city editor brought the photo back to Bishop's desk. "We can't do this," he said. "Ain't it a shame?"

He switches channels and gets Dolly Parton singing, by coincidence, "House of the Rising Sun."

At some point during each summer she'll say: "Why did you and my mother split up?"

"It was your fault," he answers. "Yours. You made too much noise, as a kid, I couldn't work." His ex-wife had once told Katie this as an explanation for the divorce, and he'll repeat it until its untruth is marble, a monument.

His ex-wife is otherwise very sensible, and thrifty, too.

Why do I live this way? Best I can do.

Walking down West Broadway on a Saturday afternoon. Barking art caged in the high white galleries, don't go inside or it'll get you, leap into your lap and cover your face with kisses. Some goes to the other extreme, snarls and shows its brilliant teeth. O art I won't hurt you if you don't hurt me. Citizens parading, plump-faced and bone-faced, lightly clad. A young black boy toting a Board of Education trombone case. A fellow with oddly cut hair the color of marigolds and a roll of roofing felt over his shoulder.

Bishop in the crowd, thirty dollars in his pocket in case he has to buy a pal a drink.

Into a gallery because it must be done. The artist's hung twenty EVERLAST heavy bags in rows of four, you're invited to have a bash. People are giving the bags every kind of trouble. Bishop, unable to resist, bangs one with his fabled left, and hurts his hand.

Bloody artists.

Out on the street again, he is bumped into by a man, then another man, then a woman. And here's Harry in lemon pants with his Britisher friend, Malcolm.

"Harry, Malcolm."

"Professor," Harry says ironically (he is a professor, Bishop is not).

Harry's got not much hair and has lost weight since he split with Tom. Malcolm is the single most cheerful individual Bishop has ever met.

Harry's university has just hired a new president who's thirty-two. Harry can't get over it.

"*Thirty-two!* I mean I don't think the board's got both oars in the water."

Standing behind Malcolm is a beautiful young woman.

"This is Christie," Malcolm says. "We've just given her lunch. We've just eaten all the dim sum in the world."

Bishop is immediately seized by a desire to cook for Christie—either his Eight-Bean Soup or his Crash Cassoulet.

She's telling him something about her windows.

"I don't care but why under my windows?"

She's wearing a purple shirt and is deeply tanned with black hair—looks like an Indian, in fact, the one who sells Mazola on TV.

Harry is still talking about the new president. "I mean he did his dissertation on *bathing trends*."

"Well maybe he knows where the big bucks are."

There's some leftover duck in the refrigerator he can use for the cassoulet.

"Well," he says to Christie, "are you hungry?"

"Yes," she says, "I am."

"We just ate," Harry says. "You can't be hungry. You can't possibly be hungry."

"Hungry hungry hungry," she says, taking Bishop's arm, which is, can you believe it, sticking out.

Putting slices of duck in bean water while Christie watches *The Adventures of Robin Hood,* with Errol Flynn and Basil Rathbone, on the kitchen TV. At the same time Hank Williams, Jr., is singing on the FM.

"I like a place where I can take my shoes off," she says, as Errol Flynn throws a whole dead deer on the banquet table.

Bishop, chopping parsley, is taking quick glances at her to see what she looks like with a glass of wine in her hand. Some people look good with white wine, some don't.

He makes a mental note to buy some Mazola—a case, maybe.

"Here's sixty seconds on fenders," says the radio.

"Do you live with anybody?" Christie asks.

"My daughter is here sometimes. Summers and Christmas." A little tarragon into the bean water. "How about you?"

"There's this guy."

But there had to be. Bishop chops steadfastly with his Three Sheep brand Chinese chopper, made in gray Fushan.

"He's an artist."

As who is not? "What kind of an artist?"

"A painter. He's in Seattle. He needs rain."

He throws handfuls of sliced onions into the water, then a can of tomato paste.

"How long does this take?" Christie asks. "I'm not rushing you. I'm just curious."

"Another hour."

"Then I'll have a little vodka. Straight. Ice. If you don't mind." Bishop loves women who drink.

Maybe she smokes!

"Actually I can't stand artists," she says.

"Like who in particular?"

"Like that woman who puts chewing gum on her stomach—"

"She doesn't do that anymore. And the chewing gum was not poorly placed."

"And that other one who cuts off parts of himself, *whittles* on himself, that fries my ass."

"It's supposed to."

"Yeah," she says, shaking the ice in her glass. "I'm reacting like a bozo."

She gets up and walks over to the counter and takes a Lark from his pack.

Very happily, Bishop begins to talk. He tells her that the night before he had smelled smoke, had gotten up and checked the apartment, knowing that a pier was on fire over by the river and suspecting it was that. He had turned on the TV to get the all-news channel and while dialing had encountered the opening credits of a Richard Widmark cop film called *Brock's Last Case* which he had then sat down and watched, his faithful Scotch at his side, until five o'clock in the morning. Richard Widmark was one of his favorite actors in the whole world, he told her, because of the way in which Richard Widmark was able to convey, what was the word, resilience. You could knock Richard Widmark down, he said, you could even knock Richard Widmark down repeatedly, but you had better bear in mind while knocking Richard Widmark down that Richard Widmark was pretty damn sure going to bounce back up and batter your conk—

"Redford is the one I like," she says.

Bishop can understand this. He nods seriously.

"The thing I like about Redford is," she says, and for ten minutes she tells him about Robert Redford.

He tastes the cassoulet with a long spoon. More salt.

It appears that she is also mighty fond of Clint Eastwood.

Bishop has the sense that the conversation has strayed, like a bad cow, from the proper path.

"Old Clint Eastwood," he says, shaking his head admiringly. "We're ready."

He dishes up the cassoulet and fetches hot bread from the oven.

"Tastes like real cassoulet," she says.

"That's the ox-tail soup mix." Why is he serving her cassoulet in summer? It's hot.

He's opened a bottle of Robert Mondavi table red.

"*Very* good," she says. "I mean I'm surprised. Really."

"Maybe could have had more tomato."

"No, really." She tears off a fistful of French bread. "Men are quite odd. I saw this guy at the farmer's market on Union Square this morning? He was standing in front of a table full of greens and radishes and corn and this and that, behind a bunch of other people, and he was staring at this farmer-girl who was wearing cutoffs and a tank top and every time she leaned over to grab a cabbage or whatnot he was getting a shot of her breasts, which were, to be fair, quite pretty—I mean how much fun can that be?"

"Moderate amount of fun. Some fun. Not much fun. What can I say?"

"And that plug I live with."

"What about him?"

"He gave me a book once."

"What was it?"

"Book about how to fix home appliances. The dishwasher was broken. Then he bought me a screwdriver. This really nice screwdriver."

"Well."

"I *fixed* the damned dishwasher. Took me two days."

"Would you like to go to bed now?"

"No," Christie says, "not yet."

Not yet! Very happily, Bishop pours more wine.

Now he's sweating, little chills at intervals. He gets a sheet from the bedroom and sits in the kitchen with the sheet draped around him, guru-style. He can hear Katie turning restlessly on the couch.

He admires the way she organizes her life—that is, the way she gets done what she wants done. A little wangling, a little nagging, a little let's-go-take-a-look and Bishop has sprung for a new pair of boots, handsome ankle-height black diablo numbers that she'll wear with black ski pants. . . .

Well, he doesn't give her many presents.

Could he bear a Scotch? He thinks not.

He remembers a dream in which he dreamed that his nose was as dark and red as a Bing cherry. As would be appropriate.

"Daddy?"

Still wearing the yellow sheet, he gets up and goes into the other room.

"I can't sleep."

"I'm sorry."

"Talk to me."

Bishop sits again on the edge of the couch. How large she is!

He gives her his Art History lecture.

"Then you get *Mo*-net and *Ma*-net, that's a little tricky, *Mo*-net was the one did all the water lilies and shit, his colors were blues and greens, *Ma*-net was the one did Bareass on the Grass and shit, his colors were browns and greens. Then you get Bonnard, he did all the interiors and shit, amazing light, and then you get Van Guk, he's the one with the ear and shit, and Say-zanne, he's the one with the apples and shit, you get Kandinsky, a bad mother, all them pick-up-sticks pictures, you get my man Mondrian, he's the one with the rectangles and shit, his colors were red yellow and blue, you get Moholy-Nagy, he did all the plastic thingummies and shit, you get Mar-cel Duchamp, he's the devil in human form. . . ."

She's asleep.

Bishop goes back into the kitchen and makes himself a drink.

It's five-thirty. Faint light in the big windows.

Christie's in Seattle, and plans to stay.

Looking out of the windows in the early morning he can sometimes see the two old ladies who live in the apartment whose garden backs up to his building having breakfast by candlelight. He can never figure out whether they are terminally romantic or whether, rather, they're trying to save electricity.

THE WOUND

He sits up again. He makes a wild grab for his mother's hair. The hair of his mother! But she neatly avoids him. The cook enters with the roast beef. The mother of the torero tastes the sauce, which is presented separately, in a silver dish. She makes a face. The torero, ignoring the roast beef, takes the silver dish from his mother and sips from it, meanwhile maintaining intense eye contact with his mistress. The torero's mistress hands the camera to the torero's mother and reaches for the silver dish. "What is all this nonsense with the dish?" asks the famous aficionado who is sitting by the bedside. The torero offers the aficionado a slice of beef, carved from the roast with a sword, of which there are perhaps a dozen on the bed. "These fellows with their swords, they think they're so fine," says one of the *imbéciles* to another, quietly. The second *imbécil* says, "We would all think ourselves fine if we could. But we can't. Something prevents us."

The torero looks with irritation in the direction of the *imbéciles*. His mistress takes the 8-mm movie camera from his mother and begins to film something outside the window. The torero has been gored in the foot. He is, in addition, surrounded by *imbéciles, idiotas,* and *bobos*. He shifts uncomfortably in his bed. Several swords fall to the floor. A telegram is delivered. The mistress of the torero puts down the camera and removes her shirt. The mother of the torero looks angrily at the *imbéciles*. The famous aficionado reads the telegram aloud. The telegram suggests the torero is a clown and a *cucaracha* for allowing himself to be gored in the foot, thus both insulting the noble profession of which he is such a poor representative and irrevocably ruining the telegram sender's Sunday afternoon, and that, furthermore, the telegram sender is even now on his way to the Church of Our Lady of the Several Sorrows to pray *against* the torero, whose future, he cordially hopes, is a thing of the past. The torero's head flops forward into the cupped hands of an adjacent *bobo*.

The mother of the torero turns on the television set, where the goring of the foot of the torero is being shown first at normal speed, then in exquisite slow motion. The torero's head remains in the cupped hands of the *bobo*. "My foot!" he shouts. Someone turns off the television. The beautiful breasts of the torero's mistress are appreciated by the aficionado, who is also an aficionado of breasts. The *imbéciles* and *idiotas* are afraid to look. So they do not. One *idiota* says to another *idiota*, "I would greatly like some of that roast beef." "But it has not been offered to us," his companion replies, "because we are so insignificant." "But no one else is eating it," the first says. "It simply sits there, on the plate." They regard the attractive roast of beef.

The torero's mother picks up the movie camera that his mistress has relinquished and begins filming the torero's foot, playing with the zoom lens. The torero, head still in the hands of the *bobo*, reaches into a drawer in the bedside table and removes from a box there a Cuban cigar of the first quality. Two *bobos* and an *imbécil* rush to light it for him, bumping into each other in the process. "Lysol," says the mother of the torero. "I forgot the application of the Lysol." She puts down the camera and looks around for the Lysol bottle. But the cook has taken it away. The mother of the torero leaves the room, in search of the Lysol bottle. He, the torero, lifts his head and follows her exit. More pain?

His mother reenters the room carrying a bottle of Lysol. The torero places his bandaged foot under a pillow, and both hands, fingers spread wide, on top of the pillow. His mother unscrews the top of the bottle of Lysol. The Bishop of Valencia enters with attendants. The Bishop is a heavy man with his head cocked permanently to the left—the result of years of hearing confessions in a confessional whose right-hand box was said to be inhabited by vipers. The torero's mistress hastily puts on her shirt. The *imbéciles* and *idiotas* retire into the walls. The Bishop extends his hand. The torero kisses the Bishop's ring. The famous aficionado does likewise. The Bishop asks if he may inspect the wound. The torero takes his foot out from under the pillow. The torero's mother unwraps the bandage. There is the foot, swollen almost twice normal size. In the center of the foot, the wound, surrounded by angry flesh. The Bishop shakes his head, closes his eyes, raises his head (on the diagonal), and murmurs a short prayer. Then he opens his eyes and looks about him for a chair. An *idiota* rushes forward with a chair. The Bishop seats himself by the bedside. The torero offers the Bishop some cold roast beef. The Bishop begins to talk about his psychoanalysis: "I am a different man now," the Bishop says. "Gloomier, duller, more fearful. In the name of the Holy Ghost, you would not believe what I see under the bed, in the middle of the night." The Bishop laughs heartily. The torero joins him. The torero's mistress is filming the Bishop. "I was happier with my whiskey," the Bishop says, laughing even harder. The laughter of the Bishop threatens the chair he is sitting in. One *bobo* says to another *bobo,* "The privileged classes can afford psychoanalysis and whiskey. Whereas all we get is sermons and sour wine. This is manifestly unfair. I protest, silently." "It is because we are no good," the second *bobo* says. "It is because we are nothings."

The torero opens a bottle of Chivas Regal. He offers a shot to the Bishop, who graciously accepts, and then pours one for himself. The torero's mother edges toward the bottle of Chivas Regal. The torero's mistress films his mother's surreptitious approach. The Bishop and the torero discuss whiskey and psychoanalysis. The torero's mother has a hand on the neck of the bottle. The torero makes a sudden wild grab for her hair. The hair of his mother! He misses and she scuttles off into a corner of the room, clutching the bottle.

The torero picks a killing sword, an *estoque,* from the half-dozen still on the bed. The Queen of the Gypsies enters.

The Queen hurries to the torero, little tufts of dried grass falling from her robes as she crosses the room. "Unwrap the wound!" she cries. "The wound, the wound, the wound!" The torero recoils. The Bishop sits severely. His attendants stir and whisper. The torero's mother takes a swig from the Chivas Regal bottle. The famous aficionado crosses himself. The torero's mistress looks down through her half-open blouse at her breasts. The torero quickly reaches into the drawer of the bedside table and removes the cigar box. He takes from the cigar box the ears and tail of a bull he killed, with excellence and emotion, long ago. He spreads them out on the bedcovers, offering them to the Queen. The ears resemble bloody wallets, the tail the hair of some long-dead saint, robbed from a reliquary. "No," the Queen says. She grasps the torero's foot and begins to unwrap the bandages. The torero grimaces but submits. The Queen withdraws from her belt a sharp knife. The torero's mistress picks up a violin and begins to play an air by Valdéz. The Queen whacks off a huge portion of roast beef, which she stuffs into her mouth while bent over the wound—gazing deeply into it, savoring it. Everyone shrinks—the torero, his mother, his mistress, the Bishop, the aficionado, the *imbéciles, idiotas,* and *bobos.* An ecstasy of shrinking. The Queen says, "I want this wound. *This one.* It is mine. Come, pick him up." Everyone present takes a handful of the torero and lifts him high above their heads (he is screaming). But the doorway is suddenly blocked by the figure of an immense black bull. The bull begins to ring, like a telephone.

AT THE TOLSTOY MUSEUM

At the Tolstoy Museum we sat and wept. Paper streamers came out of our eyes. Our gaze drifted toward the pictures. They were placed too high on the wall. We suggested to the director that they be lowered six inches at least. He looked unhappy but said he would see to it. The holdings of the Tolstoy Museum consist principally of some thirty thousand pictures of Count Leo Tolstoy.

After they had lowered the pictures we went back to the Tolstoy Museum. I don't think you can peer into one man's face too long—for too long a period. A great many human passions could be discerned, behind the skin.

Tolstoy means "fat" in Russian. His grandfather sent his linen to Holland to be washed. His mother *did not know* any bad words. As a youth he shaved off his eyebrows, hoping they would grow back bushier. He first contracted gonorrhea in 1847. He was once bitten on the face by a bear. He became a vegetarian in 1885. To make himself interesting, he occasionally bowed backward.

I was eating a sandwich at the Tolstoy Museum. The Tolstoy Museum is made of stone—many stones, cunningly wrought. Viewed from the street, it has the aspect of three stacked boxes: the first, second, and third levels. These are of increasing size. The first level is, say, the size of a shoebox, the second level the size of a case of whiskey, and the third level the size of a box that contained a new overcoat. The amazing cantilever of the third level has been much talked about. The glass floor there allows one to look straight down and provides a "floating" feeling. The entire building, viewed from the street, suggests that it is about to fall on you. This the architects relate to Tolstoy's moral authority.

Tolstoy's Coat

In the basement of the Tolstoy Museum carpenters uncrated new pictures of Count Leo Tolstoy. The huge crates stenciled FRAGILE in red ink . . .

The guards at the Tolstoy Museum carry buckets in which there are stacks of clean white pocket handkerchiefs. More than any other museum, the Tolstoy Museum induces weeping. Even the bare title of a Tolstoy work, with its burden of love, can induce weeping— for example, the article titled "Who Should Teach Whom to Write, We the Peasant Children or the Peasant Children Us?" Many people stand before this article, weeping. Too, those who are caught by Tolstoy's eyes, in the various portraits, room after room after room, are not unaffected by the experience. It is like, people say, committing a small crime and being discovered at it by your father, who stands in four doorways, looking at you.

I was reading a story of Tolstoy's at the Tolstoy Museum. In this story a bishop is sailing on a ship. One of his fellow-passengers tells the Bishop about an island on which three hermits live. The hermits are said to be extremely devout. The Bishop is seized with a desire to see and talk with the hermits. He persuades the captain of the ship to anchor near the island. He goes ashore in a small boat. He speaks to the hermits. The hermits tell the Bishop how they worship God. They have a prayer that goes: "Three of You, three of us, have mercy on us." The Bishop feels that this is a prayer prayed in the wrong way. He undertakes to teach the hermits the Lord's Prayer. The hermits learn the Lord's Prayer but with the greatest difficulty. Night has fallen by the time they have got it correctly.

The Bishop returns to his ship, happy that he has been able to assist the hermits in their worship. The ship sails on. The Bishop sits alone on deck, thinking about the experiences of the day. He sees a light in the sky, behind the ship. The light is cast by the three hermits floating over the water, hand in hand, without moving their feet. They catch up with the ship, saying: "We have forgotten, servant of God, we have forgotten your teaching!" They ask him to teach them again. The Bishop crosses himself. Then he tells the

Tolstoy as a Youth

At Starogladkovskaya, About 1852

Tiger Hunt, Siberia

hermits that their prayer, too, reaches God. "It is not for me to teach you. Pray for us sinners!" The Bishop bows to the deck. The hermits fly back over the sea, hand in hand, to their island.

The story is written in a very simple style. It is said to originate in a folk tale. There is a version of it in St. Augustine. I was incredibly depressed by reading this story. Its beauty. Distance.

At the Tolstoy Museum, sadness grasped the 741 Sunday visitors. The Museum was offering a series of lectures on the text "Why Do Men Stupefy Themselves?" The visitors were made sad by these eloquent speakers, who were probably right.

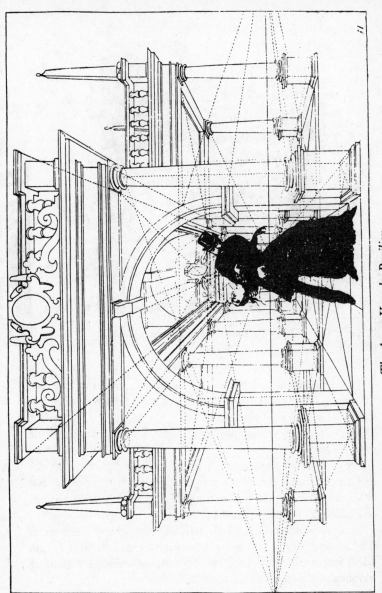

The Anna-Vronsky Pavilion

At the Disaster (Arrow Indicates Tolstoy)

People stared at tiny pictures of Turgenev, Nekrasov, and Fet. These and other small pictures hung alongside extremely large pictures of Count Leo Tolstoy.

In the plaza, a sinister musician played a wood trumpet while two children watched.

We considered the 640,086 pages (Jubilee Edition) of the author's published work. Some people wanted him to go away, but other people were glad we had him. "He has been a lifelong source of inspiration to me," one said.

I haven't made up my mind. Standing here in the "Summer in the Country" Room, several hazes passed over my eyes. Still, I think I will march on to "A Landlord's Morning." Perhaps something vivifying will happen to me there.

Museum Plaza With Monumental Head (Closed Mondays)

THE FLIGHT OF PIGEONS
FROM THE PALACE

IN the abandoned palazzo, weeds and old blankets filled the rooms. The palazzo was in bad shape. We cleaned the abandoned palazzo for ten years. We scoured the stones. The splendid architecture was furbished and painted. The doors and windows were dealt with. Then we were ready for the show.

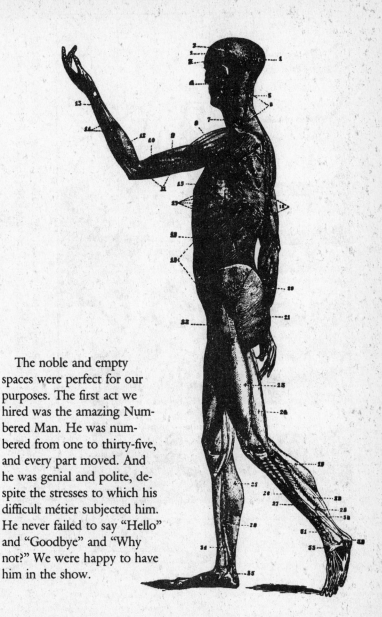

The noble and empty spaces were perfect for our purposes. The first act we hired was the amazing Numbered Man. He was numbered from one to thirty-five, and every part moved. And he was genial and polite, despite the stresses to which his difficult métier subjected him. He never failed to say "Hello" and "Goodbye" and "Why not?" We were happy to have him in the show.

Then, the Sulking Lady was obtained. She showed us her back. That was the way she felt. She had always felt that way, she said. She had felt that way since she was four years old.

We obtained other attractions—a Singing Sword and a Stone Eater. Tickets and programs were prepared. Buckets of water were placed about, in case of fire. Silver strings tethered the loud-roaring strong-stinking animals.

The lineup for opening night included:

> A startlingly handsome man
> A Grand Cham
> A tulip craze
> The Prime Rate
> Edgar Allan Poe
> A colored light

We asked ourselves: How can we improve the show?

We auditioned an explosion.

There were a lot of situations where men were being evil to women—dominating them and eating their food. We put those situations in the show.

In the summer of the
show, grave robbers appeared
in the show. Famous graves
were robbed, before your
eyes. Winding-sheets were
unwound and things best forgotten were remembered. Sad
themes were played by the
band, bereft of its mind by
the death of its tradition. In
the soft evening of the show,
a troupe of agoutis performed
tax evasion atop tall, swaying
yellow poles. Before your
eyes.

The trapeze artist with
whom I had an understand-
ing . . . The moment when
she failed to catch me . . .

Did she really try? I can't
recall her ever failing to catch
anyone she was really fond of.
Her great muscles are too
deft for that. Her great muscles at which we gaze through
heavy-lidded eyes . . .

We recruited fools for the show. We had spots for a number of fools (and in the big all-fool number that occurs immediately after the second act, some specialties). But fools are hard to find. Usually they don't like to admit it. We settled for gowks, gulls, mooncalfs. A few babies, boobies, sillies, simps. A barmie was engaged, along with certain dum-dums and beefheads. A noodle. When you see them all wandering around, under the colored lights, gibbering and performing miracles, you are surprised.

I put my father in the show, with his cold eyes. His segment was called My Father Concerned About His Liver.

Performances flew thick and fast.

We performed The Sale of the Public Library.

We performed Space Monkeys Approve Appropriations.

We did Theological Novelties and we did Cereal Music (with its raisins of beauty) and we did not neglect Piles of Discarded Women Rising from the Sea.

There was faint applause. The audience huddled together. The people counted their sins.

Scenes of domestic life were put in the show.

We used The Flight of Pigeons from the Palace.

It is difficult to keep the public interested.

The public demands new wonders piled on new wonders.

Often we don't know where our next marvel is coming from.

The supply of strange ideas is not endless.

The development of new wonders is not like the production of canned goods. Some things appear to be wonders in the beginning, but when you become familiar with them, are not wonderful at all. Sometimes a seventy-five-foot highly paid cacodemon will raise only the tiniest *frisson*. Some of us have even thought of folding the show—closing it down. That thought has been gliding through the hallways and rehearsal rooms of the show.

The new volcano we have just placed under contract seems very promising. . . .

A FEW MOMENTS
OF SLEEPING AND WAKING

EDWARD woke up. Pia was already awake.

"What did you dream?"

"You were my brother," Pia said. "We were making a film. You were the hero. It was a costume film. You had a cape and a sword. You were jumping about, jumping on tables. But in the second half of the film you had lost all your weight. You were thin. The film was ruined. The parts didn't match."

"I was your brother?"

Scarlatti from the radio. It was Sunday. Pete sat at the breakfast table. Pete was a doctor on an American nuclear submarine, a psychiatrist. He had just come off patrol, fifty-eight days under the water. Pia gave Pete scrambled eggs with mushrooms, *wienerbrød*, salami with red wine in it, bacon. Pete interpreted Pia's dream.

"Edward was your brother?"

"Yes."

"And your real brother is going to Italy, you said."

"Yes."

"It may be something as simple as a desire to travel."

Edward and Pia and Pete went for a boat ride, a tour of the Copenhagen harbor. The boat held one hundred and twenty tourists. They sat, four tourists abreast, on either side of the aisle. A guide spoke into a microphone in Danish, French, German, and English, telling the tourists what was in the harbor.

"I interpreted that dream very sketchily," Pete said to Edward.

"Yes."

"I could have done a lot more with it."

"Don't."

"This is the Danish submarine fleet," the guide said into the microphone. Edward and Pia and Pete regarded the four black submarines. There had been a flick every night on Pete's submarine. Pete discussed the fifty-eight flicks he had seen. Pete sat on Edward's couch discussing *The Sound of Music*. Edward made drinks. Rose's Lime Juice fell into the gimlet glasses. Then Edward and Pia took Pete to the airport. Pete flew away. Edward bought *The Interpretation of Dreams*.

Pia dreamed that she had journeyed to a great house, a castle, to sing. She had found herself a bed in a room overlooking elaborate gardens. Then another girl appeared, a childhood friend. The new girl demanded Pia's bed. Pia refused. The other girl insisted. Pia refused. The other girl began to sing. She sang horribly. Pia asked her to stop. Other singers appeared, demanding that Pia surrender the bed. Pia refused. People stood about the bed, shouting and singing.

Edward smoked a cigar. "Why didn't you just give her the bed?"

"My honor would be hurt," Pia said. "You know, that girl is not like that. Really she is very quiet and not asserting—asserting?— asserting herself. My mother said I should be more like her."

"The dream was saying that your mother was wrong about this girl?"

"Perhaps."

"What else?"

"I can't remember."

"Did you sing?"

"I can't remember," Pia said.

Pia's brother Søren rang the doorbell. He was carrying a pair of trousers. Pia sewed up a split in the seat. Edward made instant coffee. Pia explained *blufaerdighedskraenkelse*. "If you walk with your trousers open," she said. Søren gave Edward and Pia *The Joan Baez Songbook*. "It is a very good one," he said in English. The doorbell rang. It was Pia's father. He was carrying a pair of shoes Pia had left at the farm. Edward made more coffee. Pia sat on the floor cutting a dress out of blue, red, and green cloth. Ole arrived. He was carrying his guitar. He began to play something from *The Joan Baez Songbook*. Edward regarded Ole's Mowgli hair. We be of one blood, thee and I. Edward read *The Interpretation of Dreams*. "In cases where not my ego but only a strange person appears in the dream-content, I may safely assume that by means of identification my ego is concealed behind that person. I am permitted to supplement my ego."

Edward sat at a sidewalk café drinking a beer. He was wearing his brown suède shoes, his black dungarees, his black-and-white-checked shirt, his red beard, his immense spectacles. Edward regarded his hands. His hands seemed old. "I am thirty-three." Tiny girls walked past the sidewalk café wearing skintight black pants. Then large girls in skintight white pants.

Edward and Pia walked along Frederiksberg Allé, under the queer box-cut trees. "Here I was knocked off my bicycle when I was seven," Pia said. "By a car. In a snowstorm."

Edward regarded the famous intersection. "Were you hurt?"

"My bicycle was demolished utterly."

Edward read *The Interpretation of Dreams*. Pia bent over the sewing machine, sewing blue, red, and green cloth.

"Freud turned his friend R. into a disreputable uncle, in a dream."

"Why?"

"He wanted to be an assistant professor. He was bucking for assistant professor."

"So why was it not allowed?"

"They didn't know he was Freud. They hadn't seen the movie."

"You're joking."

"I'm trying."

Edward and Pia talked about dreams. Pia said she had been dreaming about unhappy love affairs. In these dreams, she said, she was very unhappy. Then she woke, relieved.

"How long?"

"For about two months, I think. But then I wake up and I'm happy. That it is not so."

"Why are they *unhappy* love affairs?"

"I don't know."

"Do you think it means you want new love affairs?"

"Why should I want unhappy love affairs?"

"Maybe you want to have love affairs but feel guilty about wanting to have love affairs, and so they become unhappy love affairs."

"That's subtle," Pia said. "You're insecure."

"Ho!" Edward said.

"But why then am I happy when I wake up?"

"Because you don't have to feel guilty anymore," Edward said glibly.

"Ho!" Pia said.

Edward resisted *The Interpretation of Dreams*. He read eight novels by Anthony Powell. Pia walked down the street in Edward's blue sweater. She looked at herself in a shop window. Her hair was rotten. Pia went into the bathroom and played with her hair for one hour. Then she brushed her teeth for a bit. Her hair was still rotten. Pia sat down and began to cry. She cried for a quarter hour, without making any noise. Everything was rotten.

Edward bought *Madam Cherokee's Dream Book*. Dreams in alphabetical order. If you dream of black cloth, there will be a death in the family. If you dream of scissors, a birth. Edward and Pia saw three films by Jean-Luc Godard. The landlord came and asked Edward to pay Danish income tax. "But I don't make any money in Denmark," Edward said. Everything was rotten.

Pia came home from the hairdresser with black varnish around her eyes.

"How do you like it?"

"I hate it."

Pia was chopping up an enormous cabbage, a cabbage big as a basketball. The cabbage was of an extraordinary size. It was a big cabbage.

"That's a big cabbage," Edward said.

"Big," Pia said.

They regarded the enormous cabbage God had placed in the world for supper.

"Is there vinegar?" Edward asked. "I like . . . vinegar . . . with my . . ." Edward read a magazine for men full of colored photographs of naked girls living normal lives. Edward read the *New Statesman,* with its letters to the editor. Pia appeared in her new blue, red, and green dress. She looked wonderful.

"You look wonderful."

"Tak."

"Tables are women," Edward said. "You remember you said I was jumping on tables, in your dream. Freud says that tables are figures for women. You're insecure."

"La vache!" Pia said.

Pia reported a new dream. "I came home to a small town where I was born. First, I ran around as a tourist with my camera. Then a boy who was selling something—from one of those little wagons?—asked me to take his picture. But I couldn't find him in the photo *apparat.* In the view glass. Always other people got in the way. Everyone in this town was divorced. Everybody I knew. Then I went to a ladies' club, a place where the women asked the men to dance. But there was only one man there. His picture was on an advertisement outside. He was the gigolo. Gigolo? Is that right? Then I called up people I knew, on the telephone. But they were all divorced. Everybody was divorced. My mother and father were divorced. Helle and Jens were divorced. Everybody. Everybody was floating about in a strange way."

Edward groaned. A palpable groan. "What else?"

"I can't remember."

"Nothing else?"

"When I was on my way to the ladies' club, the boy I had tried to take a picture of came up and took my arm. I was surprised but I said to myself something like, *It's necessary to have friends here.*"

"What else?"

"I can't remember."

"Did you sleep with him?"

"I don't remember."

"What did the ladies' club remind you of?"

"It was in a cellar."

"Did it remind you of anything?"

"It was rather like a place at the university. Where we used to dance."

"What is connected with that place in your mind?"

"Once a boy came through a window to a party."

"Why did he come through the window?"

"So he didn't pay."

"Who was he?"

"Someone."

"Did you dance with him?"

"Yes."

"Did you sleep with him?"

"Yes."

"Very often?"

"Twice."

Edward and Pia went to Malmö on the flying boat. The hydrofoil leaped into the air. The feeling was that of a plane laboring down an interminable runway.

"I dreamed of a roof," Pia said. "Where corn was kept. Where it was stored."

"What does that—" Edward began.

"Also I dreamed of rugs. I was beating a rug," she went on. "And I dreamed about horses, I was riding."

"Don't," Edward said.

Pia silently rehearsed three additional dreams. Edward regarded the green leaves of Malmö. Edward and Pia moved through the rug department of a department store. Surrounded by exciting rugs: Rya rugs, Polish rugs, rag rugs, straw rugs, area rugs, wall-to-wall rugs, rug remnants. Edward was thinking about one that cost five hundred crowns, in seven shades of red, about the size of an opened-up *Herald Tribune,* Paris edition.

"It is too good for the floor, clearly," Pia said. "It is to be hung on the wall."

Edward had four hundred dollars in his pocket. It was supposed to last him two months. The hideously smiling rug salesman pressed closer. They burst into the street. Just in time. "God knows they're beautiful, however," Edward said.

"What did you dream last night?" Edward asked. "What did you dream? What?"

"I can't remember."

Edward decided that he worried too much about the dark side of Pia. Pia regarded as a moon. Edward lay in bed trying to remember a dream. He could not remember. It was eight o'clock. Edward climbed out of bed to see if there was mail on the floor, if mail had fallen through the door. No. Pia awoke.

"I dreamed of beans."

Edward looked at her. *Madam Cherokee's Dream Book* flew into his hand.

"To dream of beans is, in all cases, very unfortunate. Eating them means sickness, preparing them means that the married state will be a very difficult one for you. To dream of *beets* is on the other hand a happy omen."

Edward and Pia argued about *Mrs. Miniver*. It was not written by J. B. Priestley, Edward said.

"I remember it very well," Pia insisted. "Errol Flynn was her husband, he was standing there with his straps, his straps"—Pia made a holding-up-trousers gesture—"hanging, and she said that she loved Walter Pidgeon."

"Errol Flynn was not even in the picture. You think J. B. Priestley wrote everything, don't you? Everything in English."

"I don't."

"Errol Flynn was not even in the picture." Edward was drunk. He was shouting. "Errol Flynn was not even . . . *in* . . . the goddamn *picture!*"

Pia was not quite asleep. She was standing on a street corner. Women regarded her out of the corners of their eyes. She was holding a string bag containing strawberries, beer, razor blades, turnips. An old lady rode up on a bicycle and stopped for the traffic light. The old lady straddled her bicycle, seized Pia's string bag, and threw it into the gutter. Then she pedaled away, with the changing light. People crowded around. Someone picked up the string bag. Pia shook her head. "No," she said. "She just . . . I have never seen her before." Someone asked Pia if she wanted him to call a policeman. "What for?" Pia said. Her father was standing there smiling. Pia thought, *These things have no significance really.* Pia thought, *If this is to be my dream for tonight, then I don't want it.*

THE TEMPTATION
OF ST. ANTHONY

Yes, the saint was underrated quite a bit, then, mostly by people who didn't like things that were ineffable. I think that's quite understandable—that kind of thing can be extremely irritating, to some people. After all, everything is hard enough without having to deal with something that is not tangible and clear. The higher orders of abstraction are just a nuisance, to some people, although to others, of course, they are quite interesting. I would say that on the whole, people who didn't like this kind of idea, or who refused to think about it, were in the majority. And some were actually angry at the idea of sainthood—not at the saint himself, whom everyone liked, more or less, except for a few, but about the idea he represented, especially since it was not in a book or somewhere, but actually present, in the community. Of course some people went around saying that he "thought he was better than everybody else," and you had to take these people aside and tell them that they had misperceived the problem, that it wasn't a matter of simple conceit, with which we are all familiar, but rather something pure and mystical, from the realm of the extraordinary, as it were; unearthly. But a lot of people don't like things that are unearthly, the things of this earth are good enough for them, and they don't mind telling you so. "If he'd just go out and get a job, like everybody else, then he could be saintly all day long, if he wanted to"—that was a common theme. There is a sort of hatred going around for people who have lifted their sights above the common run. Probably it has always been this way.

For this reason, in any case, people were always trying to see the inside of the saint's apartment, to find out if strange practices were being practiced there, or if you could discern, from the arrangement of the furniture and so on, if any had been, lately. They would ring the bell and pretend to be in the wrong apartment, these people, but St. Anthony would let them come in anyhow, even though he knew very well what they were thinking. They would stand around, perhaps a husband-and-wife team, and stare at the rug, which was ordinary beige wall-to-wall carpet from Kaufman's, and then at the coffee table and so on, they would sort of slide into the kitchen to see what he had been eating, if anything. They were always surprised to see that he ate more or less normal foods, perhaps a little heavy on the fried foods. I guess they expected roots and grasses. And of course there was a big unhealthy interest in the bedroom, the door to which was usually kept closed. People seemed to think he should, in pursuit of whatever higher goals he had in mind, sleep on the floor; when they discovered there was an ordinary bed in there, with a brown bedspread, they were slightly shocked. By now St. Anthony had made a cup of coffee for them, and told them to sit down and take the weight off their feet, and asked them about their work and if they had any children and so forth: they went away thinking, He's just like anybody else. That was, I think, the way he wanted to present himself, at that time.

Later, after it was all over, he moved back out to the desert.

I didn't have any particular opinion as to what was the right thing to think about him. Sometimes you have to take the long way round to get to a sound consensus, and of course you have to keep the ordinary motors of life running in the meantime. So, in that long year that saw the emergence of his will as one of its major landmarks, in our city, I did whatever I could to help things along, to direct the stream of life experience at him in ways he could handle. I wasn't a disciple, that would be putting it far too strongly; I was sort of like a friend. And there were things I could do. For example, this town is pretty goodsized, more than a hundred thousand, and in any such town—maybe more so than in the really small ones, where everyone is scratching to survive—you run into people with nothing much to do who don't mind causing a little trouble, if that would be diverting, for someone who is unusual in any way. So the example that Elaine and I set, in more or less just treating him like any one of our other friends, probably helped to normalize things, and very likely protected him, in a sense, from some of the unwelcome attentions he might otherwise have received. As men in society seem to feel that the problem is to get all opinions squared away with all other opinions, or at least in recognizable congruence with the main opinion, as if the world were a jury room that no one could leave until everybody agreed (and keeping in mind the ever-present threat of a mistrial), so the men, and the women too, of the city (which I won't name to spare possible embarrassment to those of the participants who still live here) tried to think about St. Anthony, and by extension saintliness, in the approved ways of their time and condition.

The first thing to do, then, was to prove that he was a fake. Strange as it may sound in retrospect, that was the original general opinion, because who could believe that the reverse was the case? Because it wasn't easy, in the midst of all the other things you had to think about, to imagine the marvelous. I don't mean that he went around doing tricks or anything like that. It was just a certain—"ineffable" is the only word I can think of, and I have never understood exactly what it means, but you get a kind of feeling from it, and that's what you got, too, from the saint, on good days. (He had his ups and downs.) Anyhow, it was pretty savage, in the beginning, the way the local people went around trying to get something on him. I don't mean to impugn the honesty of these doubters; doubt is real enough in most circumstances. Especially so, perhaps, in cases where what is at issue is some principle of action: if you believe something, then you logically have to act accordingly. If you decided that St. Anthony actually was a saint, then you would have to act a certain way toward him, pay attention to him, be reverent and attentive, pay homage, perhaps change your life a bit.

St. Anthony's major temptation, in terms of his living here, was maybe this: ordinary life.

Not that he proclaimed himself a saint in so many words. But his actions, as the proverb says, spoke louder. There was the ineffableness I've already mentioned, and there were certain things that he did. He was mugged, for example. That doesn't happen too often here, but it happened to him. It was at night, somebody jumped on him from behind, grabbed him around the neck and began going through his pockets. The man only got a few dollars, and then he threw St. Anthony down on the sidewalk (he put one leg in front of the saint's legs and shoved him) and then began to run away. St. Anthony called after him, held up his hand, and said, "Don't you want the watch?" It was a good watch, a Bulova. The man was thunderstruck. He actually came back and took the watch off St. Anthony's wrist. He didn't know what to think. He hesitated for a minute and then asked St. Anthony if he had bus fare home. The saint said it didn't matter, it wasn't far, he could walk. Then the mugger ran away again. I know somebody who saw it (and of course did nothing to help, as is common in such cases). Opinion was divided as to whether St. Anthony was saintly, or simple-minded. I myself thought it was kind of dumb of him. But St. Anthony explained to me that somebody had given him the watch in the first place, and he only wore it so as not to hurt that person's feelings. He never looked at it, he said. He didn't care what time it was.

Parenthetically. In the desert, where he is now, it's very cold at night. He won't light a fire. People leave things for him, outside the hut. We took out some blankets but I don't know if he uses them. People bring him the strangest things, electric coffeepots (even though there's no electricity out there), comic books, even bottles of whiskey. St. Anthony gives everything away as fast as he can. I have seen him, however, looking curiously at a transistor radio. He told me that in his youth, in Memphis (that's not Memphis, Tennessee, but the Memphis in Egypt, the ruined city) he was very fond of music. Elaine and I talked about giving him a flute or a clarinet. We thought that might be all right, because performing music, for the greater honor and glory of God, is an old tradition, some of our best music came about that way. The whole body of sacred music. We asked him about it. He said no, it was very kind of us but it would be a distraction from contemplation and so forth. But sometimes, when we drive out to see him, maybe with some other people, we all sing hymns. He appears to enjoy that. That appears to be acceptable.

A funny thing was that, toward the end, the only thing he'd say, the only word was . . . "Or." I couldn't understand what he was thinking of. That was when he was still living in town.

The famous temptations, that so much has been written about, didn't occur all that often while he was living amongst us, in our city. Once or twice. I wasn't ever actually present during a temptation but I heard about it. Mrs. Eaton, who lived upstairs from him, had actually drilled a hole in the floor, so that she could watch him! I thought that was fairly despicable, and I told her so. Well, she said, there wasn't much excitement in her life. She's fifty-eight and both her boys are in the Navy. Also some of the wood shavings and whatnot must have dropped on the saint's floor when she drilled the hole. She bought a brace-and-bit specially at the hardware store, she told me. "I'm shameless," she said. God knows that's true. But the saint must have known she was up there with her fifty-eight-year-old eye glued to the hole. Anyhow, she claims to have seen a temptation. I asked her what form it took. Well, it wasn't very interesting, she said. Something about advertising. There was this man in a business suit talking to the saint. He said he'd "throw the account your way" if the saint would something something. The only other thing she heard was a mention of "annual billings in the range of five to six mil." The saint said no, very politely, and the man left, with cordialities on both sides. I asked her what she'd been expecting and she looked at me with a gleam in her eye and said: "Guess." I suppose she meant women. I myself was curious, I admit it, about the fabulous naked beauties he is supposed to have been tempted with, and all of that. It's hard not to let your imagination become salacious, in this context. It's funny that we never seem to get enough of sexual things, even though Elaine and I have been very happily married for nine years and have a very good relationship, in bed and out of it. There never seems to be enough sex in a person's life, unless you're exhausted and worn out, I suppose—that is a curiosity, that God made us that way, that I have never understood. Not that I don't enjoy it, in the abstract.

After he had returned to the desert, we dropped by one day to see if he was home. The door of his hut was covered with an old piece of sheepskin. A lot of ants and vermin were crawling over the surface of the sheepskin. When you go through the door of the hut you have to move very fast. It's one of the most unpleasant things about going to see St. Anthony. We knocked on the sheepskin, which is stiff as a board. Nobody answered. We could hear some scuffling around inside the hut. Whispering. It seemed to me that there was more than one voice. We knocked on the sheepskin again; again nobody answered. We got back into the Pontiac and drove back to town.

Of course he's more mature now. Taking things a little easier, probably.

I don't care if he put his hand on her leg or did not put his hand on her leg.

Everyone felt the town had done something wrong, really wrong, but by that time it was too late to make up for it.

Somebody got the bright idea of trying out Camilla on him. There are some crude people in this town. Camilla is well-known. She's very aristocratic, in a way, if "aristocratic" means that you don't give a damn what kind of damn foolishness, or even evil, you lend yourself to. Her folks had too much money, that was part of it, and she was too beautiful—she was beautiful, it's the only word— that was the other part. Some of her friends put her up to it. She went over to his place wearing those very short pants they wore for a while, and all of that. She has beautiful breasts. She's very intelligent, went to the Sorbonne and studied some kind of phi- losophy called "structure" with somebody named Levy who is sup- posed to be very famous. When she came back there was nobody she could talk about it to. She smokes a lot of dope, it's well- known. But in a way, she is not uncompassionate. She was inter- ested in the saint for his own personality, as well as his being an anomaly, in our local context. The long and short of it is that she claimed he tried to make advances to her, put his hand on her leg and all that. I don't know if she was lying or not. She could have been. She could have been telling the truth. It's hard to say. Anyhow, a great hue was raised about it and her father said he was going to press charges, although in the event, he did not. She stopped talking about it, the next day. Probably something happened but I don't necessarily think it was what she said it was. She became a VISTA volunteer later and went to work in the inner city of Detroit.

Anyhow, a lot of people talked about it. Well, what if he *had* put his hand on her leg, some people said—what was so wrong about that? They were both unmarried adult human beings, after all. Sexuality is as important as saintliness, and maybe as beautiful, in the sight of God, or else why was it part of the Divine plan? You always have these conflicts of ideas between people who think one thing and people who think another. I don't give a damn if he put his hand on her leg or did not put his hand on her leg. (I would prefer, of course, that he had not.) I thought it was kind of a cheap incident and not really worth talking about, especially in the larger context of the ineffable. There really was something to that. In the world of mundanity in which he found himself, he *shone*. It was unmistakable, even to children.

Of course they were going to run him out of town, by subtle pressures, after a while. There is a lot of anticlericalism around, still. We visit him, in the desert, anyhow, once or twice a month. We missed our visits last month because we were in Florida.

He told me that, in his old age, he regarded the temptations as "entertainment."

SENTENCE

Or a long sentence moving at a certain pace down the page aiming for the bottom—if not the bottom of this page then of some other page—where it can rest, or stop for a moment to think about the questions raised by its own (temporary) existence, which ends when the page is turned, or the sentence falls out of the mind that holds it (temporarily) in some kind of an embrace, not necessarily an ardent one, but more perhaps the kind of embrace enjoyed (or endured) by a wife who has just waked up and is on her way to the bathroom in the morning to wash her hair, and is bumped into by her husband, who has been lounging at the breakfast table reading the newspaper, and didn't see her coming out of the bedroom, but, when he bumps into her, or is bumped into by her, raises his hands to embrace her lightly, transiently, because he knows that if he gives her a real embrace so early in the morning, before she has properly shaken the dreams out of her head and got her duds on, she won't respond, and may even become slightly angry, and say something wounding, and so the husband invests in this embrace not so much physical or emotional pressure as he might, because he doesn't want to waste anything—with this sort of feeling, then, the sentence passes through the mind more or less, and there is another way of describing the situation too, which is to say that the sentence crawls through the mind like something someone says to you while you're listening very hard to the FM radio, some rock group there, with its thrilling sound, and so, with your attention or the major part of it at least already awarded, there is not much mind room you can give to the remark, especially considering that you have probably just quarreled with that person, the maker of the remark, over the radio being too loud, or something like that, and the view you take, of the remark, is that you'd really rather not hear it, but if you have to hear it, you want to listen to it for the smallest possible length of time, and during a commercial, because immediately after the commercial they're going to play a new rock song by your favorite group, a cut that has never been aired before, and you want to hear it and respond to it in a new way, a way that accords with whatever you're feeling at the moment, or might feel, if the threat of new experience could be (temporarily) overbalanced by the promise of possible positive benefits, or what the mind construes as such, remembering that these are often, really, disguised defeats (not that such defeats are not, at times, good for your character, teaching you that it is not by success alone that one surmounts life, but that setbacks, too, contribute to that roughening of the personality that, by providing a textured surface to place against that of life, enables you to leave slight traces, or smudges, on the face of human history—your mark) and after all, benefit-seeking always has something of the smell of raw vanity about it, as if you wished to decorate your own brow with laurel, or wear your medals to a cookout, when the invitation had said nothing about them, and although the ego is always hungry (we are told) it is well to remember that ongoing success is nearly as meaningless as ongoing lack of success, which can make you sick, and that it is good to leave a few crumbs on the table for the rest of your brethren, not to sweep it all into the little beaded purse of your soul but to allow others, too, part of the gratification, and if you share in this way you will find the clouds smiling on you, and the postman bringing you letters, and bicycles available when you want to rent them, and many other signs, however guarded and limited, of the community's (temporary) approval of you, or at least of its willingness to let you believe (temporarily) that it finds you not so lacking in commendable virtues as it had previously allowed you to think, from its scorn of your merits, as it might be put, or anyway its consistent refusal to recognize your basic humanness and its secret blackball of the project of your remaining alive, made in executive session by its ruling bodies, which, as everyone knows, carry out concealed programs of reward and punishment, under the rose, causing faint alterations of the status quo, behind your back, at various points along the periphery of community life, together with other enterprises not dissimilar in tone, such as producing films that have special qualities, or attributes, such as a film where the second half of it is a holy mystery, and girls and women are not permitted to see it, or writing novels in which the final chapter is a plastic bag filled with water, which you can touch, but not drink: in this way, or ways, the underground mental life of the collectivity is botched, or denied, or turned into something else never imagined by the planners, who, returning from the latest seminar in crisis management and being asked what they have learned, say they have learned how to throw up their hands; the sentence meanwhile, although not insensible of these considerations, has a festering conscience of its own, which persuades it to follow its star, and to move with all deliberate speed from one place to another, without losing any of the "riders" it may have picked up just by being there, on the page, and turning this way and that, to see what is over there, under that oddly shaped tree, or over there, reflected in the rain barrel of the imagination, even though it is true that in our young manhood we were taught that short, punchy sentences were best (but what did he mean? doesn't "punchy" mean punch-drunk? I think he probably intended to say "short, *punching* sentences," meaning sentences that lashed out at you, bloodying your brain if possible, and looking up the word just now I came across the nearby "punkah," which is a large fan suspended from the ceiling in India, operated by an attendant pulling a rope—that is what I want for my sentence, to keep it cool!) we are mature enough now to stand the shock of learning that much of what we were taught in our youth was wrong, or improperly understood by those who

were teaching it, or perhaps shaded a bit, the shading resulting from
the personal needs of the teachers, who as human beings had a
tendency to introduce some of their heart's blood into their work,
and sometimes this may not have been of the first water, this heart's
blood, and even if they thought they were moving the "knowledge"
out, as the Board of Education had mandated, they could have
noticed that their sentences weren't having the knockdown power
of the new weapons whose bullets tumble end over end (but it is
true that we didn't have these weapons at that time) and they might
have taken into account the fundamental dubiousness of their project (but all the intelligently conceived projects have been eaten up
already, like the moon and the stars), leaving us, in our best clothes,
with only things to do like conducting vigorous wars of attrition
against our wives, who have now thoroughly come awake, and
slipped into their striped bells, and pulled sweaters over their torsi,
and adamantly refused to wear any bras under the sweaters, carefully
explaining the political significance of this refusal to anyone who
will listen, or look, but not touch, because that has nothing to do
with it, so they say; leaving us with only things to do like floating
sheets of Reynolds Wrap around the room, trying to find out how
many we can keep in the air at the same time, which at least gives
us a sense of participation, as though we were the Buddha, looking
down at the mystery of your smile, which needs to be investigated,
and I think I'll do that right now, while there's still enough light,
if you'll sit down over there, in the best chair, and take off all your
clothes, and put your feet in that electric toe caddy (which prevents
pneumonia) and slip into this permanent-press white hospital gown,
to cover your nakedness—why, if you do all that, we'll be ready to
begin! after I wash my hands, because you pick up an amazing
amount of exuviae in this city, just by walking around in the open
air, and nodding to acquaintances, and speaking to friends, in the
ordinary course (and death to our enemies! by the by)—but I'm
getting a little uptight, just about washing my hands, because I
can't find the soap, which somebody has used and not put back in
the soap dish, all of which is extremely irritating, if you have a
beautiful patient sitting in the examining room, naked inside her

gown, and peering at her moles in the mirror, with her immense brown eyes following your every movement (when they are not watching the moles, expecting them, as in a Disney nature film, to exfoliate) and her immense brown head wondering what you're going to do to her, the pierced places in the head letting that question leak out, while the therapist decides just to wash his hands in plain water, and hang the soap! and does so, and then looks around for a towel, but all the towels have been collected by the towel service, and are not there, so he wipes his hands on his pants, in the back (so as to avoid suspicious stains on the front) thinking: what must she think of me? and, all this is very unprofessional and at-sea looking! trying to visualize the contretemps from her point of view, if she has one (but how can she? she is not in the washroom) and then stopping, because it is finally his own point of view that he cares about and not hers, and with this firmly in mind, and a light, confident step, such as you might find in the works of Bulwer-Lytton, he enters the space she occupies so prettily and, taking her by the hand, proceeds to tear off the stiff white hospital gown (but no, we cannot have that kind of pornographic *merde* in this majestic and high-minded sentence, which will probably end up in the Library of Congress) (that was just something that took place inside his consciousness, as he looked at her, and since we know that consciousness is always consciousness *of* something, she is not entirely without responsibility in the matter) so, then, taking her by the hand, he falls into the stupendous white purée of her abyss, no, I mean rather that he asks her how long it has been since her last visit, and she says a fortnight, and he shudders, and tells her that with a condition like hers (she is an immensely popular soldier, and her troops win all their battles by pretending to be forests, the enemy discovering, at the last moment, that those trees they have eaten their lunch under have eyes and swords) (which reminds me of the performance, in 1845, of Robert-Houdin, called *The Fantastic Orange Tree,* wherein Robert-Houdin borrowed a lady's handkerchief, rubbed it between his hands and passed it into the center of an egg, after which he passed the egg into the center of a lemon, after which he passed the lemon into the center of an orange, then pressed the orange between his hands, making it smaller and smaller, until only a powder remained, whereupon he asked for a small potted orange tree and sprinkled the powder thereupon, upon which the tree burst into blossom, the blossoms turning into oranges, the oranges turning into butterflies, and the butterflies turning into beautiful young ladies, who then married members of the audience), a condition so damaging to real-time social intercourse of any kind, the best thing she can do is give up, and lay down her arms, and he will lie down in them, and together they will permit themselves a bit of the old slap and tickle, she wearing only her Mr. Christopher medal, on its silver chain, and he (for such is the latitude granted the professional classes) worrying about the sentence, about its thin wires of dramatic tension, which have been omitted, about whether we should write down some natural events occurring in the sky (birds, lightning bolts), and about a possible coup d'état within the sentence, whereby its chief verb would be—but at this moment a messenger rushes into the sentence, bleeding from a hat of thorns he's wearing, and cries out: "You don't know what you're doing! Stop making this sentence, and begin to make Moholy-Nagy cocktails, for those are what we really need, on the frontiers of bad behavior!" and then he falls to the floor, and a trapdoor opens under him, and he falls through that, into a damp pit where a blue narwhal waits, its horn poised (but maybe the weight of the messenger, falling from such a height, will break off the horn)—thus, considering everything carefully, in the sweet light of the ceremonial axes, in the run-mad skimble-skamble of information sickness, we must make a decision as to whether we should proceed, or go back, in the latter case enjoying the pathos of eradication, in the former case reading an erotic advertisement which begins, *How to Make Your Mouth a Blowtorch of Excitement* (but wouldn't that overtax our mouthwashes?), attempting, during the pause, while our burned mouths are being smeared with fat, to imagine a better sentence, worthier, more meaningful, like those in the Declaration of Independence, or a bank statement showing that you have seven thousand kroner more than you thought you had—a statement summing up the unreasonable demands that you make on life, and one that also asks the question, if you can imagine these demands, why are they not routinely met, tall fool? but of course it is not that query that this infected sentence has set out to answer (and hello! to our girlfriend, Rosetta Stone, who has stuck by us through thin and thin) but some other query that we shall some day discover the nature of, and here comes Ludwig, the expert on sentence construction we have borrowed from the Bauhaus, who will—"Guten Tag, Ludwig!"—probably find a way to cure the sentence's sprawl, by using the improved ways of thinking developed in Weimar—"I am sorry to inform you that the Bauhaus no longer exists, that all of the great masters who formerly thought there are either dead or retired, and that I myself have been reduced to constructing books on how to pass the examination for police sergeant"—and Ludwig falls through the Tugendhat House into the history of man-made objects; a disappointment, to be sure, but it reminds us that the sentence itself is a man-made object, not the one we wanted of course, but still a construction of man, a structure to be treasured for its weakness, as opposed to the strength of stones

PEPPERONI

FINANCIALLY, the paper is quite healthy. The paper's timber-lands, mining interests, pulp and paper operations, book, magazine, corrugated-box, and greeting-card divisions, film, radio, television, and cable companies, and data-processing and satellite-communi-cations groups are all flourishing, with overall return on invested capital increasing at about eleven percent a year. Compensation of the three highest-paid officers and directors last year was $399,500, $362,700, and $335,400 respectively, exclusive of profit-sharing and pension-plan accruals.

But top management is discouraged and saddened, and middle management is drinking too much. Morale in the newsroom is fair, because of the recent raises, but the shining brows of the copy boys, traditional emblems of energy and hope, have begun to display odd, unattractive lines. At every level, even down into the depths of the pressroom, where the pressmen defiantly wear their square dirty folded-paper caps, people want management to stop what it is doing before it is too late.

The new VDT machines have hurt the paper, no doubt about it. The people in the newsroom don't like the machines. (A few say they like the machines but these are the same people who like the washrooms.) When the machines go down, as they do, not infrequently, the people in the newsroom laugh and cheer. The executive editor has installed one-way glass in his office door, and stands behind it looking out over the newsroom, fretting and groaning. Recently the paper ran the same stock tables every day for a week. No one noticed, no one complained.

Middle management has implored top management to alter its course. Top management has responded with postdated guarantees, on a sliding scale. The Guild is off in a corner, whimpering. The pressmen are holding an unending series of birthday parties commemorating heroes of labor. Reporters file their stories as usual, but if they are certain kinds of stories they do not run. A small example: the paper did not run a Holiday Weekend Death Toll story after Labor Day this year, the first time since 1926 no Holiday Weekend Death Toll story appeared in the paper after Labor Day (and the total was, although not a record, a substantial one).

Some elements of the staff are not depressed. The paper's very creative real-estate editor has been a fountain of ideas, and his sections, full of color pictures of desirable living arrangements, are choked with advertising and make the Sunday paper fat, fat, fat. More food writers have been hired, and more clothes writers, and more furniture writers, and more plant writers. The bridge, whist, skat, cribbage, domino, and *vingt-et-un* columnists are very popular.

The Editor's Caucus has once again applied to middle management for relief, and has once again been promised it (but middle management has Glenfiddich on its breath, even at breakfast). Top management's polls say that sixty-five percent of the readers "want movies," and feasibility studies are being conducted. Top management acknowledges, over long lunches at good restaurants, that the readers are wrong to "want movies" but insists that morality cannot be legislated. The newsroom has been insulated (with products from the company's Echotex division) so that the people in the newsroom can no longer hear the sounds in the streets.

The paper's editorials have been subcontracted to Texas Instruments, and the obituaries to Nabisco, so that the staff will have "more time to think." The foreign desk is turning out language lessons (*"Yo temo que Isabel no venga,"* "I am afraid that Isabel will not come"). There was an especially lively front page on Tuesday. The No. 1 story was pepperoni—a useful and exhaustive guide. It ran right next to the slimming-your-troublesome-thighs story, with pictures.

Top management has vowed to stop what it is doing—not now but soon, soon. A chamber orchestra has been formed among the people in the newsroom, and we play Haydn until the sun comes up.

SOME OF US
HAD BEEN THREATENING
OUR FRIEND COLBY

Some of us had been threatening our friend Colby for a long time, because of the way he had been behaving. And now he'd gone too far, so we decided to hang him. Colby argued that just because he had gone too far (he did not deny that he had gone too far) did not mean that he should be subjected to hanging. Going too far, he said, was something everybody did sometimes. We didn't pay much attention to this argument. We asked him what sort of music he would like played at the hanging. He said he'd think about it but it would take him a while to decide. I pointed out that we'd have to know soon, because Howard, who is a conductor, would have to hire and rehearse the musicians and he couldn't begin until he knew what the music was going to be. Colby said he'd always been fond of Ives's Fourth Symphony. Howard said that this was a "delaying tactic" and that everybody knew that the Ives was almost impossible to perform and would involve weeks of rehearsal, and that the size of the orchestra and chorus would put us way over the music budget. "Be reasonable," he said to Colby. Colby said he'd try to think of something a little less exacting.

Hugh was worried about the wording of the invitations. What if one of them fell into the hands of the authorities? Hanging Colby was doubtless against the law, and if the authorities learned in advance what the plan was they would very likely come in and try to mess everything up. I said that although hanging Colby was almost certainly against the law, we had a perfect *moral* right to do so because he was *our* friend, *belonged* to us in various important senses, and he had after all gone too far. We agreed that the invitations would be worded in such a way that the person invited could not know for $ure what he was being invited to. We decided to refer to the event as "An Event Involving Mr. Colby Williams." A handsome script was selected from a catalogue and we picked a cream-colored paper. Magnus said he'd see to having the invitations printed, and wondered whether we should serve drinks. Colby said he thought drinks would be nice but was worried about the expense. We told him kindly that the expense didn't matter, that we were after all his dear friends and if a group of his dear friends couldn't get together and do the thing with a little bit of *éclat,* why, what was the world coming to? Colby asked if he would be able to have drinks, too, before the event. We said, "Certainly."

The next item of business was the gibbet. None of us knew too much about gibbet design, but Tomás, who is an architect, said he'd look it up in old books and draw the plans. The important thing, as far as he recollected, was that the trapdoor function perfectly. He said that just roughly, counting labor and materials, it shouldn't run us more than four hundred dollars. "Good God!" Howard said. He said what was Tomás figuring on, rosewood? No, just a good grade of pine, Tomás said. Victor asked if unpainted pine wouldn't look kind of "raw," and Tomás replied that he thought it could be stained a dark walnut without too much trouble.

I said that although I thought the whole thing ought to be done really well and all, I also thought four hundred dollars for a gibbet, on top of the expense for the drinks, invitations, musicians, and everything, was a bit steep, and why didn't we just use a tree—a nice-looking oak, or something? I pointed out that since it was going to be a June hanging the trees would be in glorious leaf and that not only would a tree add a kind of "natural" feeling but it was also strictly traditional, especially in the West. Tomás, who had been sketching gibbets on the backs of envelopes, reminded us that an outdoor hanging always had to contend with the threat of rain. Victor said he liked the idea of doing it outdoors, possibly on the bank of a river, but noted that we would have to hold it some distance from the city, which presented the problem of getting the guests, musicians, etc., to the site and then back to town.

At this point everybody looked at Harry, who runs a car-and-truck-rental business. Harry said he thought he could round up enough limousines to take care of that end but that the drivers would have to be paid. The drivers, he pointed out, wouldn't be friends of Colby's and couldn't be expected to donate their services, any more than the bartender or the musicians. He said that he had about ten limousines, which he used mostly for funerals, and that he could probably obtain another dozen by calling around to friends of his in the trade. He said also that if we did it outside, in the open air, we'd better figure on a tent or awning of some kind to cover at least the principals and the orchestra, because if the hanging was being rained on he thought it would look kind of dismal. As between gibbet and tree, he said, he had no particular preferences and he really thought that the choice ought to be left up to Colby, since it was his hanging. Colby said that everybody went too far, sometimes, and weren't we being a little Draconian? Howard said rather sharply that all that had already been discussed, and which did he want, gibbet or tree? Colby asked if he could have a firing squad. No, Howard said, he could not. Howard said a firing squad would just be an ego trip for Colby, the blindfold and last-cigarette bit, and that Colby was in enough hot water already without trying to "upstage" everyone with unnecessary theatrics. Colby said he was sorry, he hadn't meant it that way, he'd take the tree. Tomás crumpled up the gibbet sketches he'd been making, in disgust.

Then the question of the hangman came up. Pete said did we really need a hangman? Because if we used a tree, the noose could be adjusted to the appropriate level and Colby could just jump off something—a chair or stool or something. Besides, Pete said, he very much doubted if there were any free-lance hangmen wandering around the country, now that capital punishment has been done away with absolutely, temporarily, and that we'd probably have to fly one in from England or Spain or one of the South American countries, and even if we did that how could we know in advance that the man was a professional, a real hangman, and not just some money-hungry amateur who might bungle the job and shame us all, in front of everybody? We all agreed then that Colby should just jump off something and that a chair was not what he should jump off of, because that would look, we felt, extremely tacky— some old kitchen chair sitting out there under our beautiful tree. Tomás, who is quite modern in outlook and not afraid of innovation, proposed that Colby be standing on a large round rubber ball ten feet in diameter. This, he said, would afford a sufficient "drop" and would also roll out of the way if Colby suddenly changed his mind after jumping off. He reminded us that by not using a regular hangman we were placing an awful lot of the responsibility for the success of the affair on Colby himself, and that although he was sure Colby would perform creditably and not disgrace his friends at the last minute, still, men have been known to get a little irresolute at times like that, and the ten-foot-round rubber ball, which could probably be fabricated rather cheaply, would insure a "bang-up" production right down to the wire.

At the mention of "wire," Hank, who had been silent all this time, suddenly spoke up and said he wondered if it wouldn't be better if we used wire instead of rope—more efficient and in the end kinder to Colby, he suggested. Colby began looking a little green, and I didn't blame him, because there is something extremely distasteful in thinking about being hanged with wire instead of rope—it gives you a sort of a revulsion, when you think about it. I thought it was really quite unpleasant of Hank to be sitting there talking about wire, just when we had solved the problem of what Colby was going to jump off of so neatly, with Tomás's idea about the rubber ball, so I hastily said that wire was out of the question, because it would injure the tree—cut into the branch it was tied to when Colby's full weight hit it—and that in these days of increased respect for the environment, we didn't want that, did we? Colby gave me a grateful look, and the meeting broke up.

Everything went off very smoothly on the day of the event (the music Colby finally picked was standard stuff, Elgar, and it was played very well by Howard and his boys). It didn't rain, the event was well attended, and we didn't run out of Scotch, or anything. The ten-foot rubber ball had been painted a deep green and blended in well with the bucolic setting. The two things I remember best about the whole episode are the grateful look Colby gave me when I said what I said about the wire, and the fact that nobody has ever gone too far again.

LIGHTNING

Edward Connors, on assignment for *Folks,* set out to interview nine people who had been struck by lightning. "Nine?" he said to his editor, Penfield. "Nine, ten," said Penfield, "doesn't matter, but it has to be more than eight." "Why?" asked Connors, and Penfield said that the layout was scheduled for five pages and they wanted at least two people who had been struck by lightning per page plus somebody pretty sensational for the opening page. "Slightly wonderful," said Penfield, "nice body, I don't have to tell you, somebody with a special face. Also, struck by lightning."

Connors advertised in *The Village Voice* for people who had been struck by lightning and would be willing to talk for publication about the experience and in no time at all was getting phone calls. A number of the callers, it appeared, had great-grandfathers or grandmothers who had also been struck by lightning, usually knocked from the front seat of a buckboard on a country road in 1910. Connors took down names and addresses and made appointments for interviews, trying to discern from the voices if any of the women callers might be, in the magazine's terms, wonderful.

Connors had been a reporter for ten years and a free-lancer for five, with six years in between as a PR man for Topsy Oil in Midland-Odessa. As a reporter he had been excited, solid, underpaid, in love with his work, a specialist in business news, a scholar of the regulatory agencies and their eternal gavotte with the Seven Sisters, a man who knew what should be done with natural gas, with nuclear power, who knew crown blocks and monkey boards and Austin chalk, who kept his own personal hard hat ("Welltech") on top of a filing cabinet in his office. When his wife pointed out, eventually, that he wasn't making enough money (absolutely true!) he had gone with Topsy, whose PR chief had been dropping handkerchiefs in his vicinity for several years. Signing on with Topsy, he had tripled his salary, bought four moderately expensive suits, enjoyed (briefly) the esteem of his wife, and spent his time writing either incredibly dreary releases about corporate doings or speeches in praise of free enterprise for the company's CEO, E. H. ("Bug") Ludwig, a round, amiable, commanding man of whom he was very fond. When Connors's wife left him for a racquetball pro attached to the Big Spring Country Club he decided he could afford to be poor again and departed Topsy, renting a dismal rear apartment on Lafayette Street in New York and patching an income together by writing for a wide variety of publications, classical record reviews for *High Fidelity*, *Times* Travel pieces ("Portugal's Fabulous Beaches") exposés for *Penthouse* ("Inside the Trilateral Commission"). To each assignment he brought a good brain, a good eye, a tenacious thoroughness, gusto. He was forty-five, making a thin living, curious about people who had been struck by lightning.

The first man he interviewed was a thirty-eight-year-old tile setter named Burch who had been struck by lightning in February 1978 and had immediately become a Jehovah's Witness. "It was the best thing that ever happened to me," said Burch, "in a way." He was a calm, rather handsome man with pale blond hair cut short, military style, and an elegantly spare (deep grays and browns) apartment in the West Twenties which looked, to Connors, as if a decorator had been involved. "I was coming back from a job in New Rochelle," said Burch, "and I had a flat. It was clouding up pretty good and I wanted to get the tire changed before the rain started. I had the tire off and was just about to put the spare on when there was this just terrific crash and I was flat on my back in the middle of the road. Knocked the tire tool 'bout a hundred feet, I found it later in a field. Guy in a VW van pulled up right in front of me, jumped out and told me I'd been struck. I couldn't hear what he was saying, I was deafened, but he made signs. Took me to a hospital and they checked me over, they were amazed—no burns, nothing, just the deafness, which lasted about forty-eight hours. I figured I owed the Lord something, and I became a Witness. And let me tell you my life since that day has been—" He paused, searching for the right word. "*Serene*. Truly serene." Burch had had a great-grandfather who had also been struck by lightning, knocked from the front seat of a buckboard on a country road in Pennsylvania in 1910, but no conversion had resulted in that case, as far as he knew. Connors arranged to have a *Folks* photographer shoot Burch on the following Wednesday and, much impressed—rarely had he encountered serenity on this scale—left the apartment with his pockets full of Witness literature.

Connors next talked to a woman named MacGregor who had been struck by lightning while sitting on a bench on the Cold Spring, New York, railroad platform and had suffered third-degree burns on her arms and legs—she had been wearing a rubberized raincoat which had, she felt, protected her somewhat, but maybe not, she couldn't be sure. Her experience, while lacking a religious dimension per se, had made her think very hard about her life, she said, and there had been some important changes (*Lightning changes things,* Connors wrote in his notebook). She had married the man she had been seeing for two years but had been slightly dubious about, and on the whole, this had been the right thing to do. She and Marty had a house in Garrison, New York, where Marty was in real estate, and she'd quit her job with Estée Lauder because the commute, which she'd been making since 1975, was just too tiring. Connors made a date for the photographer. Mrs. MacGregor was pleasant and attractive (fawn-colored suit, black clocked stockings) but, Connors thought, too old to start the layout with.

The next day he got a call from someone who sounded young. Her name was Edwina Rawson, she said, and she had been struck by lightning on New Year's Day, 1980, while walking in the woods with her husband, Marty. (*Two Martys in the same piece?* thought Connors, scowling.) Curiously enough, she said, her great-grandmother had also been struck by lightning, knocked from the front seat of a buggy on a country road outside Iowa City in 1911. "But I don't want to be in the magazine," she said. "I mean, with all those rock stars and movie stars. Olivia Newton-John I'm not. If you were writing a book or something—"

Connors was fascinated. He had never come across anyone who did not want to appear in *Folks* before. He was also slightly irritated. He had seen perfectly decent colleagues turn amazingly ugly when refused a request for an interview. "Well," he said, "could we at least talk? I promise I won't take up much of your time, and, you know, this is a pretty important experience, being struck by lightning—not many people have had it. Also you might be interested in how the others felt. . . ." "Okay," she said, "but off the record unless I decide otherwise." "Done," said Connors. *My God, she thinks she's the State Department.*

Edwina was not only slightly wonderful but also mildly superb, worth a double-page spread in anybody's book, *Vogue, Life, Elle, Ms., Town & Country,* you name it. Oh Lord, thought Connors, there are ways and ways to be struck by lightning. She was wearing jeans and a parka and she was beautifully, beautifully black—a considerable plus, Connors noted automatically, the magazine conscientiously tried to avoid lily-white stories. She was carrying a copy of *Variety* (not an actress, he thought, *please* not an actress) and was not an actress but doing a paper on *Variety* for a class in media studies at NYU. "God, I love *Variety,*" she said. "The stately march of the grosses through the middle pages." Connors decided that "Shall we get married?" was an inappropriate second remark to make to one newly met, but it was a very tough decision.

They were in a bar called Bradley's on University Place in the Village, a bar Connors sometimes used for interviews because of its warmth, geniality. Edwina was drinking a Beck's and Connors, struck by lightning, had a feeble paw wrapped around a vodka-tonic. Relax, he told himself, go slow, we have half the afternoon. There was a kid, she said, two-year-old boy, Marty's, Marty had

split for California and a job as a systems analyst with Warner
Communications, good riddance to bad rubbish. Connors had no
idea what a systems analyst did: go with the flow? The trouble with
Marty, she said, was that he was immature, a systems analyst, and
white. She conceded that when the lightning hit he had given her
mouth-to-mouth resuscitation, perhaps saved her life; he had taken
a course in CPR at the New School, which was entirely consistent
with his cautious, be-prepared, white-folks' attitude toward life. She
had nothing against white folks, Edwina said with a warm smile,
or rabbits, as black folks sometimes termed them, but you had to
admit that, qua folks, they sucked. Look at the Trilateral Commission, she said, a perfect example. Connors weighed in with some
knowledgeable words about the Commission, detritus from his
Penthouse piece, managing to hold her interest through a second
Beck's.

"Did it change your life, being struck?" asked Connors. She
frowned, considered. "Yes and no," she said. "Got rid of Marty,
that was an up. Why I married him I'll never know. Why he married
me I'll never know. A minute of bravery, never to be repeated."
Connors saw that she was much aware of her own beauty, her
hauteur about appearing in the magazine was appropriate—who
needed it? People would dig slant wells for this woman, go out
into a producing field with a tank truck in the dead of night and
take off five thousand gallons of somebody else's crude, write fan-
ciful checks, establish Pyramid Clubs with tony marble-and-gold
headquarters on Zurich's Bahnhofstrasse. What did he have to offer?

"Can you tell me a little bit more about how you felt when it
actually hit you?" he asked, trying to keep his mind on business.
"Yes," Edwina said. "We were taking a walk—we were at his mother's place in Connecticut, near Madison—and Marty was talking
about whether or not he should take a SmokeEnders course at the
Y, he smoked Kents, miles and miles of Kents. I was saying, yes,
yes, do it! and whammo! the lightning. When I came to, I felt like
I was burning inside, inside my chest, drank seventeen glasses of
water, chug-a-lugged them, thought I was going to bust. Also, my
eyebrows were gone. I looked at myself in the mirror and I had zip

eyebrows. Looked really funny, maybe improved me." Regarding her closely Connors saw that her eyebrows were in fact dark dramatic slashes of eyebrow pencil. "Ever been a model?" he asked, suddenly inspired. "That's how I make it," Edwina said, "that's how I keep little Zachary in britches, look in the Sunday *Times Magazine*, I do Altman's, Macy's, you'll see me and three white chicks, usually, lingerie ads. . . ."

The soul burns, Connors thought, having been struck by lightning. Without music, Nietzsche said, the world would be a mistake. Do I have that right? Connors, no musician (although a scholar of fiddle music from Pinchas Zukerman to Eddie South, "dark angel of the violin," 1904–62), agreed wholeheartedly. Lightning an attempt at music on the part of God? Does get your attention, Connors thought, *attempt* wrong by definition because God is perfect by definition. . . . Lightning at once a *coup de théâtre* and career counseling? Connors wondered if he had a song to sing, one that would signify to the burned beautiful creature before him.

"The armadillo is the only animal other than man known to contract leprosy," Connors said. "The slow, friendly armadillo. I picture a leper armadillo, white as snow, with a little bell around its neck, making its draggy scamper across Texas from El Paso to Big Spring. My heart breaks."

Edwina peered into his chest where the cracked heart bumped around in its cage of bone. "Man, you are one sentimental taxpayer."

Connors signaled the waiter for more drinks. "It was about 1880 that the saintly armadillo crossed the Rio Grande and entered Texas," he said, "seeking to carry its message to that great state. Its message was, squash me on your highways. Make my nine-banded shell into beautiful lacquered baskets for your patios, decks, and mobile homes. Watch me hayfoot-strawfoot across your vast savannas enriching same with my best-quality excreta. In some parts of South America armadillos grow to almost five feet in length and are allowed to teach at the junior-college level. In Argentina—"

"You're crazy, baby," Edwina said, patting him on the arm.

"Yes," Connors said, "would you like to go to a movie?"

The movie was *Moscow Does Not Believe in Tears,* a nifty item.

Connors, Edwina inhabiting both the right and left sides of his brain, next interviewed a man named Stupple who had been struck by lightning in April 1970 and had in consequence joined the American Nazi Party, specifically the Horst Wessel Post #66 in Newark, which had (counting Stupple) three members. *Can't use him,* thought Connors, *wasting time,* nevertheless faithfully inscribing in his notebook pages of viciousness having to do with the Protocols of Zion and the alleged genetic inferiority of blacks. *Marvelous, don't these guys ever come up with anything new?* Connors remembered having heard the same routine, almost word for word, from an Assistant Grand Dragon of the Shreveport (La.) Klan, a man somewhat dumber than a bathtub, in 1967 at the Dew Drop Inn in Shreveport, where the ribs in red sauce were not bad. Stupple, who had slipped a Nazi armband over the left sleeve of his checked flannel shirt for the interview, which was conducted in a two-room apartment over a failing four-lane bowling alley in Newark, served Connors Danish aquavit frozen into a block of ice with a very good Japanese beer, Kirin, as a chaser. "Won't you need a picture?" Stupple asked at length, and Connors said, evasively, "Well, you know, lots of people have been struck by lightning. . . ."

Telephoning Edwina from a phone booth outside the Port Authority Terminal, he learned that she was not available for dinner. "How do you feel?" he asked her, aware that the question was imprecise—he really wanted to know whether having been struck by lightning was an ongoing state or, rather, a one-time illumination—and vexed by his inability to get a handle on the story. "Tired," she said, "Zach's been yelling a lot, call me tomorrow, maybe we can do something. . . ."

Penfield, the *Folks* editor, had a call on Connors's service when he got back to Lafayette Street. "How's it coming?" Penfield asked. "I don't understand it yet," Connors said, "how it works. It changes people." "What's to understand?" said Penfield, "wham-bam-thank-you-ma'am, you got anybody I can use for the opening? We've got these terrific shots of individual bolts, I see a four-way bleed with the text reversed out of this saturated purple sky and this tiny but absolutely wonderful face looking up at the bolt—" "She's black," said Connors, "you're going to have trouble with the purple, not enough contrast." "So it'll be subtle," said Penfield excitedly, "rich and subtle. The bolt will give it enough snap. It'll be nice."

Nice, thought Connors, what a word for being struck by lightning.

Connors, trying to get at the core of the experience—did being struck exalt or exacerbate pre-existing tendencies, states of mind, and what was the relevance of electroshock therapy, if it was a therapy?—talked to a Trappist monk who had been struck by lightning in 1975 while working in the fields at the order's Piffard, New York, abbey. Having been given permission by his superior to speak to Connors, the small, bald monk was positively loquacious. He told Connors that the one deprivation he had felt keenly, as a member of a monastic order, was the absence of rock music. "Why?" he asked rhetorically. "I'm too old for this music, it's for kids, I know it, you know it, makes no sense at all. But I love it, I simply love it. And after I was struck the community bought me this Sony Walkman." Proudly he showed Connors the small device with its delicate earphones. "A special dispensation. I guess they figured I was near-to-dead, therefore it was all right to bend the Rule a bit. I simply love it. Have you heard the Cars?" Standing in a beet field with the brown-habited monk Connors felt the depth of the man's happiness and wondered if he himself ought to rethink his attitude toward Christianity. It would not be so bad to spend one's days pulling beets in the warm sun while listening to the Cars and then retire to one's cell at night to read St. Augustine and catch up on Rod Stewart and the B-52s.

"The thing is," Connors said to Edwina that night at dinner, "I don't understand precisely what effects the change. Is it pure fright? Gratitude at having survived?" They were sitting in an Italian restaurant called Da Silvano on Sixth near Houston, eating tortellini in a white sauce. Little Zachary, a good-looking two-year-old, sat in a high chair and accepted bits of cut-up pasta. Edwina had had a shoot that afternoon and was not in a good mood. "The same damn thing," she said, "me and three white chicks, you'd think somebody'd turn it around just once." She needed a *Vogue* cover and a fragrance campaign, she said, and then she would be sitting pretty. She had been considered for *Hashish* some time back but didn't get it and there was a question in her mind as to whether her agency (Jerry Francisco) had been solidly behind her. "Come along," said Edwina, "I want to give you a back rub, you look a tiny bit peaked."

Connors subsequently interviewed five more people who had been struck by lightning, uncovering some unusual cases, including a fellow dumb from birth who, upon being struck, began speaking quite admirable French; his great-grandfather, as it happened, had also been struck by lightning, blasted from the seat of a farm wagon in Brittany in 1909. In his piece Connors described the experience as "ineffable," using a word he had loathed and despised his whole life long, spoke of lightning-as-grace, and went so far as to mention the Descent of the Dove. Penfield, without a moment's hesitation, cut the whole paragraph, saying (correctly) that the *Folks* reader didn't like "funny stuff" and pointing out that the story was running long anyway because of the extra page given to Edwina's opening layout, in which she wore a Mary McFadden pleated tube and looked, in Penfield's phrase, approximately fantastic.

THE CATECHIST

In the evenings, usually, the catechist approaches.

"Where have you been?" he asks.

"In the park," I say.

"Was she there?" he says.

"No," I say.

The catechist is holding a book. He reads aloud: *"The chief reason for Christ's coming was to manifest and teach God's love for us. Here the catechist should find the focal point of his instruction."* On the word "manifest" the catechist places the tip of his right forefinger upon the tip of his left thumb, and on the word "teach" the catechist places the tip of his right forefinger upon the tip of his left forefinger.

Then he says: "And the others?"

I say: "Abusing the mothers."

"The guards?"

"Yes. As usual."

The catechist reaches into his pocket and produces a newspaper clipping. "Have you heard the news?" he asks.

"No," I say.

He reads aloud: *"Vegetable Oil Allowed in Three Catholic Rites."*

He pauses. He looks at me. I say nothing. He reads aloud: *"Rome, March 2nd. Reuters."* He looks at me. I say nothing. *"Reuters,"* he repeats. *"Roman Catholic sacramental anointings may in the future be performed with any vegetable oil, according to a new Vatican ruling that lifts the Church's age-old—"* He pauses. *"Age-old,"* he emphasizes.

I think: Perhaps she is at ease. Looking at her lake.

The catechist reads: *". . . that lifts the Church's age-old insistence on the use of olive oil. New paragraph. Under Catholic ritual, holy oil previously blessed by a bishop is used symbolically in the sacraments of confirmation, baptism, and the anointing of the sick, formerly extreme unction. New paragraph. Other vegetable oils are cheaper and considerably easier to obtain than olive oil in many parts of the world, Vatican observers noted."* The catechist pauses. "You're a priest. I'm a priest," he says. "Now I ask you."

I think: Perhaps she is distressed and looking at the lake does nothing to mitigate the distress.

He says: "Consider that you are dying. The sickroom. The bed. The plucked-at sheets. The distraught loved ones. The priest approaches. Bearing the holy viaticum, the sacred oils. The administration of the Host. The last anointing. And what is it you're given? You, the dying man? Peanut oil."

I think: Peanut oil.

The catechist replaces the clipping in his pocket. He will read it to me again tomorrow. Then he says: "When you saw the guards abusing the mothers, you—"

I say: "Wrote another letter."

"And you mailed the letter?"

"As before."

"The same mailbox?"

"Yes."

"You remembered to put a stamp—"

"A twenty-two-cent Frilled Dogwinkle."

I think: When I was young they asked other questions.

He says: "Tell me about her."

I say: "She has dark hair."

"Her husband—"

"I don't wish to discuss her husband."

The catechist reads from his book. *"The candidate should be questioned as to his motives for becoming a Christian."*

I think: My motives?

He says: "Tell me about yourself."

I say: "I'm forty. I have bad eyes. An enlarged liver."

"That's the alcohol," he says.

"Yes," I say.

"You're very much like your father, there."

"A shade more avid."

We have this conversation every day. No detail changes. He says: "But a man in your profession—"

I say: "But I don't want to discuss my profession."

He says: "Are you going back now? To the park?"

"Yes. She may be waiting."

"I thought she was looking at the lake."

"When she is not looking at the lake, then she is in the park."

The catechist reaches into the sleeve of his black robe. He produces a manifesto. He reads me the manifesto. *"All intellectual productions of the bourgeoisie are either offensive or defensive weapons against the revolution. All intellectual productions of the bourgeoisie are, objectively, obfuscating objects which are obstacles to the emancipation of the proletariat."* He replaces the manifesto in his sleeve.

I say: "But there are levels of signification other than the economic involved."

The catechist opens his book. He reads: *"A disappointing experience: the inadequacy of language to express thought. But let the catechist take courage."* He closes the book.

I think: Courage.

He says: "What do you propose to do?"

I say: "I suggested to her that I might change my profession."

"Have you had an offer?"

"A feeler."

"From whom?"

"General Foods."

"How did she respond?"

"A chill fell upon the conversation."

"But you pointed out—"

"I pointed out that although things were loosening up it would doubtless be a long time before priests were permitted to marry."

The catechist looks at me.

I think: She is waiting in the park, in the children's playground.

He says: "And then?"

I say: "I heard her confession."

"Was it interesting?"

"Nothing new."

"What were the others doing?"

"Tormenting the mothers."

"You wrote another letter?"

"Yes."

"You don't tire of this activity, writing letters?"

"One does what one can." I think: Or does not do what one can.

He says: "Let us discuss love."

I say: "I know nothing about it. Unless of course you refer to Divine love."

"I had in mind love as it is found in the works of Scheler, who holds that love is an aspect of phenomenological knowledge, and Carroll, who holds that 'tis love, 'tis love, that—"

"I know nothing about it."

The catechist opens his book. He reads: *"How to deal with the educated. Temptation and scandals to be faced by the candidate during his catechumenate."* He closes the book. There is never a day, never a day, on which we do not have this conversation. He says: "When were you ordained?"

I say: "1960."

He says: "These sins, your own, the sins we have been discussing, I'm sure you won't mind if I refer to them as sins although their magnitude, whether they are mortal or venial, I leave it to you to assess, in the secret places of your heart—"

I say: "One sits in the confessional hearing confessions, year after year, Saturday after Saturday, at four in the afternoon, twenty-one years times fifty-two Saturdays, excluding leap year—"

"One thousand and ninety-two Saturdays—"

"Figuring forty-five adulteries to the average Saturday—"

"Forty-nine thousand one hundred and forty adulteries—"

"One wonders: Perhaps there should be a redefinition? And with some adulteries there are explanations. The man is a cabdriver. He works nights. His wife wants to go out and have a good time. She tells him that she doesn't do anything wrong—a few drinks at the neighborhood bar, a little dancing. 'Now, you know, Father, and I know, Father, that where there's drinking and dancing there's bloody well something else too. So I tell her, Father, she'll stay out of that bar or I'll hit her upside the head. Well, Father, she says to me you can hit me upside the head all you want but I'm still going to that bar when I want and you can hit me all day long and it won't stop me. Now, what can I do, Father? I got to be in this cab every night of the week except Mondays and sometimes I work Mondays to make a little extra. So I hit her upside the head a few times but it don't make any difference, she goes anyhow. So I figure, Father, she's getting it outside the home, why not me? I'm always sorry after, Father, but what can I do? If I had a day job it would be different and now she just laughs at me and what can I do, Father?' "

"What do you say?"

"I advise self-control."

The catechist pokes about in his pockets. He pokes in his right-hand pocket for a time and then pokes in his left-hand pocket. He produces at length a tiny Old Testament, a postage-stamp Old Testament. He opens the postage-stamp Old Testament. *"Miserable comforters are ye all."* He closes the postage-stamp Old Testament. "Job 16:2." He replaces the postage-stamp Old Testament in his left-hand pocket. He pokes about in his right-hand pocket and produces a button on which the word LOVE is printed. He pins the button on my cassock, above the belt, below the collar. He says: "But you'll go there again."

I say: "At eleven. The children's playground."

He says: "The rain. The trees."

I say: "All that rot."

He says: "The benches damp. The seesaw abandoned."

I say: "All that garbage."

He says: "Sunday the day of rest and worship is hated by all classes of men in every country to which the Word has been carried. Hatred of Sunday in London approaches one hundred percent. Hatred of Sunday in Rio produces suicides. Hatred of Sunday in Madrid is only appeased by the ritual slaughter of large black animals, in rings. Hatred of Sunday in Munich is the stuff of legend. Hatred of Sunday in Sydney is considered by the knowledgeable to be hatred of Sunday at its most exquisite."

I think: She will press against me with her hands in the back pockets of her trousers.

The catechist opens his book. He reads: *"The apathy of the listeners. The judicious catechist copes with the difficulty."* He closes the book.

I think: Analysis terminable and interminable. I think: Then she will leave the park looking backward over her shoulder.

He says: "And the guards, what were they doing?"

I say: "Abusing the mothers."

"You wrote a letter?"

"Another letter."

"Would you say, originally, that you had a vocation? Heard a call?"

"I heard many things. Screams. Suites for unaccompanied cello. I did not hear a call."

"Nevertheless—"

"Nevertheless I went to the clerical-equipment store and purchased a summer cassock and a winter cassock. The summer cassock has short sleeves. I purchased a black hat."

"And the lady's husband?"

"He is a psychologist. He works in the limits of sensation. He is attempting to define precisely the two limiting sensations in the sensory continuum, the upper limit and the lower limit. He is often at the lab. He is measuring vanishing points."

"An irony."

"I suppose."

There is no day on which this conversation is not held and no detail of this conversation which is not replicated on any particular day on which this conversation is held.

The catechist produces from beneath his cloak a banner. He unfurls the banner and holds the unfurled banner above his head with both hands. The banner says, YOU ARE INTERRUPTED IN THE MIDST OF MORE CONGENIAL WORK? BUT THIS IS GOD'S WORK. The catechist refurls the banner. He replaces the banner under his cloak. He says: "But you'll go there again?"

I say: "Yes. At eleven."

He says: "But the rain . . ."

I say: "With her hands in the back pockets of her trousers."

He says: *"Deo gratias."*

PORCUPINES
AT THE UNIVERSITY

"AND now the purple dust of twilight time / steals across the meadows of my heart," the Dean said.

His pretty wife, Paula, extended her long graceful hands full of Negronis.

A scout burst into the room, through the door. "Porcupines!" he shouted.

"Porcupines what?" the Dean asked.

"Thousands and thousands of them. Three miles down the road and coming fast!"

"Maybe they won't enroll," the Dean said. "Maybe they're just passing through."

"You can't be sure," his wife said.

"How do they look?" he asked the scout, who was pulling porcupine quills out of his ankles.

"Well, you know. Like porcupines."

"Are you going to bust them?" Paula asked.

"I'm tired of busting people," the Dean said.

"They're not people," Paula pointed out.

"De bustibus non est disputandum," the scout said.

"I suppose I'll have to do something," the Dean said.

*   *   *

Meanwhile the porcupine wrangler was wrangling the porcupines across the dusty and overbuilt West.

Dust clouds. Yips. The lowing of porcupines.

"Git along theah li'l porcupines."

And when I reach the great porcupine canneries of the East, I will be rich, the wrangler reflected. I will sit on the front porch of the Muehlebach Hotel in New York City and smoke me a big seegar. Then, the fancy women.

"All right you porcupines step up to that yellow line."

There was no yellow line. This was just an expression the wrangler used to keep the porcupines moving. He had heard it in the Army. The damn-fool porcupines didn't know the difference.

The wrangler ambled along reading the ads in a copy of *Song Hits* magazine. PLAY HARMONICA IN 5 MINS. and so forth.

The porcupines scuffled along making their little hops. There were four-five thousand in the herd. Nobody had counted exactly.

An assistant wrangler rode in from the outskirts of the herd. He too had a copy of *Song Hits* magazine, in his hip pocket. He looked at the head wrangler's arm, which had a lot of little holes in it.

"Hey Griswold."

"Yeah?"

"How'd you get all them little holes in your arm?"

"You ever try to slap a brand on a porky-pine?"

Probably the fancy women will be covered with low-cut dresses and cheap perfume, the wrangler thought. Probably there will be hundreds of them, hundreds and hundreds. All after my medicine bundle containing my gold and my lucky drill bit. But if they try to rush me I will pull out my guitar. And sing them a song of prairie virility.

"Porcupines at the university," the Dean's wife said. "Well, why not?"

"We don't have *facilities* for four or five thousand porcupines," the Dean said. "I can't get a dial tone."

"They could take Alternate Life Styles," Paula said.

"We've already got too many people in Alternate Life Styles," the Dean said, putting down the telephone. "The hell with it. I'll bust them myself. Single-handed. Ly."

"You'll get hurt."

"Nonsense, they're only porcupines. I'd better wear my old clothes."

"Bag of dirty shirts in the closet," Paula said.

The Dean went into the closet.

Bags and bags of dirty shirts.

"Why doesn't she ever take these shirts to the laundry?"

Griswold, the wrangler, wrote a new song in the saddle.

> *Fancy woman fancy woman*
> *How come you don't do right*
> *I oughta rap you in the mouth*
>   *for the way you acted*
> *In the porte cochère of the Trinity River*
>   *Consolidated General High last Friday*
> *Nite.*

I will sit back and watch it climbing the charts, he said to himself. As recorded by Merle Travis. First, it will be a Bell Ringer. Then, the Top Forty. Finally a Golden Oldie.

"All right you porcupines. Git along."

The herd was moving down a twelve-lane trail of silky-smooth concrete. Signs along the trail said things like NEXT EXIT 5 MI. and RADAR IN USE.

"Griswold, some of them motorists behind us is gettin' awful pissed."

"I'm runnin' this-here porky-pine drive," Griswold said, "and I say we better gettum off the road."

The herd was turned onto a broad field of green grass. Green grass with white lime lines on it at ten-yard intervals.

The Sonny and Cher show, the wrangler thought. Well, Sonny, how I come to write this song, I was on a porky-pine drive. The last of the great porky-pine drives you might say. We had four-five thousand head we'd fatted up along the Tuscalora and we was headin' for New York City.

*   *   *

The Dean loaded a gleaming Gatling gun capable of delivering 360 rounds a minute. The Gatling gun sat in a mule-drawn wagon and was covered with an old piece of canvas. Formerly it had sat on a concrete slab in front of the ROTC Building.

First, the Dean said to himself, all they see is this funky old wagon pulled by this busted-up old mule. Then, I whip off the canvas. There stands the gleaming Gatling gun capable of delivering 360 rounds a minute. My hand resting lightly, confidently on the crank. They shall not pass, I say. Ils ne passeront pas. Then, the porcupine hide begins to fly.

I wonder if these rounds are still good?

The gigantic Gatling gun loomed over the herd like an immense piece of bad news.

"Hey Griswold."

"What?"

"He's got a gun."

"I *see* it," Griswold said. "You think I'm blind?"

"What we gonna do?"

"How about vamoose-ing?"

"But the herd . . ."

"Them li'l porcupines can take care of their own selves," Griswold said. "Goddamn it, I guess we better parley." He got up off the grass, where he had been stretched full-length, and walked toward the wagon.

"What say potner?"

"Look," the Dean said. "You can't enroll those porcupines. It's out of the question."

"That so?"

"It's out of the question," the Dean repeated. "We've had a lot of trouble around here. The cops won't even speak to me. We can't *take* any more trouble." The Dean glanced at the herd. "That's a mighty handsome herd you have there."

"Kind of you," Griswold said. "That's a mighty handsome mule *you* got."

They both gazed at the Dean's terrible-looking mule.

Griswold wiped his neck with a red bandanna. "You don't want no porky-pines over to your place, is that it?"

"That's it."

"Well, we don't *go* where we ain't wanted," the wrangler said. "No call to throw down on us with that . . . *machine* there."

The Dean looked embarrassed.

"You don't know Mr. Sonny Bono, do you?" Griswold asked. "He lives around here somewheres, don't he?"

"I haven't had the pleasure," the Dean said. He thought for a moment. "I know a booker in Vegas, though. He was one of our people. He was a grad student in comparative religion."

"Maybe we can do a deal," the wrangler said. "Which-a-way is New York City?"

"Well?" the Dean's wife asked. "What were their demands?"

"I'll tell you in a minute," the Dean said. "My mule is double-parked."

The herd turned onto the Cross Bronx Expressway. People looking out of their cars saw thousands and thousands of porcupines. The porcupines looked like badly engineered vacuum-cleaner attachments.

Vegas, the wrangler was thinking. Ten weeks at Caesar's Palace at a sock 15 Gs a week. The Ballad of the Last Drive. Leroy Griswold singing his smash single, The Ballad of the Last Drive.

"Git along theah, li'l porcupines."

The citizens in their cars looked at the porcupines, thinking: What is wonderful? Are these porcupines wonderful? Are they significant? Are they what I need?

SAKRETE

On our street, fourteen garbage cans are now missing. The garbage cans from One Seventeen and One Nineteen disappeared last night. This is not a serious matter, but on the other hand we can't sit up all night watching over our garbage cans. It is probably best described as an annoyance. One Twelve, One Twenty-two, and One Thirty-one have bought new plastic garbage cans at Barney's Hardware to replace those missing. We are thus down eleven garbage cans, net. Many people are using large dark plastic garbage bags. The new construction at the hospital at the end of the block has displaced a number of rats. Rats are not much bothered by plastic garbage bags. In fact, if I were ordered to imagine what might most profitably be invented by a committee of rats, it would be the dark plastic garbage bag. The rats run up and down our street all night long.

If I were ordered to imagine who is stealing our garbage cans, I could not do it. I very much doubt that my wife is doing it. Some of the garbage cans on our street are battered metal, others are heavy green plastic. Heavy green plastic or heavy black plastic predominates. Some of the garbage cans have the numbers of the houses they belong to painted on their sides or lids, with white paint. Usually by someone with only the crudest sense of the art of lettering. One Nineteen, which has among its tenants a gifted commercial artist, is an exception. No one excessively famous lives on our street, to my knowledge, therefore the morbid attention that the garbage of the famous sometimes attracts would not be a factor. The Precinct says that no other street within the precinct has reported similar problems.

If my wife is stealing the garbage cans, in the night, while I am drunk and asleep, what is she doing with them? They are not in the cellar, I've looked (although I don't like going down to the cellar, even to replace a blown fuse, because of the rats). My wife has a yellow Pontiac convertible. No one has these anymore but I can imagine her lifting garbage cans into the back seat of the yellow Pontiac convertible, at four o'clock in the morning, when I am dreaming of being on stage, dreaming of having to perform a drum concerto with only one drumstick. . . .

On our street, twenty-one garbage cans are now missing. New infamies have been announced by One Thirty-one through One Forty-three—seven in a row, and on the same side of the street. Also, depredations at One Sixteen and One Sixty-four. We have put out dozens of cans of D-Con but the rats ignore them. Why should they go for the D-Con when they can have the remnants of Ellen Busse's Boeuf Rossini, for which she is known for six blocks in every direction? We eat well, on this street, there's no denying it. Except for the nursing students at One Fifty-eight, and why should they eat well, they're students, are they not? My wife cooks soft-shell crabs, in season, breaded, dusted with tasty cayenne, deep-fried. Barney's Hardware has run out of garbage cans and will not get another shipment until July. Any new garbage cans will have to be purchased at Budget Hardware, far, far away on Second Street.

Petulia, at Custom Care Cleaners, asks why my wife has been acting so peculiar lately. "Peculiar?" I say. "In what way do you mean?" Dr. Maugham, who lives at One Forty-four where he also has his office, has formed a committee. Mr. Wilkens, from One Nineteen, Pally Wimber, from One Twenty-nine, and my wife are on the committee. The committee meets at night, while I sleep, dreaming, my turn in the batting order has come up and I stand at the plate, batless. . . .

There are sixty-two houses on our street, four-story brownstones

for the most part. Fifty-two garbage cans are now missing. Rats
riding upon the backs of other rats gallop up and down our street,
at night. The committee is unable to decide whether to call itself
the Can Committee or the Rat Committee. The City has sent an
inspector who stood marveling, at midnight, at the activity on our
street. He is filing a report. He urges that the remaining garbage
cans be filled with large stones. My wife has appointed me a sub-
committee of the larger committee with the task of finding large
stones. Is there a peculiar look on her face as she makes the ap-
pointment? Dr. Maugham has bought a shotgun, a twelve-gauge
over-and-under. Mr. Wilkins has bought a Chase bow and two dozen
hunting arrows. I have bought a flute and an instruction book.

If I were ordered to imagine who is stealing our garbage cans,
the Louis Escher family might spring to mind, not as culprits but
as proximate cause. The Louis Escher family has a large income
and a small apartment, in One Twenty-one. The Louis Escher family
is given to acquiring things, and given the size of the Louis Escher
apartment, must dispose of old things in order to accommodate
new things. Sometimes the old things disposed of by the Louis
Escher family are scarcely two weeks old. Therefore, the garbage
at One Twenty-one is closely followed in the neighborhood, in the
sense that the sales and bargains listed in the newspapers are closely
followed. The committee, which feels that the garbage of the Louis
Escher family may be misrepresenting the neighborhood to the
criminal community, made a partial list of the items disposed of by
the Louis Escher family during the week of August eighth: one
mortar & pestle, majolica ware; one English cream maker (cream
is made by mixing unsalted sweet butter and milk); one set green
earthenware geranium leaf plates; one fruit ripener designed by
scientists at the University of California, Plexiglas; one nylon um-
brella tent with aluminum poles; one combination fountain pen
and clock with LED readout; one mini hole-puncher-and-confetti-
maker; one pistol-grip spring-loaded flyswatter; one cast-iron tor-
tilla press; one ivory bangle with elephant-hair accent; and much,
much more. But while I do not doubt that the excesses of the Louis
Escher family are misrepresenting the neighborhood to the criminal
community, I cannot bring myself to support even a resolution of

censure, since the excesses of the Louis Escher family have given us much to talk about and not a few sets of green earthenware geranium leaf plates over the years.

I reported to my wife that large stones were hard to come by in the city. "Stones," she said. *"Large stones."* I purchased two hundred pounds of Sakrete at Barney's Hardware, to make stones with. One need only add water and stir, and you have made a stone as heavy and brutish as a stone made by God himself. I am temporarily busy, in the basement, shaping Sakrete to resemble this, that, and the other, but mostly stones—a good-looking stone is not the easiest of achievements. Ritchie Beck, the little boy from One Ten who is always alone on the sidewalk during the day, smiling at strangers, helps me. I once bought him a copy of *Mechanix Illustrated,* which I myself read avidly as a boy. Harold, who owns Custom Care Cleaners and also owns a Cessna, has offered to fly over our street at night and drop bombs made of lethal dry-cleaning fluid on the rats. There is a channel down the Hudson he can take (so long as he stays under eleven hundred feet), a quick left turn, the bombing run, then a dash back up the Hudson. They will pull his ticket if he's caught, he says, but at that hour of the night . . . I show my wife the new stones. "I don't like them," she says. "They don't look like real stones." She is not wrong, they look, in fact, like badly thrown pots, as if they had been done by a potter with no thumbs. The committee, which has named itself the Special Provisional Unnecessary-Rat Team (SPURT), has acquired armbands and white steel helmets and is discussing a secret grip by which its members will identify themselves to each other.

There are now no garbage cans on our street—no garbage cans left to steal. A committee of rats has joined with the Special Provisional committee in order to deal with the situation, which, the rats have made known, is attracting unwelcome rat elements from other areas of the city. Members of the two committees exchange secret grips, grips that I know not of. My wife drives groups of rats here and there in her yellow Pontiac convertible, attending important meetings. The crisis, she says, will be a long one. She has never been happier.

CAPTAIN BLOOD

Wʜᴇɴ Captain Blood goes to sea, he locks the doors and windows of his house on Cow Island personally. One never knows what sort of person might chance by, while one is away.

When Captain Blood, at sea, paces the deck, he usually paces the foredeck rather than the afterdeck—a matter of personal preference. He keeps marmalade and a spider monkey in his cabin, and four perukes on stands.

When Captain Blood, at sea, discovers that he is pursued by the Dutch Admiral Van Tromp, he considers throwing the women overboard. So that they will drift, like so many giant lotuses in their green, lavender, purple, and blue gowns, across Van Tromp's path, and he will have to stop and pick them up. Blood will have the women fitted with life jackets under their dresses. They will hardly be in much danger at all. But what about the jaws of sea turtles? No, the women cannot be thrown overboard. Vile, vile! What an idiotic idea! What could he have been thinking of? Of the patterns they would have made floating on the surface of the water, in the moonlight, a cerise gown, a silver gown . . .

Captain Blood presents a façade of steely imperturbability.

He is poring over his charts, promising everyone that things will get better. There has not been one bit of booty in the last eight months. Should he try another course? Another ocean? The men have been quite decent about the situation. Nothing has been said. Still, it's nerve-wracking.

When Captain Blood retires for the night (leaving orders that he be called instantly if something comes up) he reads, usually. Or smokes, thinking calmly of last things.

His hideous reputation should not, strictly speaking, be painted in the horrible colors customarily employed. Many a man walks the streets of Panama City, or Port Royal, or San Lorenzo, alive and well, who would have been stuck through the gizzard with a rapier, or smashed in the brain with a boarding pike, had it not been for Blood's swift, cheerful intervention. Of course, there are times when severe measures are unavoidable. At these times he does not flinch, but takes appropriate action with admirable steadiness. There are no two ways about it: when one looses a seventy-four-gun broadside against the fragile hull of another vessel, one gets carnage.

Blood at dawn, a solitary figure pacing the foredeck.

No other sail in sight. He reaches into the pocket of his blue velvet jacket trimmed with silver lace. His hand closes over three round, white objects: mothballs. In disgust, he throws them over the side. One *makes* one's luck, he thinks. Reaching into another pocket, he withdraws a folded parchment tied with ribbon. Unwrapping the little packet, he finds that it is a memo that he wrote to himself ten months earlier. "*Dolphin,* Captain Darbraunce, 120 tons, cargo silver, paprika, bananas, sailing Mar. 10 Havana. *Be there!*" Chuckling, Blood goes off to seek his mate, Oglethorpe— that laughing blond giant of a man.

Who will be aboard this vessel which is now within cannon-shot? wonders Captain Blood. Rich people, I hope, with pretty gold and silver things aplenty.

"Short John, where is Mr. Oglethorpe?"

"I am not Short John, sir. I am John-of-Orkney."

"Sorry, John. Has Mr. Oglethorpe carried out my instructions?"

"Yes, sir. He is forward, crouching over the bombard, lit cheroot in hand, ready to fire."

"Well, fire then."

"Fire!"

BAM!

"The other captain doesn't understand what is happening to him!"

"He's not heaving to!"

"He's ignoring us!"

"The dolt!"

"Fire again!"

BAM!

"That did it!"

"He's turning into the wind!"

"He's dropped anchor!"

"He's lowering sail!"

"Very well, Mr. Oglethorpe. You may prepare to board."

"Very well, Peter."

"And Jeremy—"

"Yes, Peter?"

"I know we've had rather a thin time of it these last few months."

"Well it hasn't been so bad, Peter. A little slow, perhaps—"

"Well, before we board, I'd like you to convey to the men my appreciation for their patience. Patience and, I may say, tact."

"We knew you'd turn up something, Peter."

"Just tell them for me, will you?"

Always a wonderful moment, thinks Captain Blood. Preparing to board. Pistol in one hand, naked cutlass in the other. Dropping lightly to the deck of the engrappled vessel, backed by one's grinning, leering, disorderly, rapacious crew who are nevertheless under the strictest buccaneer discipline. There to confront the little band of fear-crazed victims shrinking from the entirely possible carnage. Among them, several beautiful women, but one really spectacular beautiful woman who stands a bit apart from her sisters, clutching a machete with which she intends, against all reason, to—

When Captain Blood celebrates the acquisition of a rich prize, he goes down to the galley himself and cooks *tallarínes a la catalána* (noodles, spare ribs, almonds, pine nuts) for all hands. The name of the captured vessel is entered in a little book along with the names of all the others he has captured in a long career. Here are some of them: the *Oxford*, the *Luis*, the *Fortune*, the *Lambe*, the *Jamaica Merchant*, the *Betty*, the *Prosperous*, the *Endeavor*, the *Falcon*, the *Bonadventure*, the *Constant Thomas*, the *Marquesa*, the *Señora del Carmen*, the *Recovery*, the *María Gloriosa*, the *Virgin Queen*, the *Esmeralda*, the *Havana*, the *San Felipe*, the *Steadfast* . . .

The true buccaneer is not persuaded that God is not on his side, too—especially if, as is often the case, he turned pirate after some monstrously unjust thing was done to him, such as being press-ganged into one or another of the Royal Navies when he was merely innocently having a drink at a waterfront tavern, or having been confined to the stinking dungeons of the Inquisition just for making some idle, thoughtless, light remark. Therefore, Blood feels himself to be devout *in his own way,* and has endowed candles burning in churches in most of the great cities of the New World. Although not under his own name.

Captain Blood roams ceaselessly, making daring raids. The average raid yields something like 20,000 pieces-of-eight, which is apportioned fairly among the crew, with wounded men getting more according to the gravity of their wounds. A cut ear is worth two pieces, a cut-*off* ear worth ten to twelve. The scale of payments for injuries is posted in the forecastle.

When he is on land, Blood is confused and troubled by the life of cities, where every passing stranger may, for no reason, assault him, if the stranger so chooses. And indeed, the stranger's mere presence, multiplied many times over, is a kind of assault. Merely having to *take into account* all these hurrying others is a blistering occupation. This does not happen on a ship, or on a sea.

An amusing incident: Captain Blood has overhauled a naval vessel, has caused her to drop anchor (on this particular voyage he is sailing with three other ships under his command and a total enlistment of nearly one thousand men), and is now interviewing the arrested captain in his cabin full of marmalade jars and new perukes.

"And what may your name be, sir? If I may ask?"

"Jones, sir."

"What kind of a name is that? English, I take it?"

"No, it's American, sir."

"American? What is an American?"

"America is a new nation among the nations of the world."

"I've not heard of it. Where is it?"

"North of here, north and west. It's a very small nation, at present, and has only been a nation for about two years."

"But the name of your ship is French."

"Yes it is. It is named in honor of Benjamin Franklin, one of our American heroes."

"*Bon Homme Richard*? What has that to do with Benjamin or Franklin?"

"Well it's an allusion to an almanac Dr. Franklin published called—"

"You weary me, sir. You are captured, American or no, so tell me—do you surrender, with all your men, fittings, cargo, and whatever?"

"Sir, I have not yet begun to fight."

"Captain, this is madness. We have you completely surrounded. Furthermore there is a great hole in your hull below the waterline where our warning shot, which was slightly miscalculated, bashed in your timbers. You are taking water at a fearsome rate. And still you wish to fight?"

"It is the pluck of us Americans, sir. We are just that way. Our tiny nation has to be pluckier than most if it is to survive among the bigger, older nations of the world."

"Well, bless my soul, Jones, you are the damnedest goatsucker I ever did see. Stab me if I am not tempted to let you go scot-free, just because of your amazing pluck."

"No sir, I insist on fighting. As founder of the American naval tradition, I must set a good example."

"Jones, return to your vessel and be off."

"No, sir, I will fight to the last shred of canvas, for the honor of America."

"Jones, even in America, wherever it is, you must have encountered the word 'ninny.' "

"Oh. I see. Well then. I think we'll be weighing anchor, Captain, with your permission."

"Choose your occasions, Captain. And God be with you."

Blood, at dawn, a solitary figure pacing the foredeck. The world of piracy is wide, and at the same time, narrow. One can be gallant all day long, and still end up with a spider monkey for a wife. And what does his mother think of him?

The favorite dance of Captain Blood is the grave and haunting Catalonian *sardana*, in which the participants join hands facing each other to form a ring which gradually becomes larger, then smaller, then larger again. It is danced without smiling, for the most part. He frequently dances this with his men, in the middle of the ocean, after lunch, to the music of a single silver trumpet.

110 WEST SIXTY-FIRST STREET

Paul gave Eugenie a very large swordfish steak for her birthday. It was wrapped in red-and-white paper. The paper was soaked with swordfish juices in places but Eugenie was grateful nevertheless. He had tried. Paul and Eugenie went to a film. Their baby had just died and they were trying not to think about it. The film left them slightly depressed. The child's body had been given to the hospital for medical experimentation. "But what about life after death?" Eugenie's mother had asked. "There isn't any," Eugenie said. "Are you positive?" her mother asked. "No," Eugenie said. "How can I be positive? But that's my opinion."

Eugenie said to Paul: "This is the best birthday I've ever had." "The hell it is," Paul said. Eugenie cooked the swordfish steak wondering what the hospital had done to Claude. Claude had been two years old when he died. *That goddamn kid!* she thought. Looking around her, she could see the places where he had been—the floor, mostly. Paul thought: My swordfish-steak joke was not successful. He looked at the rather tasteless swordfish on his plate. Eugenie touched him on the shoulder.

Paul and Eugenie went to many erotic films. But the films were not erotic. Nothing was erotic. They began looking at each other and thinking about other people. The back wall of the apartment was falling off. Contractors came to make estimates. A steel I-beam would have to be set into the wall to support the floor of the apartment above, which was sagging. The landlord did not wish to pay the four thousand dollars the work would cost. One could see daylight between the back wall and the party wall. Paul and Eugenie went to his father's place in Connecticut for a day. Paul's father was a will lawyer—a lawyer specializing in wills. He showed them a flyer advertising do-it-yourself wills. DO YOU HAVE A WILL? *Everyone should. Save on legal fees—make your own will with Will Forms Kit. Kit has 5 will forms, a 64-page book on wills, a guide to the duties of the executor, and forms for recording family assets. $1.98.* Eugenie studied the third-class mail. "What are our family assets?" she asked Paul. Paul thought about the question. Paul's sister Debbie had had a baby at fifteen, which had been put up for adoption. Then she had become a nun. Paul's brother Steve was in the Secret Service and spent all of his time guarding the widow of a former President. "Does Debbie still believe in a life after death?" Eugenie asked suddenly. "She believes, so far as I can determine, in life *now,*" Paul's father said. Eugenie remembered that Paul had told her that his father had been fond, when Debbie was a child, of beating her on her bare buttocks with a dog leash. "She believes in social action," Paul's bent father continued. "Probably she is right. That seems to be the trend among nuns."

Paul thought: Barbados. There we might recover what we have lost. I wonder if there is a charter flight through the Bar Association?

Paul and Eugenie drove back to the city.

"This is a lot of depressing crud that we're going through right now," Paul said as they reached Port Chester, N.Y. "But later it will be better." No it won't, Eugenie thought. "Yes it will," Paul said.

"You are extremely self-righteous," Eugenie said to Paul. "That is the one thing I can't stand in a man. Sometimes I want to scream." "You are a slut without the courage to go out and be one," Paul replied. "Why don't you go to one of those bars and pick up somebody, for God's sake?" "It wouldn't do any good," Eugenie said. "I know that," Paul said. Eugenie remembered the last scene of the erotic film they had seen on her birthday, in which the girl had taken a revolver from a drawer and killed her lover with it. At the time she had thought this a poor way to end the film. Now she wished she had a revolver in a drawer. Paul was afraid of having weapons in the house. "They fire themselves," he always said. "You don't have anything to do with it."

Mason came over and talked. Paul and Mason had been in the Army together. Mason, who had wanted to be an actor, now taught speech at a junior college on Long Island. "How are you bearing up?" Mason asked, referring to the death of Claude. "Very well," Paul said. "I am bearing up very well but she is not." Mason looked at Eugenie. "Well, I don't blame her," he said. "She should be an alcoholic by now." Eugenie, who drank very little, smiled at Mason. Paul's jokes were as a rule better than Mason's jokes. But Mason had compassion. His compassion is real, she thought. Only he doesn't know how to express it.

Mason told a long story about trivial departmental matters. Paul and Eugenie tried to look interested. Eugenie had tried to give Claude's clothes to her friend Julia, who also had a two-year-old. But Julia had said no. "You would always be seeing them," she said. "You should give them to a more distant friend. Don't you have any distant friends?" Paul was promoted. He became a full partner in his law firm. "This is a big day," he said when he came home. He was slightly drunk. "There is no such thing as a big day," Eugenie said. "Once, I thought there was. Now I know better. I sincerely congratulate you on your promotion, which I really believe was well deserved. You are talented and you have worked very hard. Forgive me for that remark I made last month about your self-righteousness. What I said was true—I don't retreat from that position—but a better wife would have had the tact not to mention it." "No," Paul said. "You were right to mention it. It is true. You should tell the truth when you know it. And you should go out and get laid if you feel like it. The veneer of politesse we cover ourselves with is not in general good for us." "No," Eugenie said. "Listen. I want to get pregnant again. You could do that for me. It's probably a bad idea but I want to do it. In spite of everything." Paul closed his eyes. "No no no no no," he said.

Eugenie imagined the new child. This time, a girl. A young

woman, she thought, eventually. Someone I could talk to. With
Claude, we made a terrible mistake. We should have had a small
coffin, a grave. We were sensible. We were unnatural. Paul emerged
from the bathroom with a towel wrapped around his waist. There
was some water on him still. Eugenie touched him on the shoulder.
Paul and Eugenie had once taken a sauna together, in Norway.
Paul had carried a glass of brandy into the sauna and the glass had
become so hot that he could not pick it up. The telephone rang.
It was Eugenie's sister in California. "We are going to have another
child," Eugenie said to her sister. "Are you pregnant?" her sister
asked. "Not yet," Eugenie said. "Do you think about him?" her
sister asked. "I still see him crawling around the floor," Eugenie
said. "Under the piano. He liked to screw around under the piano."

In the days that followed, Paul discovered a pair of gold cuff
links, oval in shape, at the bottom of a drawer. Cuff links, he
thought. Could I ever have worn cuff links? In the days that followed, Eugenie met Tiger. Tiger was a black artist who hated white
people so much he made love only to white women. "I am color-
blind, Tiger," Eugenie said to Tiger, in bed. "I really am." "The
hell you are," Tiger said. "You want to run a number on somebody,
go ahead. But don't jive *me*." Eugenie admired Tiger's many fine
qualities. Tiger "turned her head around," she explained to Paul.
Paul tried to remain calm. His increased responsibilities were wearing out his nerve ends. He was guiding a bus line through bankruptcy. Paul asked Eugenie if she was using contraceptives. "Of
course," she said.

"How'd it happen?" Tiger asked Eugenie, referring to the death
of Claude. Eugenie told him. "That don't make me happy," Tiger
said. "Tiger, you are an egocentric mushbrain monster," she said.
"You mean I'm a *mean nigger*," Tiger said. He loved to say "nigger"
because it shook the white folks so. "I mean you're an imitation
wild man. You're about as wild as a can of Campbell's Chicken with
Rice soup." Tiger then hit her around the head a few times to
persuade her of his authenticity. But she was relentless. "When you
get right down to it," she said, holding on to him and employing
the dialect, "you ain't no better than a *husband*."

Tiger fell away into the bottomless abyss of the formerly known.

Paul smiled. He had not known it would come to this, but now that it had come to this, he was pleased. The bus line was safely parked in the great garage of Section 112 of the Bankruptcy Act. Time passed. Eugenie's friend Julia came over for coffee and brought her three-year-old son, Peter. Peter walked around looking for his old friend Claude. Eugenie told Julia about the departure of Tiger. "He snorted coke but he would never give me any," she complained. "He said he didn't want to get me started." "You should be grateful," Julia said. "You can't afford it." There was a lot of noise from the back room where workmen were putting in the steel I-beam, finally. Paul was promoted from bus-line bankruptcies to railroad bankruptcies. "Today is a big day," he told Eugenie when he got home. "Yes, it is," she said. "They gave me the Cincinnati & West Virginia. The whole thing. It's all mine." "That's wonderful," Eugenie said. "I'll make you a drink." Then they went to bed, he masturbating with long slow strokes, she masturbating with quick light touches, kissing each other passionately all the while.

THE FILM

THINGS have never been better, except that the child, one of the stars of our film, has just been stolen by vandals, and this will slow down the progress of the film somewhat, if not bring it to a halt. But might not this incident, which is not without its own human drama, be made part of the story line? Julie places a hand on the child's head, in the vandal camp. "The fever has broken." The vandals give the child a wood doll to play with, until night comes. And suddenly I blunder into a landing party from our ships— forty lieutenants all in white, all holding their swords in front of their chins, in salute. The officer in charge slams his blade into its scabbard several times, in a gesture either decisive or indecisive. Yes, he will help us catch the vandals. No, he has no particular plan. Just general principles, he says. The Art of War itself.

The idea of the film is that it not be like other films.

I heard a noise outside. I looked out of the window. An old woman was bent over ·my garbage can, borrowing some of my garbage. They do that all over the city, old men and old women. They borrow your garbage and they never bring it back.

Thinking about the "Flying to America" sequence. This will be the film's climax. But am I capable of mounting such a spectacle? Fortunately I have Ezra to help.

"And is it not the case," said Ezra, when we first met, "that I have been associated with the production of nineteen major motion pictures of such savage originality, scalding *vérité*, and honey-warm sexual indecency that the very theaters chained their doors rather than permit exhibition of these major motion pictures on their ammonia-scented gum-daubed premises? And is it not the case," said Ezra, "that I myself with my two sinewy hands and strong-wrought God-gift brain have participated in the changing of seven high-class literary works of the first water and four of the second water and two of the third water into major muscatel? And is it not the living truth," said Ezra, "that I was the very man, I myself and none other without exception, who clung to the underside of the camera of the great Dreyer, clung with my two sinewy hands and noble thighs and cunning-muscled knees both dexter and sinister, during the cinematization of the master's *Gertrud*, clung there to slow the movement of said camera to that exquisite slowness which distinguishes this masterpiece from all other masterpieces of its water? And is it not chapter and verse," said Ezra, "that I was the comrade of all the comrades of the Dziga-Vertov group who was first in no-saying, firmest in no-saying, most final in no-saying, to all honey-sweet commercial seductions of whatever water and capitalist blandishments of whatever water and ideological incorrectitudes of whatever water whatsoever? And is it not as true as Saul become Paul," said Ezra, "that you require a man, a firm-limbed long-winded good true man, and that *I am the man* standing before you in his very blood and bones?"

"You are hired, Ezra," I said.

Whose child is it? We forgot to ask, when we sent out the casting call. Perhaps it belongs to itself. It has an air of self-possession quite remarkable in one so homely, and I notice that its paychecks are made out to it, rather than a nominee. Fortunately we have Julie to watch over it. The motor hotel in Tel Aviv is our temporary, not long-range, goal. New arrangements will probably not do the trick but we are making them anyhow: the ransom has been counted into pretty colored sacks, the film placed in round tin cans, the destroyed beams blocking the path are pushed aside. ... .

Thinking of sequences for the film.
    A frenzy of desire?
    Sensible lovers taking precautions?
    Swimming with horses?

Today we filmed fear, a distressing emotion aroused by impending danger, real or imagined. In fear you know what you're afraid of, whereas in anxiety you do not. Correlation of children's fears with those of their parents is .667 according to Hagman. We filmed the startle pattern—shrinking, blinking, all that. Ezra refused to do "inhibition of the higher nervous centers." I don't blame him. However he was very good in demonstrating the sham rage reaction and also in "panting." Then we shot some stuff in which a primitive person (my bare arm standing in for the primitive person) kills an enemy by pointing a magic bone at him. "O.K., who's got the magic bone?" The magic bone was brought. I pointed the magic bone and the actor playing the enemy fell to the ground. I had carefully explained to the actor that the magic bone would not really kill him, probably.

    Next, the thrill of fear along the buttocks. We used Julie's buttocks for this sequence. "Hope is the very sign of lack-of-happiness," said Julie, face down on the divan. "Fame is a palliative for doubt," I said. "Wealth-formation is a source of fear for both winners and losers," Ezra said. "Civilization aims at making all good things accessible even to cowards," said the actor who had played the enemy, quoting Nietzsche. Julie's buttocks thrilled.

    We wrapped, then. I took the magic bone home with me. I don't believe in it, exactly, but you never know.

Have I ever been more alert, more confident? Following the dropped handkerchiefs to the vandal camp—there, a blue and green one, hanging on a shrub! The tall vandal chief wipes his hands on his sweatshirt. Vandals, he says, have been grossly misperceived. Their old practices, which earned them widespread condemnation, were a response to specific historical situations, and not a character trait, like being good or bad. Our negative has been scratched with a pointed instrument, all 150,000 feet of it. But the vandals say they were on the other side of town that night, planting trees. It is difficult to believe them. But gazing at the neat rows of saplings, carefully emplaced and surrounded by a vetchlike gound cover . . . A beautiful job! One does not know what to think.

We have got Mark Grunion for the film; he will play the important role of George. Mark wanted many Gs in the beginning, but now that he understands the nature of the project he is working for scale, so that he can grow, as an actor and as a person. He is growing visibly, shot by shot. Soon he will be the biggest actor in the business. The other actors crowd about him, peering into his ankles. . . . *Should* this film be made? That is one of the difficult questions one has to forget, when one is laughing in the face of unclear situations, or bad weather. What a beautiful girl Julie is! Her lustrous sexuality has the vandals all agog. They follow her around trying to touch the tip of her glove, or the flounce of her gown. She shows her breasts to anyone who asks. "Amazing grace!" the vandals say.

Today we filmed the moon rocks. We set up in the Moon Rock Room, at the Smithsonian. There they were. The moon rocks. The moon rocks were the greatest thing we had ever seen in our entire lives! The moon rocks were red, green, blue, yellow, black, and white. They scintillated, sparkled, glinted, glittered, twinkled, and gleamed. They produced booms, thunderclaps, explosions, clashes, splashes, and roars. They sat on a pillow of the purest Velcro, and people who touched the pillow were able to throw away their crutches and jump in the air. Four cases of gout and eleven instances of hyperbolic paraboloidism were cured before our eyes. The air rained crutches. The moon rocks drew you toward them with a fatal irresistibility, but at the same time held you at a seemly distance with a decent reserve. Peering into the moon rocks, you could see the future and the past in color, and you could change them in any way you wished. The moon rocks gave off a slight hum, which cleaned your teeth, and a brilliant glow, which absolved you from sin. The moon rocks whistled *Finlandia,* by Jean Sibelius, while reciting *The Confessions of St. Augustine,* by I. F. Stone. The moon rocks were as good as a meaningful and emotionally rewarding seduction that you had not expected. The moon rocks were as good as listening to what the members of the Supreme Court say to each other, in the Supreme Court Locker Room. They were as good as a war. The moon rocks were better than a presentation copy of the *Random House Dictionary of the English Language* signed by Geoffrey Chaucer himself. They were better than a movie in which the President refuses to tell the people what to do to save themselves from the terrible thing that is about to happen, although he knows what ought to be done and has written a secret memorandum about it. The moon rocks were better than a good cup of coffee from an urn decorated with the change of Philomel, by the barbarous king. The moon rocks were better than a *¡huelga!* led by Mongo Santamaria, with additional dialogue by St. John of the Cross and special effects by Melmoth the Wanderer. The moon rocks surpassed our expectations. The dynamite out-of-sight very heavy and together moon rocks turned us on, to the highest degree. There was blood on our eyes, when we had finished filming them.

What if the film fails? And if it fails, will I know it?

A murdered doll floating face down in a bathtub—that will be the opening shot. A "cold" opening, but with faint intimations of the happiness of childhood and the pleasure we take in water. Then, the credits superimposed on a hanging side of beef. Samisen music, and a long speech from a vandal spokesman praising vandal culture and minimizing the sack of Rome in 455 A.D. Next, shots of a talk program in which all of the participants are whispering, including the host. Softness could certainly be considered a motif here. The child is well-behaved through the long hours of shooting. The lieutenants march nicely, swinging their arms. The audience smiles.

A vandal is standing near the window, and suddenly large cracks appear in the window. Pieces of glass fall to the floor. But I was watching him the whole time; he did nothing.

I wanted to film everything but there are things we are not getting. The wild ass is in danger in Ethiopia—we've got nothing on that. We've got nothing on intellectual elitism funded out of public money, an important subject. We've got nothing on ball lightning and nothing on the National Grid and not a foot on the core-mantle problem, the problem of a looped economy, or the interesting problem of the night brain.

I wanted to get it all but there's only so much time, so much energy. There's an increasing resistance to antibiotics worldwide and liquid metal fast-breeder reactors are subject to swelling and a large proportion of Quakers are color-blind but our film will have not a shred of material on any of these matters.

Is the film sufficiently sexual? I don't know.

I remember a brief exchange with Julie about revolutionary praxis.

"But I thought," I said, "that there had been a sexual revolution and everybody could sleep with anybody who was a consenting adult."

"In theory," Julie said. "In theory. But sleeping with someone also has a political dimension. One does not, for example, go to bed with running dogs of imperialism."

I thought: But who will care for and solace the running dogs of imperialism? Who will bring them their dog food, who will tuck the covers tight as they dream their imperialistic dreams?

We press on. But where is Ezra? He was supposed to bring additional light, the light we need for "Flying to America." The vandals hit the trail, confused as to whether they should place themselves under our protection, or fight. The empty slivovitz bottles are buried, the ashes of the cooking fires scattered. At a signal from the leader the sleek, well-cared-for mobile homes swing onto the highway. The rehabilitation of the filmgoing public through "good design," through "softness," is our secret aim. The payment of rent

for seats will be continued for a little while, but eventually abolished.
Anyone will be able to walk into a film as into a shower. Bathing
with the actors will become commonplace. Terror and terror are
our two great principles, but we have other principles to fall back
on, if these fail. "I can relate to that," Mark says. He does. We
watch skeptically.

Who had murdered the doll? We pressed our inquiry, receiv-
ing every courtesy from the Tel Aviv police, who said they had
never seen a case like it, either in their memories, or in dreams.
A few wet towels were all the evidence that remained, except for,
in the doll's hollow head, little pieces of paper on which were
written

JULIE

JULIE

JULIE

JULIE

in an uncertain hand. And now the ground has opened up and
swallowed our cutting room. One cannot really hold the vandals
responsible. And yet . . .

Now we are shooting "Flying to America."

The 112 pilots check their watches.

Ezra nowhere to be seen. Will there be enough light?

If the pilots all turn on their machines at once . . .

Flying to America.

(But did I remember to—?)

"Where is the blimp?" Marcello shouts. "I can't find the—"

Ropes dangling from the sky.

I'm using forty-seven cameras, the outermost of which is posted
in the Dover Marshes.

The Atlantic is calm in some parts, angry in others.

A blueprint four miles long is the flight plan.

Every detail coordinated with the air-sea rescue services of all
nations.

Victory through Air Power! I seem to remember that slogan from
somewhere.

Hovercraft flying to America. Flying boats flying to America. F-111s flying to America. The China Clipper!

Seaplanes, bombers, Flying Wings flying to America.

A shot of a pilot named Tom. He opens the cockpit door and speaks to the passengers. "America is only two thousand miles away now," he says. The passengers break out in smiles.

Balloons flying to America (they are painted in red and white stripes). Spads and Fokkers flying to America. Self-improvement is a large theme in flying to America. "Nowhere is self-realization more a possibility than in America," a man says.

Julie watching the clouds of craft in the air . . .

Gliders gliding to America. One man has constructed a huge paper aircraft, seventy-two feet in length. It is doing better than we had any right to expect. But then great expectations are an essential part of flying to America.

Rich people are flying to America, and poor people, and people of moderate means. This aircraft is powered by twelve rubber bands, each rubber band thicker than a man's leg—can it possibly survive the turbulence over Greenland?

Long thoughts are extended to enwrap the future American experience of the people who are flying to America.

And here is Ezra! Ezra is carrying the light we need for this part of the picture—a great bowl of light lent to us by the U.S. Navy. Now our film will be successful, or at least completed, and the aircraft illuminated, and the child rescued, and Julie will marry well, and the light from the light will fall into the eyes of the vandals, fixing them in place. Truth! That is another thing they said our film wouldn't contain. I had simply forgotten about it, in contemplating the series of triumphs that is my private life.

OVERNIGHT
TO MANY DISTANT CITIES

A group of Chinese in brown jackets preceded us through the halls of Versailles. They were middle-aged men, weighty, obviously important, perhaps thirty of them. At the entrance to each room a guard stopped us, held us back until the Chinese had finished inspecting it. A fleet of black government Citroëns had brought them, they were much at ease with Versailles and with each other, it was clear that they were being rewarded for many years of good behavior.

Asked her opinion of Versailles, my daughter said she thought it was overdecorated.

Well, yes.

Again in Paris, years earlier, without Anna, we had a hotel room opening on a courtyard, and late at night through an open window heard a woman expressing intense and rising pleasure. We blushed and fell upon each other.

Right now sunny skies in mid-Manhattan, the temperature is forty-two degrees.

In Stockholm we ate reindeer steak and I told the Prime Minister . . . That the price of booze was too high. Twenty dollars for a bottle of J&B! He (Olof Palme) agreed, most politely, and said that they financed the Army that way. The conference we were attending was held at a workers' vacation center somewhat outside the city. Shamelessly, I asked for a double bed, there were none, we pushed two single beds together. An Israeli journalist sat on the two single beds drinking our costly whiskey and explaining the devilish policies of the Likud. Then it was time to go play with the Africans. A poet who had been for a time a Minister of Culture explained why he had burned a grand piano on the lawn in front of the Ministry. "The piano," he said, "is not the national instrument of Uganda."

A boat ride through the scattered islands. A Warsaw Pact novelist asked me to carry a package of paper back to New York for him.

Woman is silent for two days in San Francisco. And walked through the streets with her arms raised high touching the leaves of the trees.

"But you're *married*!"

"But that's *not my fault*!"

Tearing into cold crab at Scoma's we saw Chill Wills at another table, doing the same thing. We waved to him.

In Taegu the air was full of the noise of helicopters. The helicopter landed on a pad, General A jumped out and walked with a firm, manly stride to the spot where General B waited—generals visiting each other. They shook hands, the honor guard with its blue scarves and chromed rifles popped to, the band played, pictures were taken. General A followed by General B walked smartly around the rigid honor guard and then the two generals marched off to the General's Mess, to have a drink.

There are eight hundred and sixty-one generals now on active service. There are four hundred and twenty-six brigadier generals, three hundred and twenty-four major generals, eighty-seven lieutenant generals, and twenty-four full generals. The funniest thing in the world is a general trying on a nickname. Sometimes they don't stick. "Howlin' Mad," "Old Hickory," "Old Blood and Guts," and "Buck" have already been taken. "Old Lacy" is not a good choice.

If you are a general in the field you will live in a general's van, which is a kind of motor home for generals. I once saw a drunk

two-star general, in a general's van, seize hold of a visiting actress—
it was Marilyn Monroe—and seat her on his lap, shrieking all the
while "R.H.I.P.!" or, Rank Has Its Privileges.

Enough of generals.

Thirty-percent chance of rain this afternoon, high in the mid-
fifties.

In London I met a man who was not in love. Beautiful shoes, black
as black marble, and a fine suit. We went to the theatre together,
matter of a few pounds, he knew which plays were the best plays,
on several occasions he brought his mother. "An American," he
said to his mother, "an American I met." "Met an American during
the war," she said to me, "didn't like him." This was reasonably
standard, next she would tell me that we had no culture. Her son
was hungry, starving, mad in fact, sucking the cuff buttons of his
fine suit, choking on the cuff buttons of his fine suit, left and right
sleeves jammed into his mouth—he was not in love, he said, "again
not in love, not in love again." I put him out of his misery with a
good book, Rilke, as I remember, and resolved never to find myself
in a situation as dire as his.

In San Antonio we walked by the little river. And ended up in
Helen's Bar, where John found a pool player who was, like John,
an ex-Marine. How these ex-Marines love each other! It is a flat
scandal. The Congress should do something about it. The IRS
should do something about it. You and I talked to each other while
John talked to his Parris Island friend, and that wasn't too bad,
wasn't too bad. We discussed twenty-four novels of normative adultery. "Can't *have* no adultery without adults," I said, and you agreed
that this was true. We thought about it, our hands on each other's
knees, under the table.

In the car on the way back from San Antonio the ladies talked
about the rump of a noted poet. "Too big," they said, "too big too
big too big." "Can you imagine going to bed with him?" they said,
and then all said, "No no no no no," and laughed and laughed and
laughed and laughed.

I offered to get out and run alongside the car, if that would allow
them to converse more freely.

In Copenhagen I went shopping with two Hungarians. I had thought they merely wanted to buy presents for their wives. They bought leather gloves, chess sets, frozen fish, baby food, lawnmowers, air conditioners, kayaks. . . . We were six hours in the department store.

"This will teach you," they said, "never to go shopping with Hungarians."

Again in Paris, the hotel was the Montalembert. . . . Anna jumped on the bed and sliced her hand open on an open watercolor tin, blood everywhere, the concierge assuring us that "In the war, I saw much worse things."

Well, yes.

But we couldn't stop the bleeding, in the cab to the American Hospital the driver kept looking over his shoulder to make sure that we weren't bleeding on his seat covers, handfuls of bloody paper towels in my right and left hands. . , . .

On another evening, as we were on our way to dinner, I kicked the kid with carefully calibrated force as we were crossing the Pont Mirabeau, she had been pissy all day, driving us crazy, her character improved instantly, wonderfully, this is a tactic that can be used exactly once.

In Mexico City we lay with the gorgeous daughter of the American ambassador by a clear, cold mountain stream. Well, that was the plan, it didn't work out that way. We were around sixteen and had run away from home, in the great tradition, hitched various long rides with various sinister folk, and there we were in the great city with about two t-shirts to our names. My friend Herman found us jobs in a jukebox factory. Our assignment was to file the slots in American jukeboxes so that they would accept the big, thick Mexican coins. All day long. No gloves.

After about a week of this we were walking one day on the street on which the Hotel Reforma is to be found and there were my father and grandfather, smiling. "The boys have run away," my father had told my grandfather, and my grandfather had said, "Hot damn, let's go get 'em." I have rarely seen two grown men enjoying themselves so much.

Ninety-two this afternoon, the stock market up in heavy trading.

In Berlin everyone stared, and I could not blame them. You were spectacular, your long skirts, your long dark hair. I was upset by the staring, people gazing at happiness and wondering whether to credit it or not, wondering whether it was to be trusted and for how long, and what it meant to them, whether they were in some way hurt by it, in some way diminished by it, in some way criticized by it, good God get it out of my sight—

I correctly identified a Matisse as a Matisse even though it was an uncharacteristic Matisse, you thought I was knowledgeable whereas I was only lucky, we stared at the Schwitters show for one hour and twenty minutes, and then lunched. *Vitello tonnato,* as I recall.

When Herman was divorced in Boston . . . Carol got the good barbecue pit. I put it in the Blazer for her. In the back of the Blazer were cartons of books, tableware, sheets and towels, plants, and oddly, two dozen white carnations fresh in their box. I pointed to the flowers. "Herman," she said, "he never gives up."

In Barcelona the lights went out. At dinner. Candles were produced and the shiny langoustines placed before us. Why do I love Barcelona above most other cities? Because Barcelona and I share a passion for walking? I was happy there? You were with me? We were celebrating my hundredth marriage? I'll stand on that. Show me a man who has not married a hundred times and I'll show you a wretch who does not deserve God's good world.

Lunching with the Holy Ghost I praised the world, and the Holy Ghost was pleased. "We have that little problem in Barcelona," He said, "the lights go out in the middle of dinner." "I've noticed," I said. "We're working on it," He said, "what a wonderful city, one of our best." "A great town," I agreed. In an ecstasy of admiration for what is we ate our simple soup.

Tomorrow, fair and warmer, warmer and fair, most fair . . .

CONSTRUCTION

I went to Los Angeles and, in due course, returned, having finished the relatively important matter of business which had taken me to Los Angeles, something to do with a contract, a noxious contract, which I signed, after the new paragraphs were inserted and initialed by all parties, tiresome business of initialing numberless copies of documents reproduced on onionskin, which does not feel happy in the hand. One of the lawyers wore a woven straw Western hat with a snake hatband. He had an excessive suntan. The hatband displayed as its centerpiece the head of a rattlesnake with its mouth stretched and the fangs touchable. Helen made a joke about it, she does something in the West Coast office, I'm not sure what it is but she is treated with considerable deference, they all seem to defer to her, an attractive woman, of course, but also one who manifests a certain authority, a quiet authority, had I had the time I would have asked someone what she was "all about," as we say, but I had to get back, one cannot spend all one's time in lawyers' offices in Los Angeles. Although it was January and there was snow, blizzarding even, elsewhere, the temperature was in the fifties and the foliage, the collection of strange-looking trees, not trees but something between a tree and a giant shrub, that distinguishes the city, that hides what is less prepossessing than the trees—I refer to the local construction—which serves as a screen or scrim between the eye and the local construction, much of it admirable no doubt, the foliage was successfully carrying out its function, making Los Angeles a pleasant, reticent, green place, which fact I noticed before my return from Los Angeles.

The flight back from Los Angeles was without event, very calm and smooth in the night. I had a cup of hot chicken noodle soup which the flight attendant was kind enough to prepare for me; I handed her the can of chicken noodle soup and she (I suppose, I don't know the details) heated it in her microwave oven and then brought me the cup of hot chicken noodle soup which I had handed her in canned form, also a number of drinks which helped make the calm, smooth flight more so. The plane was half empty, there had been a half-hour delay in getting off the ground which I spent marveling at a sentence in a magazine, the sentence reading as follows: "[Name of film] explores the issues of love and sex without ever being chaste." I marveled over this for the full half-hour we sat on the ground waiting for clearance on my return from Los Angeles, thinking of adequate responses, such as "Well we avoided *that* at least," but no response I could conjure up was equal to or could be equal to the original text which I tore out of the magazine and folded and placed, folded, in my jacket pocket for further consideration at some time in the future when I might need a giggle. Then deplaning and carrying my bag through the mostly deserted tunnels of the airport to the cab rank, I obtained a cab driven by a black man who was, he said, leaving the cab business to begin a messenger service and had that very morning taken delivery on a truck, a 1987 Toyota, for the purpose and was, as soon as his shift ended, going to not only show the 1987 Toyota to his mother but also pick up his car insurance. He asked me what I thought about the economy and I said that I thought it would continue to do well, nationally, for a time but that the local economy, by which I meant that of the whole region, would I thought not do as well, because of structural problems. He then told me a story about being in the jungle in Vietnam with a fellow who had been there for seventeen months and got a letter from his wife in which she announced that she was pregnant but (and I quote) "hadn't been doing anything," and that his colleague, in the jungle, had then gone crazy, and I said, "Seventeen months, what was he doing there for seventeen months?" the normal tour being one year, and he said, "He extended," and I said, "He extended?" and he said, "Yeah, extended," and I said, *"Then he was crazy before he got the letter,"* and he said, "Bingo!" and we both said, "Hoo hoo," in healthy fashion. He dropped me off in front of my building and I went upstairs and made a thickish cup of Hot Spiced Cider from an envelope of Hot Spiced Cider Mix that I had acquired free when I bought the bottle of Tree Top Apple Cider that was in my refrigerator, and took off my tie, and sat there, in my house, on my return from Los Angeles.

I thought about the food that I had had in Los Angeles and about what I had to do next, the next day, the next several days, and of course about the long-range plan. I sat there in the darkened room without a shirt (I had taken off my shirt) thinking about the food I had had in Los Angeles, the rather ordinary Tournedos Rossini, the rather too down-to-earth Huevos Rancheros in a very expensive place that nevertheless presented its Huevos Rancheros on a *tin plate,* and its coffee in *cracked blue enamel mugs,* the Chuck Wagon was its name. Breakfast there with Helen, who had an air of authority, one could not immediately fathom its source and I was too tired, after a long night in Los Angeles, too tired or insufficiently interested, to ask the questions, either of her associates or my associates or of Helen directly, that would have allowed me to fathom the sources of her authority in Los Angeles, Los Angeles being to me a place where one went, of necessity, at rare intervals, to sign and/or initial or renegotiate whatever needed such attention. I noticed very little about the place, the shrubs or trees, saw a bit of the ocean from my hotel-room window, saw an old woman in a green bathrobe on the balcony of the building opposite, at the same level, the eleventh floor, and wondered if she was a guest or if she was one of those persons who clean the place; if she was one of those persons who clean the place it seemed unlikely that she would come to work in a green bathrobe and I am sure that she wore a green bathrobe, but she did not resemble a guest or tenant, she had a bent broken stooped losing-the-game look of the kind that defines the person who is not winning the game. Seldom am I in error about such things, the eidetic memory as we say, saw a figure of some kind possibly female atop the Mormon temple, the figure seemed to be leading the people somewhere, onward, presumably, saw several unpainted pictures on the street, from the windows of the limousine in which I was moved from place to place, Pietàs mostly, one creature holding another creature in its arms, at bus stops, mostly. Los Angeles.

I thought about sand although I saw no sand in Los Angeles, they told me that there were beaches in the vicinity; the bit of ocean I had seen from the window of my hotel room on Wilshire implied sand but I saw no sand during my not extensive stay in Los Angeles, where I signed various documents having to do with the long-range plan, which I sat thinking about in the dank without my shirt upon my return from Los Angeles. I mentally compared our city to Los Angeles, a competition in which our city was not found inferior, you may be sure, a weighing of values in which our city was not given short weight, you may be sure. In the matter of madhouses alone we surpass Los Angeles. To say nothing of our grand boulevards and taverns (where never, never would one be served Huevos Rancheros on a tin plate) and our excellent mayor who habitually meets the City Council with a Holy Bible clenched between his teeth. But I had no desire to get into a slanging match with the city of Los Angeles, in my mind, and so turned my mind to the problem at hand, the long-range plan.

I was considering the long-range plan, pressing upon me in all its immensity, the eight-hundred-and-seventy-six-million-dollar long-range plan for which I have been repeatedly criticized by my associates and by their associates and, who knows, by associates of the associates of my associates, with particular reference to the vast underground parking facility, when my mother telephoned to ask what the left-hand page of a book is called. My mother often calls me at two o'clock in the morning because she has trouble sleeping. "Recto," I said, "it's either recto or verso, I don't remember which is which, look it up, how are you?" My mother said that she was fine except for horrible nightmares when she did manage to get to sleep, horrible nightmares involving the long-range plan. I had taken the eight-hundred-and-seventy-six-million-dollar long-range plan home to show my mother some months previously, she studied the many-hundred-page printout and then announced that, very probably, it would give her nightmares. My mother is a disciple of Schumacher, the "small" man, a disciple of Mumford, a disciple (moving backward in time) of Fourier, and a disciple most recently of François Mitterrand, she wonders why we can't have a President like that, a real Socialist who also speaks excellent French. My mother is somewhat out of touch with present realities and feels that property is theft and feels that my father taught me the wrong things (although I feel that much of what my father taught me, in his quite bold and dramatic way, his quite bold and dramatic and let it be acknowledged self-dramatizing way, was of great use to me later—the épée, the leveraged buyout, Chapter 11—although had he really loved me he would have placed more stress, perhaps, on air conditioning, the manufacture, sale, installation, and maintenance of air conditioning). My problem with the long-range plan was not ethical, like my mother's, but practical: Why am I doing this?

It is not easy, it is not the easiest thing, to go through life asking this sort of question, this sort of poignant and noxious question that poisons and makes poignant (I detest poignancy!) one's every can of chicken noodle soup or cup of Hot Spiced Cider, afflicting equally morning, noon, and night (I sleep no better than my mother does), infecting calm seriousness and the will-to-win. *For America,* I say to myself, *for America,* and that works sometimes but sometimes it does not; *for America* is better than *because I can* and not as good, not as sweetly persuasive, as *movement of historical forces,* which is itself less convincing than either *what else?* or *why not?* Where in this, I ask myself, where in all this "construction" (and the vast underground parking facility alone will extend from here to St. Louis, or very near), where in all this is the (and we do not fail to notice, do not fail to notice, the constructive associations clustering about the word "construction," the hugely affirmative and congratulatory overtones clinging like busy rust to the word "construction") answer to the question, Why am I doing this?

What else? Why not?

There remained the mystery of Helen, whose moods, her aggressive moods, her fearful moods, her celebratory, resentful, and temporizing moods, remained to be plumbed, thoroughly plumbed. Thoroughness is the key to avoidance of noxious and life-ruining questions, perplexing, noxious, and life-ruining questions which threaten the delicate principle, construction. Construction is like a little boy growing up or an old man winding down or a middle-aged man floundering in the soup, where not infrequently I find that boiling lobster, myself. The spread (margarine, disease) of the physical surround can be like a spill of mixed motives or like an irruption of the divine (New Jerusalem, vast underground parking facility) or like decay in the sense of spoliation of an existing unshrubbed unbuilt swamp or Eden, these are the three categories under which construction may be subsumed, the word "subsumed" itself sounds like a soil test. But if one spends (and on the word "spend" I wish to dwell not at all) one's time thinking about these issues one loosens one's grasp on other issues, bond issues, for example, on leverage and the honest use of materials and density and building codes which vary fearfully from locality to locality and tax wrinkles and the golden section and 1% for art and 100% locations and cul-de-sacs and the Wiener Werkstätte and seals-and-cladding and fast skinning and cure of paints and the beveling of glass and how to clinch a nail and how to sleep well, at night, in the vast *marché aux puces* of my calling. . . .

The next day, pausing only to instruct my secretary, Rip, to throw our messenger business to Hubie the former cabdriver, who had given me his card, I flew back to Los Angeles to begin understanding the mystery of Helen.

LETTERS TO THE EDITORE

*T*HE *Editor of* Shock Art *has hardly to say that the amazing fecundity of the LeDuff–Galerie Z controversy during the past five numbers has enflamed both shores of the Atlantic, at intense length. We did not think anyone would care, but apparently, a harsh spot has been touched. It is a terrible trouble to publish an international art-journal in two languages simultaneously, and the opportunities for dissonance have not been missed. We will accept solely one more correspondence on this matter, addressed to our editorial offices, 6, Viale Berenson, 20144 Milano (Italy), and that is the end. Following is a poor selection of the recent reverberations.*

Nicolai PONT
Editore

SIRS:

This is to approximate a reply to the reply of Doug LeDuff to our publicity of 29 December which appeared in your journal and raised such possibilities of anger. The fumings of Mr. LeDuff were not unanticipated by those who know. However nothing new has been proved by these vapourings, which leave our points untouched, for the most part, and limp off into casuistry and vague threats. We are not very intimidated! The matters of substantial interest in our original publicity are scatheless. Mr. LeDuff clearly has the opinion that the readers of *Shock Art* are dulls, which we do not. Our contention that the works of Mr. LeDuff the American are sheer copyings of the work of our artist Gianbello Bruno can be sustained by ruthless scholarship, of the type that Mr. LeDuff cannot, for obvious reasons, bear to produce. But the recipient of today's art-scene is qualified enough to judge for himself. We need only point to the 1978 exposition at the Galerie Berger, Paris, in which the "asterisk" series of Bruno was first inserted, to see what is afoot. The American makes the claim that he has been painting asterisks since 1975—we say, if so, where are these asterisks? In what collections? In what expositions? With what documentation? Whereas the accomplishment of the valuable Bruno is fully documented, by the facts and other printed materials, as was brought out in our original publicity. That LeDuff has infiltrated the collectors of four continents with his importunity proves nothing, so much so as to be dismissive and final.

Of course the fully American attitude of the partisans of LeDuff, that there is nothing except America, is evident here in the apparently fair evaluation of the protagonists which is in fact deeply biased in the direction of their native land. The manifestation of Mr. Ringwood Paul in your most recent number, wherein he points out (correctly) that the asterisks of LeDuff are six-pointed versus the asterisks of Bruno which have uniformly five points, is not a "knockout blow." In claiming severe plastic originality for LeDuff on this score, Mr. Paul only displays the thickness of entrenched opinion. It is easy, once one has "borrowed" a concept from another artist, to add a little small improvement, but it is not so easy to put it back again without anyone noticing! Finally, the assertion of the estimable critic (American again, we understand!) Paula Marx that the moiré effect achieved by both Bruno and LeDuff by the superimposition of many asterisks on many other asterisks is an advancement created by LeDuff alone and then adduced by Bruno, is flatly false. Must we use carbon-dating on these recent peintures to establish truth, as if we were archeologists faced with an exhausted culture? No, there are living persons among us who remember. To support this affair with references to the "idealism" of the œuvre of LeDuff is the equivalent of saying, "Yes, mostly his shirts are clean." But the clean shirt of LeDuff conceals that which can only throw skepticism on this œuvre.

> Bernardo BROWN
> H. L. AKEFELDT
> Galerie Z
> Milan

SIRS:

The whole thing is to make me smile. What do these Americans want? They come over here and everyone installs them in the best hotels with lavish napery, but still, complaints of every kind. Profiting unduly from the attentions of rich bourgeois, they then emplane once again for America, richer and thoughtful of coming again to again despoil our bourgeois. Doug LeDuff is a pig and a child, but so are his enemies.

> Pino VITT
> Rome

CARO NIKKI—

May I point out the facility of the LeDuff–Galerie Z debate that you have allowed to discolor your pages for many months now? Whether or not you were admirable in your decision to accept for publication the Galerie Z advertisings defaming LeDuff (whom I personally feel to be a monger of dampish wallpaper) is not for me to state, although you were clearly incredible, good faith notwithstanding. I can only indicate, from the womb of history, that both LeDuff and Bruno have impersonated the accomplishments of the Magdeburg Handwerker (May 14, 1938).

> Hugo TIMME
> Düsseldorf

SIRS:

The members of the SURFACE Group (Basel) are unfalteringly supportive of the immense American master, Doug LeDuff.

> Gianni ARNAN
> Michel PIK
> Zin REGALE
> Erik ZORN
> Basel

EDITORE (if any)
Shock Art
MILANO

The most powerful international interests of the gallery-critic-collector cartel have only to gain by the obfuscations of the LeDuff–Galerie Z bickerings. How come you have ignored Elaine Grasso, whose work of now many years in the field of parentheses is entirely propos?

> Magda BAUM
> Rotterdam

SIRS:

Shock Art is being used unforeseeably in this affair. The asterisk has a long provenance and is neither the formulation of LeDuff nor of Bruno either, in any case. The asterisk (from the Greek *asteriskos* or small star) presents itself in classical mythology as the sign which Hera, enraged by yet another of Zeus's manifold infidelities, placed on the god's brow while he slept, to remind him when he gazed in the mirror in the morning that he should be somewhere else. I plead with you, Sig. Pont, to publish my letter, so that people will know.

> G. PHILIOS
> Athens

CARO PONT,

It was kind of you to ask me to comment on the good fight you are making in your magazine. A poor critic is not often required to consult on these things, even though he may have much better opinions than those who are standing in the middle, because of his long and careful training in ignoring the fatigues of passionate involvement—if he has it!

Therefore, calmly and without prejudice toward either party, let us examine the issues with an unruffled eye. LeDuff's argument (in *Shock Art* #37) that an image, once floated on the international art-sea, is a fish that anyone may grab with impunity, and make it his own, would not persuade an oyster. Questions of primacy are not to be scumbled in this way, which, had he been writing from a European perspective, he would understand, and be ashamed. The brutality of the American rape of the world's exhibition spaces and organs of art-information has distanciated his senses. The historical aspects have been adequately trodden by others, but there is one category yet to be entertained—that of the psychological. The fact that LeDuff is replicated in every museum, in every journal, that one cannot turn one's gaze without bumping into this raw plethora, LeDuff, LeDuff, LeDuff (whereas poor Bruno, the true progenitor, is eating the tops of bunches of carrots)—what has this done to LeDuff himself? It has turned him into a dead artist, but the corpse yet bounces in its grave, calling attentions toward itself in the most unseemly manner. But truth cannot be swallowed forever. When the real story of low optical stimulus is indited, Bruno will be rectified.

Titus Toselli DOLLA
Palermo

GREAT DAYS

WHEN I was a little girl I made mud pies, dangled strings down crayfish holes hoping the idiot crayfish would catch hold and allow themselves to be hauled into the light. Snarled and cried, ate ice cream and sang "How High the Moon." Popped the wings off crickets and floated stray Scrabble pieces in ditch water. All perfect and ordinary and perfect.

—Featherings of ease and bliss.

—I was preparing myself. Getting ready for the great day.

—Icy day with salt on all the sidewalks.

—Sketching attitudes and forming pretty speeches.

—Pitching pennies at a line scraped in the dust.

—Doing and redoing my lustrous abundant hair.

—Man down. Center and One Eight.

—Tied flares to my extremities and wound candy canes into my lustrous, abundant hair. Getting ready for the great day.

—For I do not deny that I am a little out of temper.

—Glitches in the system as yet unapprehended.

—Oh that clown band. Oh its sweet strains.

—Most excellent and dear friend. Who the silly season's named for.

—My demands were not met. One, two, three, four.

—I admire your dash and address. But regret your fear and prudence.

—Always worth making the effort, always.

—Yes that's something we do. Our damnedest. They can't take that away from us.

—The Secretary of State cares. And the Secretary of Commerce.

—Yes they're clued in. We are not unprotected. Soldiers and policemen.

—Man down. Corner of Mercer and One Six.

—Paying lots of attention. A clear vision of what can and can't be done.

—Progress extending far into the future. Dams and aqueducts. The amazing strength of the powerful.

—Organizing our deepest wishes as a mother foresightedly visits a store that will be closed tomorrow.

—Friendship's the best thing.

—One of the best things. One of the very best.

—I performed in a hall. Alone under the burning lights.

—The hall ganged with admiring faces. Except for a few.

—Julia was there. Rotten Julia.

—But I mean you really like her don't you?

—Well I mean who doesn't like violet eyes?

—Got to make the effort, scratch where it itches, plans, schemes, directives, guidelines.

—Well I mean who doesn't like frisky knees?

—Yes she's lost her glow. Gone utterly.

—The strains of the city working upon an essentially nonurban sensibility.

—But I love the city and will not hear it traduced.

—Well, me too. But after all. But still.

—Think Julia's getting it on with Bally.

—Yeah I heard about that he's got a big mouth.

—But handsome hipbones got to give him that.

—I remember, I can feel them still, pressing into me as they once did on hot afternoons and cool nights and feverish first-thing-in-the-mornings.

—Yes, Bally is a regal memory for everyone.

—My best ghost. The one I think about, in bitter times and good.

—Trying to get my colors together. Trying to play one off against another. Trying for cancellation.

—I respect your various phases. Your sweet, even discourse.

—I spent some time away and found everyone there affable, gentle, and good.

—Nonculminating kind of ultimately affectless activity.

—Which you mime so gracefully in auditoria large and small.

—And yet with my really wizard! good humor and cheerful thoughtless mien, I have caused a lot of trouble.

—I suppose that's true. Strictly speaking.

—Bounding into the woods on all fours barking like a mother biting at whatever moves in front of me—

—Do you also save string?

—On my free evenings and paid holidays. Making the most of the time I have here on this earth. Knotting, sewing, weaving, welding.

—Naming babies, Lou, Lew, Louis.

—And his toes, wonderful toes, that man has got toes.

—Decorated with rings and rubber bands.

—Has a partiality for white. White gowns, shifts, aprons, flowers, sauces.

—He was a salty dog all right. Salty dog.

—I was out shooting with him once, pheasant, he got one, with his fancy shotgun. The bird bursting like an exploding pillow.

—Have to stand there and watch them, their keen eyes scanning the whatever. And then say "Good shot!"

—Oh I could have done better, better, I was lax.

—Or worse, don't fret about it, could have put your cute little butt in worse places, in thrall to dismaler personalities.

—I was making an effort. What I do best.

—You are excellent at it. Really first-rate.

—Never fail to knock myself out. Put pictures on the walls and pads under the rugs.

—I really admire you. I really do. To the teeth.

—Bust your ass, it's the only way.

—As we learn from studying the careers of all the great figures of the past. Heraclitus and Launcelot du Lac.

—Polish the doorknobs with Brasso and bring in the sea bass in its nest of seaweed.

—And not only that. And not only that.

—Tickling them when they want to be tickled. Abstaining, when they do not.

—Large and admirable men. Not neglecting the small and ignoble. Dealing evenhandedly with every situation on a case-by-case basis.

—Yeah yeah yeah yeah yeah.

—Knew a guy wore his stomach on his sleeve. I dealt with the problem using astrology in its medical aspects. His stomach this, his stomach that, God Almighty but it was tiresome, tiresome in the extreme. I dealt with it by using astrology in its medical aspects.

—To each his own. Handmade bread and individual attention.

—You've got to have something besides yourself. A cat, too often.

—I could have done better but I was dumb. When you're young you're sometimes dumb.

—Yeah yeah yeah yeah yeah. I remember.

—Well let's have a drink.

—Well I don't mind if I do.

—I have Goldwasser, Bombay gin, and Old Jeb.

—Well I wouldn't mind a Scotch myself.

—I have that too.

—Growing older and with age, less beautiful.

—Yeah I've noticed that. Losing your glow.

—Just gonna sit in the wrinkling house and wrinkle. Get older and worse.

—Once you lose your glow you never get it back.

—Sometimes by virtue of the sun on a summer's day.

—Wrinkling you so that you look like a roast turkey.

—As is the case with the Oni of Ife. Saw him on television.

—Let me show you this picture.

—Yes that's very lovely. What is it?

—It's *Vulcan and Maia*.

—Yes. He's got his hooks into her. She's struggling to get away.

—Vigorously? Vigorously. Yes.

—Who's the artist?

—Spranger.

—Never heard of him.

—Well.

—Yes, you may hang it. Anywhere you like. On that wall or that wall or that wall.

—Thank you.

—Probably I can get ahead by working hard, paying attention to detail.

—I thought that. Once I thought that.

—Reading a lot of books and having good ideas.

—Well that's not bad. I mean it's a means.

—Do something wonderful. I don't know what.

—Like a bass player plucking the great thick strings of his instrument with powerful plucks.

—Blood vessels bursting in my face just under the skin all the while.

—Hurt by malicious criticisms all very well grounded.

—Washing and rewashing my lustrous, abundant hair.

—For Leatherheart, I turn my back. My lustrous, abundant back.

—That cracks them up does it?

—At least they know I'm in town.

—Ease myself into bed of an evening brain jumping with hostile fluids.

—It's greens in a pot.

—It's confetti in the swimming pool.

—It's U-joints in the vichyssoise.

—It's staggers under the moon.

—He told me terrible things in the evening of that day as we sat side by side waiting for the rain to wash the watercolors from his watercolor paper. Waiting for the rain to wash the paper clean, quite clean.

—Took me by the hand and led me through all the rooms. Many rooms.

—I know all about it.

—The kitchen is especially splendid.

—Quite so.

—A dozen Filipinos with trays.

—Close to that figure.

—Trays with edibles. Wearables. Readables. Collectibles.

—Ah, you're a fool. A damned fool.

—Goodbye, madame. Dip if you will your hand in the holy-water font as you leave, and attend as well to the poor box just to the right of the door.

—Figs and kiss-me-nots. I would meet you upon this honestly.

—I went far beyond the time normally allotted for a speaker. Far.

—In Mexico City. Wearing the black jacket with the silver conchos. And trousers of fire pink.

—Visited a health club there, my rear looked like two pocketbooks, they worked on it.

—You were making an effort.

—Run in the mornings too, take green tea at noon, study household management, finance, repair of devices.

—Born with a silver hoe in your mouth.

—Yes. Got to get going, got to make some progress.

—Followed by development of head banging in the child.

—I went far beyond the time normally allotted to, or for, a speaker. It is fair to say they were enthralled. And transfixed. Inappropriate laughter at some points but I didn't mind that.

—Did the Eminence arrive?

—In a cab. In his robes of scarlet.

—He does a tough Eminence.

—Yes very tough. I was allowed to kiss the ring. He sat there, in the audience, just like another member of the audience. Just like anybody. Transfixed and enthralled.

—Whirling and jiggling in the red light and throwing veils on the floor and throwing gloves on the floor—

—One of my finest. They roared for ten minutes.

—I am so proud of you. Again and again. Proud of you.

—Oh well, yes. I agree. Quite right. Absolutely.

—What? Are you sure? Are you quite sure? Let me show you this picture.

—Yes that's quite grand. What is it?

—It's *Tancred Succored by Ermina*.

—Yes she's sopping up the blood there, got a big rag, seems a sweet girl, God he's out of it isn't he, dead or dying horse at upper left. . . . Who's the artist?

—Ricchi.

—Never heard of him.

—Well.

—I'll take it. You may stack it with the others, against that wall or that wall or that wall—

—Thank you. Where shall I send the bill?

—Send it anywhere you like. Anywhere your little heart desires.

—Well I hate to be put in this position. Bending and subservient.

—Heavens! I'd not noticed. Let me raise you up.

—Maybe in a few days. A few days or a few years.

—Lave you with bee jelly and bone oil.

—And if I have ever forgiven you your astonishing successes—

—Mine.

—And if I have ever been able to stomach your serial triumphs—

—The sky. A rectangle of gray in the foreground and behind that, a rectangle of puce. And behind that, a square of silver gilt.

—Got to get it together, get the big bucks.

—Yes I'm thinking hard, thinking hard.

—Frolic and detour.

—What's that mean?

—I don't know just a bit of legal language I picked up somewhere.

—Now that I take a long look at you—

—In the evening by the fireside—

—I find you utterly delightful. Abide with me. We'll have little cakes with smarm, yellow smarm on them—

—Yes I just feel so fresh and free here. One doesn't feel that way every day, or every week.

—Last night at two the barking dog in the apartment above stopped barking. Its owners had returned. I went into the kitchen and barked through the roof for an hour. I believe I was understood.

—Man down. Corner of Water and Eight Nine.

—Another wallow?

—I've wallowed for today thank you. Control is the thing.

—Control used to be the thing. Now, abandon.

—I'll never achieve abandon.

—Work hard and concentrate. Try Clown, Baby, Hell-hag, Witch, the Laughing Cavalier. The Lord helps those—

—Purple bursts in my face as if purple staples had been stapled there every which way—

—Hurt by malicious criticisms all very well grounded—

—Oh that clown band. Oh its sweet strains.

—The sky. A rectangle of glister. Behind which, a serene brown. A yellow bar, vertical, in the upper right.

—I love you, Harmonica, quite exceptionally.

—By gum I think you mean it. I think you do.

—It's *Portia Wounding Her Thigh*.

—It's *Wolfram Looking at His Wife Whom He Has Imprisoned with the Corpse of Her Lover*.

—If you need a friend I'm yours till the end.

—Your gracious and infinitely accommodating presence.

—Julia's is the best. Best I've ever seen. The finest.

—The muscle of jealousy is not in me. Nowhere.

—Oh it is so fine. Incomparable.

—Some think one thing, some another.

—The very damn best believe me.

—Well I don't know, I haven't seen it.

—Well, would you like to see it?

—Well, I don't know, I don't know her very well do you?

—Well, I know her well enough to ask her.

—Well, why don't you ask her if it's not an inconvenience or this isn't the wrong time or something.

—Well, probably this is the wrong time come to think of it because she isn't here and some time when she is here would probably be a better time.

—Well, I would like to see it right now because just talking about it has got me in the mood to see it. If you know what I mean.

—She told me that she didn't like to be called just for that purpose, people she didn't know and maybe wouldn't like if she did know, I'm just warning you.

—Oh.

—You see.

—I see.

—I could have done better. But I don't know how. Could have done better, cleaned better or cooked better or I don't know. Better.

—You smile. And the angels sing. La la la la la la la la la la la la.

—Blew it. Blew it.

—Had a clown at the wedding he officiated standing there in his voluptuous white costume his drum and trumpet at his feet. He said, "Do you, Harry . . ." and all that. The guests applauded, the clown band played, it was a brilliant occasion.

—Our many moons of patience and accommodation. Tricks and stunts unknown to common cunts.

—The guests applauded. Above us, a great tent with red and yellow stripes.

—The unexploded pillow and the simple, blunt sheet.

—I was fecund, savagely so.

—Painting dead women by the hundreds in passionate imitation of Delacroix.

—Sailing after lunch and after sailing, gin.

—Do not go into the red barn, he said. I went into the red barn. Julia. Swinging on a rope from hayloft to tack room. Gazed at by horses with their large, accepting eyes. They somehow looked as if they knew.

—You packed hastily reaching the station just before midnight counting the pennies in your purse.

—Yes. Regaining the city, plunged once more into activities.

—You've got to have something besides yourself. A cause, interest, or goal.

—Made myself knowledgeable in certain areas, one, two, three, four. Studied the Value Line and dipped into cocoa.

—The kind of thing you do so well.

—Acquired busts of certain notables, marble, silver, bronze. The Secretary of Defense and the Chairman of the Joint Chiefs.

—Wailed a bit now and then into the ears of friends and caverns of the telephone.

—But I rallied. Rallied.

—Made an effort. Made the effort.

—To make soft what is hard. To make hard the soft. To conceal what is black with use, under new paint. Check the tomatoes with their red times, in the manual. To enspirit the spiritless. To get me a jug and go out behind the barn sharing with whoever is out behind the barn, peasant or noble.

—Sometimes I have luck. In plazas or taverns.

—Right as rain. I mean okey-dokey.

—Unless the participant affirmatively elects otherwise.

—What does that mean?

—Damfino. Just a bit of legal language I picked up somewhere.

—You are the sunshine of my life.

—Toys toys I want more toys.

—Yes, I should think you would.

—That wallow in certainty called the love affair.

—The fading gray velvet of the sofa. He clowned with my panties in his teeth. Walked around that way for half an hour.

—What's this gunk here in this bucket?

—Bread in milk, have some.

—I think I could eat a little something.

—A mistletoe salad we whipped up together.

—Stick to it, keep after it. Only way to go is all the way.

—Want to buy a garter belt? Have one, thanks. Cut your losses, try another town, split for the tall timber.

—Well it's a clean afternoon, heavy on the azaleas.

—Yes they pride themselves on their azaleas. Have competitions, cups.

—I dashed a hope and dimmed an ardor. Promises shimmering like shrimp in light just under the surface of the water.

—Peered into his dental arcade noting the health of his pink tissue.

—Backed into a small table which overturned with a scattering of ashtrays and back copies of important journals.

—What ought I to do? What do you advise me? Should I try to see him? What will happen? Can you tell me?

—Yes it's caring and being kind. We have corn dodgers too and blood sausage.

—Lasciviously offered a something pure and white.

—But he hastily with an embarrassed schottische of the hands covered you up again.

—Much like that. Every day. I don't mind doing the work if I get the results.

—We had a dog because we thought it would keep us together. A plain dog.

—Did it?

—Naw it was just another of those dumb ideas we had we thought would keep us together.

—Bone ignorance.

—Saw him once more, he was at a meeting I was at, had developed an annoying habit of coughing into his coat collar whenever he—

—Coughed.

—Yes he'd lift his coat collar and cough into it odd mannerism very annoying.

—Then the candles going out one by one—

—The last candle hidden behind the altar—

—The tabernacle door ajar—

—The clapping shut of the book.

—I got ready for the great day. The great day came, several times in fact.

—Each time with memories of the last time.

—No. These do not in fact intrude. Maybe as a slight patina of the over-and-done-with. Each great day is itself, with its own war machines, rattles, and green lords. There is the hesitation that the particular day won't be what it is meant to be. Mostly it is. That's peculiar.

—He told me terrible things in the evening of that day as we sat side by side waiting for the rain to wash his watercolor paper clean. Waiting for the rain to wash the watercolors from his watercolor paper.

—What do the children say?

—There's a thing the children say.

—What do the children say?

—They say: Will you always love me?

—Always.

—Will you always remember me?

—Always.

—Will you remember me a year from now?

—Yes, I will.

—Will you remember me two years from now?

—Yes, I will.

—Will you remember me five years from now?

—Yes, I will.

—Knock knock.

—Who's there?

—You see?

THE BABY

THE first thing the baby did wrong was to tear pages out of her books. So we made a rule that each time she tore a page out of a book she had to stay alone in her room for four hours, behind the closed door. She was tearing out about a page a day, in the beginning, and the rule worked fairly well, although the crying and screaming from behind the closed door were unnerving. We reasoned that that was the price you had to pay, or part of the price you had to pay. But then as her grip improved she got to tearing out two pages at a time, which meant eight hours alone in her room, behind the closed door, which just doubled the annoyance for everybody. But she wouldn't quit doing it. And then as time went on we began getting days when she tore out three or four pages, which put her alone in her room for as much as sixteen hours at a stretch, interfering with normal feeding and worrying my wife. But I felt that if you made a rule you had to stick to it, had to be consistent, otherwise they get the wrong idea. She was about fourteen months old or fifteen months old at that point. Often, of course, she'd go to sleep, after an hour or so of yelling, that was a mercy. Her room was very nice, with a nice wooden rocking horse and practically a hundred dolls and stuffed animals. Lots of things to do in that room if you used your time wisely, puzzles and things.

Unfortunately sometimes when we opened the door we'd find that she'd torn more pages out of more books while she was inside, and these pages had to be added to the total, in fairness.

The baby's name was Born Dancin'. We gave the baby some of our wine, red, white, and blue, and spoke seriously to her. But it didn't do any good.

I must say she got real clever. You'd come up to her where she was playing on the floor, in those rare times when she was out of her room, and there'd be a book there, open beside her, and you'd inspect it and it would look perfectly all right. And then you'd look closely and you'd find a page that had one little corner torn, could easily pass for ordinary wear-and-tear, but I knew what she'd done, she'd torn off this little corner and swallowed it. So that had to count and it did. They will go to any lengths to thwart you. My wife said that maybe we were being too rigid and that the baby was losing weight. But I pointed out to her that the baby had a long life to live and had to live in the world with others, had to live in a world where there were many, many rules, and if you couldn't learn to play by the rules you were going to be left out in the cold with no character, shunned and ostracized by everyone. The longest we ever kept her in her room consecutively was eighty-eight hours, and that ended when my wife took the door off its hinges with a crowbar even though the baby still owed us twelve hours because she was working off twenty-five pages. I put the door back on its hinges and added a big lock, one that opened only if you put a magnetic card in a slot, and I kept the card.

But things didn't improve. The baby would come out of her room like a bat out of hell and rush to the nearest book, *Goodnight Moon* or whatever, and begin tearing pages out of it hand over fist. I mean there'd be thirty-four pages of *Goodnight Moon* on the floor in ten seconds. Plus the covers. I began to get a little worried. When I added up her indebtedness, in terms of hours, I could see that she wasn't going to get out of her room until 1992, if then. Also, she was looking pretty wan. She hadn't been to the park in weeks. We had more or less of an ethical crisis on our hands.

I solved it by declaring that it was *all right* to tear pages out of

books, and moreover, that it was all right to *have torn* pages out of
books in the past. That is one of the satisfying things about being
a parent—you've got a lot of moves, each one good as gold. The
baby and I sit happily on the floor, side by side, tearing pages out
of books, and sometimes, just for fun, we go out on the street and
smash a windshield together.

JANUARY

*T*HE *interview took place, appropriately enough, on St. Thomas in the U.S. Virgin Islands. Thomas Brecker was renting a small villa, before which a bougainvillaea bloomed, on the outskirts of Charlotte Amalie. Brecker was wearing an orange-red tie with a light blue cotton shirt and seemed very much at ease. He has a leg brace because of an early bout with polio but it does not seem to inhibit his movement, which is vigorous, athletic. At sixty-five, he has published seven books, from* Christianity and Culture *(1964) to, most recently,* The Possibility of Belief, *for which he won the Van Baaren Prize awarded annually by Holland's Groningen Foundation. While we talked, on a sultry day in June 1986, a houseboy attended us, bringing cool drinks on a brown plastic tray of the sort found in cafeterias. From time to time we were interrupted by Brecker's son Patrick, six, who seemed uncomfortable when out of sight of his father.*

INTERVIEWER

You were a journalist when you began, I believe. Can you tell us something about those years?

BRECKER

I wasn't much of a journalist, or I wasn't a journalist for very long, two or three years. This was on a small paper in California, a middle-sized daily, a Knight-Ridder paper in San Jose. I started out doing all the routine things, courts, police, city hall, then they made me the religion writer. I did that for two years. It was not a choice assignment, it was very much looked down upon, one step above being an obituary writer, what we called the mort man. Also, in those days it was very difficult to print anything that might be construed as critical of any given religion, even when you were dealing with the problems a particular church might be having. So many things couldn't be talked about: abortion, mental illness among the clergy, fratricidal behavior among churches of the same denomination. Now that's all changed.

INTERVIEWER

And that got you interested in religion.

BRECKER

Yes. It was very good experience and I'm grateful for it. I began to think of religion in a much more practical sense than I'd ever thought about it before, what the church offered or could offer to people, what people got from the church in a day-to-day sense, and especially what it did to the clergy. I saw people wrestling with terrible dilemmas, gay priests, ministers who had to counsel people against abortion when abortion was obviously the only sane solution to, say, the problem of a pregnant thirteen-year-old, women who could only be nurses or teachers when they felt they had a very powerful vocation for the priesthood itself— I came to theoretical concerns by way of very practical ones.

INTERVIEWER

You did your undergraduate work at UCLA, I remember.

BRECKER

Yes. In chemistry, of all things. My undergraduate degree was in chemical engineering, but when I got out there were no jobs so I took the first thing that was offered, which was this fifty-dollar-a-week newspaper thing in San Jose. So after working on the paper, I went back to the university and studied first philosophical anthropology and then religion. I ended up at the Harvard Divinity School. That would be the late forties.

INTERVIEWER

You did your dissertation with Tillich.

BRECKER

No. I knew him and of course he was of enormous importance to all of us. He was at Harvard until '62, I believe. He had an apartment on Chauncy Street in Cambridge, on the second floor, he used to have informal seminars at home, some of which I attended. But he wasn't my dissertation director, a man named Howard Cadmus was.

INTERVIEWER

Your dissertation dealt with acedia.

BRECKER

In the forties that sort of topic was more or less in the air. And of course it's interesting, that sort of sickness, torpor, one wonders how it arises and how it's dealt with, and it's real and it has a relation, albeit a negative one, to religion. The topic was maybe too fashionable but I still think the dissertation was respectable, a respectable piece of work if not brilliant.

INTERVIEWER

What was the burden of the argument?

BRECKER

The thesis was that acedia is a turning toward something rather than, as it's commonly conceived of, a turning away from something. I argued that acedia is a positive reaction to extraordinary demand, for example, the demand that one embrace the *good news* and become one with the mystical body of Christ. The demand is extraordinary because it's so staggering in terms of changing your life—out of the ordinary, out of the common run. Acedia is often conceived of as a kind of sullenness in the face of existence; I tried to locate its positive features. For example, it precludes certain kinds of madness, crowd mania, it precludes a certain kind of error. You're not an enthusiast and therefore you don't go out and join a lynch mob—rather you languish on a couch with your head in your hands. I was trying to stake out a position for the uncommitted which still, at the same time, had something to do with religion. I may have been right or wrong, it doesn't much matter now, but that's what I was trying to do.

Acedia refuses certain kinds of relations with others. Of course there's a concomitant loss—of being with others, intersubjectivity. In literature, someone like Huysmans exemplifies the type. You could argue that he was just a 19th Century dandy of a certain kind but that misses the point, which is that something brought him to this position. As ever, fear comes into it. I argued that acedia was a manifestation of fear and I think that's true. Here it would be a fear of the need to submit, of joining the culture, of losing that much of the self to the culture.

INTERVIEWER

The phrase "the need to submit"—you're consistently critical of that.

BRECKER

It has parts, just like anything else. There's a relief in submission to authority and that's a psychological good. At the same time, we consider submission a diminishment of the individual, a ceding of individual being, which we criticize. It's a paradox which has to do with competing goods. For example, how much of your own autonomy do you cede to duly constituted authority, whether civil or churchly? And this is saying you're not coerced. We pay taxes because there's a fairly efficient system of coercion involved, but how much fealty do you give a government which is very often pursuing schemes which you, as an individual, using your best judgment, consider quite mad? And how much submission to a church, quite possibly the very wrongheaded temporary management of a church, whether it's a local vestry with ten deacons of suspect intelligence or Rome itself? Christ tells us not to throw the first stone, and that's beautiful, but at some point somebody has to stand up and say that such-and-such is nonsense—which is equivalent to throwing stones.

On the other hand, how much value should be attached to individual being? I take a clue from the fact that we *are* individual beings, that we're constructed that way, we're unique beings. That's also the root of many of our problems, of course.

INTERVIEWER

You're well-known for critiques of contemporary religion, but also for what might be called an esthetic distaste for some aspects of modern religion.

BRECKER

If you're talking about television evangelism and that sort of thing, it's a waste of time to be critical. I begin speaking from the position that I'm a fool and an ignoramus, which is true enough and not just a rhetorical device, and having said that, I can also say that these performances give me very little to think about. There's so little content that there's almost nothing to talk about. A sociologist might profitably study the phenomenon but that's about it. You note the sadness in the fact that so many people draw some kind of nourishment from what is really a very thin version of religion. On the other hand, people like Harvey Cox, who speaks about "people's religion," by which I take him to mean religion in nontraditional forms or mixed traditions or even what might be called bastard forms, have a point too—it can't be disregarded, it has to be thought about. Not that Cox was talking about television specifically. He's thinking, after Tillich, about the theology of culture as a whole. His generosity is what's admirable, and I don't mean that as a way of saying that his thought is not.

INTERVIEWER

Still, the whole thing, the millions of people watching and mailing in their money, is an example of what you characterize as the need to submit.

BRECKER

It's that, certainly. But I'd rather talk about submission at the other end of the scale—say the Catholic bishops in regard to Rome, or St. Augustine, any of the classic saints, very strong figures, bending to what they think or feel to be the will of God. Here you have the most sophisticated people imaginable, people for whom religion has been a central concern all their lives, people who have in every sense earned the right to speak on this sort of question, and you find a joyous submission. The other end of the scale from what we were speaking of as the madness of crowds. That's got to be respected but at the same time it can be examined, because the final effect is precisely submission. What is to be said of this kind of very informed, very sophisticated submission? That it reflects a proper, even admirable humility? It does. Or is it an abdication of responsibility? It's that too, or can be.

INTERVIEWER

The question is one of degree, then. How much you give up.

BRECKER

The question is, rather, what is proper to man? The right way to proceed in regard to these matters can be argued in so many ways, and has been, that the individual can be forgiven for chucking the whole business, giving up religion entirely, and many people do. Still, the question remains. Is a particular position a reasoned position or is it rather a matter of personality, or even pride, the *non serviam*? If it is a reasoned position, how do you deal with the finitude of human reason? What should be trusted, reason or authority? Authority or the individual cast of mind?

INTERVIEWER

To get back to fear, why is it so central in your schema?

BRECKER

It has to do with the problem of finitude, of which fear is an aspect. A mind without limit would have no fear, not even the fear of death. There'd be nothing to fear. Death, for example, would be understood so perfectly that it could contain nothing that could perturb the mind. It's the kind of thing the Eastern religions aim at. Obviously, we'll never get there, to this kind of serenity, because of the limits of human understanding.

But we are most ingenious, most ingenious. One of the finest religious inventions is the concept of absolution. I fall into error, confess it, and you give me absolution, or somebody gives me absolution. That cleansing—itself a very human idea, the washing-away—is of interest. It prevents us from being worse and worse, from in some sense stewing in our own juices. It makes new directions possible. It's just a bloody marvelous conception, and there are others just as good, of which the idea of life after death is merely the first example. Life-after-death may be seen as coercive, or as providing hope, or as pure metaphor, or as absolute fact. What's the truth of the matter? I don't know.

INTERVIEWER

But people can get that from psychiatry, absolution. Admittedly, with greater difficulty.

BRECKER

And perhaps greater efficacy. But as an immediate thing, the fact of absolution is inspired. Although there's a downside to that too, in that it restores one to the ranks of the blessed and the idea of there being a class of persons whom we agree to call blessed is a bit worrisome. There's something psychologically worrisome about there being *the blessed*. I like better the notion that we are all sinners, from a psychological point of view. A sinner who knows himself to be a sinner is always tense, cautious, morally speaking.

INTERVIEWER

What influence would you say your books have had? What do you consider your audience?

BRECKER

Books are dealt with in different ways by professionals in a particular discipline and by ordinary readers. I try to write for both. Let's say I write a book, a book dealing with the kinds of things we've been talking about. And you sit down to read my book. But let's also say that you're a specialist and you turn at once to the index—more or less to see where my book originated, if that's the right word. And going through the index you note, say, references to Alfred Adler, Hannah Arendt, Martin Buber, Dostoevsky, Huizinga, Konrad Lorenz, Otto Rank, Max Weber, and Gregory Zilboorg. So you feel you've read my book or at least have a pretty good sense of where it's coming from, as people say nowadays. You might, with great courtesy, then skim the text in search of unfamiliar ideas, etc. etc. Or to see what I got wrong.

As for influence, I think it's very slight, tiny. I've yet to meet anyone who's been influenced in any important way by my books. I've met lots of people who want to argue particular points, which leaves me at a bit of a disadvantage. I'm not so much interested in resolving varying Christologies or in debating specific religious ideas, techniques of atonement, for example.

INTERVIEWER

Can you accept a disinterested objectivity as finally normative, in regard to historical Christianity?

BRECKER

I've never found a disinterested objectivity. You have to view each tradition in the context of its own historical particularity, and these invariably militate against what might be called a disinterested stance. Very often people establish validity through the construction of a criterion, or a series of criteria, which they then satisfy. The criteria can be very elaborate. It's a neat way of proceeding.

The "good news" is always an announcement of a reconcilation of the particular into the universal. I have a lifelong tendency not to want to be absorbed into the universal, which amounts to saying a lifelong resistance to the forms of religion. But not to religious thought, which I consider of the greatest importance. It's a paradox, maybe a fruitful one, I don't know. Looking at myself, I say, hubris, maybe, the sin of pride, again, but this feeling exists and at least I can look at it, try to understand it, try to figure out how widespread it is. That is, are there others who feel this way? Again a paradox, a movement toward the universal: I don't want to be the only one who wants to be out on a limb. Or I'm seeking validation from outside, etc. etc.

INTERVIEWER

On the question of—

BRECKER

Remember that I was the opposite of a charismatic figure, not a leader, not even a preacher. Perhaps because I had polio and was on crutches and all that. Polio might be said, by a shrink, to be the basis of my psyche in that it set me apart, involuntarily, and it may be that that apartness persisted, as a habit of mind. It would be curious if that accounted for my career, so-called. There are just too many variables to enable you to judge the quality of your own thought. Truth rests with God alone, and a little bit with me, as the proverb says.

Also, there's no progress in my field, there's adding-on but nothing that can truthfully be described as progress. Religion is not susceptible to *aggiornamento,* to being brought up to date, although in terms of intellectual effort the impulse is not shoddy either. It's one of the pleasures of the profession that you are always in doubt.

BRECKER

I think about my own death quite a bit, mostly in the way of noticing possible symptoms—a biting in the chest—and wondering, Is this it? It's a function of being over sixty, and I'm maybe more concerned by how than when. That's a . . . I hate to abandon my children. I'd like to live until they're on their feet. I had them too late, I suppose.

BRECKER

Heraclitus said that religion is a disease, but a noble disease. I like that.

BRECKER

Teaching of any kind is always open to error. Suppose I taught my children a little mnemonic for the days of the month and it went like this: "Thirty days hath September, April, June, and November, all the rest have thirty-one, except for January, which has none." And my children taught this to their children and other people, and it came to be the conventional way of thinking about the days of the month. Well, there'd be a little problem there, right?

BRECKER

I can do without certitude. I would have liked to have had faith.

BRECKER

The point of my career is perhaps how little I achieved. We speak of someone as having had "a long career" and that's usually taken to be admiring, but what if it's thirty-five years of persistence in error? I don't know what value to place on what I've done, perhaps none at all is right. If I'd done something with soybeans, been able to increase the yield of an acre of soybeans, then I'd know I'd done something. I can't say that.